Frances Ruiz is a native of Asheville, NC. She holds a degree in Creative Writing with an Additional Major in Spanish from Carnegie Mellon University. She has traveled to and lived in several different countries, including Argentina, Spain, and Austria.

Fairy Senses

Book One
of
The Key to Embralia

Frances Ruiz

Hinterland Sky Press

Cover Design: Frances Ruiz
Cover Art: © Frances Ruiz

First Edition: 2008

This is a work of fiction. All characters and events are products of the author's imagination and are used fictitiously. Any resemblance to actual events or persons, living or dead, is entirely coincidental and not intended by the author.

© 2008, by Frances Ruiz

All rights reserved. No part of this book may be used or reproduced in any manner whatsoever without written permission from the copyright holders, except in the case of brief quotations embodied in critical articles and reviews.

Hinterland Sky Press
37 W. Black Oak Drive
Asheville, NC, 28804
www.hinterlandsky.com

Printed in the United States of America

ISBN-10: 0-9818880-0-3
ISBN-13: 978-0-9818880-0-2

Library of Congress Control Number: 2008931893

Thanks to my family for all of their love and support, and to Quique for his insight into Galiza.

Contents

Chapter 1
An Unexpected Discovery
11

Chapter 2
The Miasmonians
27

Chapter 3
The Offer
41

Chapter 4
Transformation
50

Chapter 5
A New Plan
59

Chapter 6
Glendenland
69

Chapter 7
Miasmos's Search
94

Chapter 8
The Key to Embralia
123

Chapter 9
Thomas's Secret
139

Chapter 10
The Council Meeting
152

Chapter 11
Queimada
173

Chapter 12
Breaking Point
189

Chapter 13
Face to Face
203

Chapter 14
Return to Humanland
223

Chapter 1
An Unexpected Discovery

Kelly reached for the light switch but then thought better of it. Instead she carefully started to feel her way down the stairs. The sound came again – a faint crackling like plastic wrap moving. When the sound had first started, she had tried to ignore it, huddling under her covers and pretending she hadn't heard anything. But the rustling noises had gone on for at least ten minutes. Kelly paused halfway down the stairs, experiencing a mixture of curiosity and dread. She told herself it was probably just the wind from an open window blowing over a plastic grocery bag. She took a deep breath and resumed her tiptoed descent down the stairs.

Kelly followed the intermittent sounds towards the kitchen. Peeking through the doorway, she noticed that the refrigerator door was slightly ajar. A pale artificial light leaked out of it and cast an eerie glow in the far corner of the room. *That's odd*, Kelly thought. The kitchen looked empty, although Kelly's view was partially obscured by the counter island in the room's center. She stood absolutely still and listened. For a few seconds there was silence, but then the sounds resumed. They were coming from inside the refrigerator. She cautiously approached the island and crouched down behind it. Inching herself up to its edge, she was soon able to peer around it, and the entire length of the refrigerator came into view. The sight that met her eyes surprised Kelly so much that she jumped back to her feet and a half-gasp, half-squeal escaped her throat.

Inside the refrigerator the chocolate cake her mother had baked for her birthday sat exposed. The plastic wrap had been pulled over to one side and something, or perhaps more exactly, someone, was crouching beside it. The creature had stopped moving when it heard the sound Kelly had made. Kelly was now standing still as well, transfixed by the creature. It looked like a miniature man, about a foot tall. He was fat, and there were wings coming out of his back. The wings were unlike anything Kelly had ever seen. They weren't like butterfly wings, or bird wings either. They were closest to drawings she had seen of bat wings or of the wings of medieval dragons, with pointed joints and what looked to be a thin membranous texture. It took Kelly a moment to notice that the little man with wings was transparent; she could see part of the cake through his miniature T-shirt. Just then the little man's wings twitched, and Kelly felt her hand grasp a wooden spoon that had been left out on the counter.

"What, I mean, who are you?" she asked him, holding the spoon to his back. The little man cringed at being addressed. He hunched his back and peeked over his shoulder, one eye open. He had cake smeared all over his round, ruddy face.

"Hey, that's my cake!" She waved the spoon threateningly, which wasn't difficult considering the birthday cake her mother had so lovingly baked and decorated in preparation for her birthday sat mutilated beside him. The little man jumped up into the air and hovered over Kelly's head, just out of her reach. He munched on a handful of cake and stared down at her with wide eyes. His wings beat regularly, causing him to bobble up and down slightly as he hovered above her.

"I asked you a question. Who are you?"

"You can see me? I can't believe it. Not possible, not possible." He suddenly swooped down until he was only inches from her face. He snapped his fingers. He lost the transparent quality and was immediately solid. Kelly could no longer see through him. He snapped his fingers again. He became transparent. He repeated this snapping transformation two or three times, ending in the transparent form.

Kelly had the urge to laugh but she controlled herself. "What are you doing?" Kelly asked. "How do you make yourself go transparent like that?"

"Transparent you say? Not invisible? Most strange, most strange." He flew over to the basket of fruit on the counter, muttering to himself. He picked up a grape, which for his size was about as large as a honeydew melon. He reached his fist inside the hole at the top of the grape where the stem had once been attached, pulled out a fistful of pulp and started stuffing his mouth with it. Kelly watched him. He seemed to have forgotten she was there.

"Hmm, hmm," Kelly cleared her throat.

The little man looked up. "You're telling me you can see me?" he asked.

"Obviously I can see you. I'm talking to you aren't I?"

"But humans can't see us, unless we want to be seen."

"Us?" Kelly asked.

"Fairies of course."

"Fairies?" This miniature fat man with dragon wings stealing all of her food was a fairy? "You're kind of bigger than I would have imagined," she found herself saying.

"I'm just big boned!" He flung the grape to the floor. Obviously she had hit a sore point.

"I didn't mean like that. I just thought, you know, if they existed, fairies would be smaller, like a few inches tall."

"Doesn't surprise me. Those stupid moving drawings on that moving picture box give the wrong idea. Tinsy tiny twinky tinkly fake flimsy fairies those are. Real fairies are like me. I'm a perfect specimen." The fairy puffed out his chest and sucked in his stomach at these words, then twirled around in the air 360 degrees.

"A fine specimen indeed," Kelly said. The fairy didn't seem to pick up on the sarcasm in her voice. "So how come I can see you?"

"Maybe something's wrong with my magic. But no, before I came here there was a man in the street and he didn't see me. And just two days ago I was here, and you didn't see me." He had started flying back and forth a few feet at a time in front of her, what Kelly guessed must be a fairy equivalent to pacing. He stroked his chin pensively as he fluttered back and forth.

"And I haven't felt sick. I haven't really used any magic lately though, let's see..." He pulled something out of the cloth bag he wore over his shoulder. The object bore a striking resemblance to a toothpick. He pointed it at the grape that was now on the floor. A tiny spark flew from the toothpick and hit the grape. The grape exploded, spraying juice in all directions. Kelly was too shocked to say anything. The fairy smiled and put the toothpick back in his shoulder bag. "Looks like my powers are intact. Well then, let me see. You couldn't see me a few days ago but now you can, so that means—" The fairy's eyes grew wide and he abruptly swirled around to look at Kelly.

"That cake, that cake was birthday cake! Wasn't it? Birthday cake!" he shouted.

"Yes," Kelly said.

"How old are you?"

"If it's after midnight I'm fourteen."

The fairy gasped. "Fourteen, dear me, dear me. Of course. That's the only explanation. Fourteen, dear me. Myself, me, meeting one of you, I can't believe it."

"One of me, what do you mean?"

But the fairy wasn't listening. He had started to fly all around Kelly, darting here and there very fast. She could hear a faint hum as his wings beat faster and faster. He kept repeating "Fourteen, fourteen," and "Dear me, dear me," over and over again.

"Would you stop it, please," Kelly said forcefully. He was making her dizzy. The fairy stopped and looked at her, surprised. Then he turned and zoomed off into the living room. Kelly followed just in time to see him wriggle through a slit in the screen of one of the open windows. She ran to the window but there was no sign of him. He had disappeared into the night.

She was flying in the air, darting through the branches. There were no leaves on the trees; they were all dead. She was cold. Her entire body shivered but she felt an urgency propelling her to go on. Suddenly she felt a sharp pain in her back between her shoulder blades. She couldn't keep herself aloft anymore and she fell, hitting a few branches on the way down before she cleared the treetops and there was nothing between her and the ground except thirty feet of air. The wind whistled in her ears as she hurtled downwards.

Kelly sat up, breathing fast. It was 9:30 a.m. Her heart was racing from the dream's vividness. All of the sensations that had gone along with the flying, and later with the falling, had felt incredibly real. No doubt the dream had been inspired by last night's kitchen encounter. She lay in bed and replayed the event in her mind. Why had she been able to see the fairy when other people couldn't? What had he meant when he had called her "one of you"? She hoped he would come back soon to answer these questions.

After a few minutes Kelly heard her mother singing a song downstairs, and that coupled with the brightening morning sunshine that glared through the cracks in her bedroom curtains drew her mind back to everyday matters. She stretched, postponing the moment she would have to go downstairs and join her mother in this year's summer project of Christmas tree ornament production. Around this time of year, at the start of summer vacation, Kelly always wished her mother Mindy wasn't a schoolteacher. As a schoolteacher Mindy had summers off too, and it never took her long to find labor-intensive moneymaking projects to drag her daughter into. Kelly was already spending several hours daily crafting Christmas tree ornaments to be sold come wintertime, and she highly doubted that she would get the day off just because it was her birthday. She rolled out of bed and took a long shower, then spent at least fifteen extra minutes blow-drying her shoulder-length, jet-black hair in front of the bathroom mirror. She was pleased to see that the dark circles that had appeared under her bright green eyes early in the school year had at last started to disappear.

15

"Hi mom," Kelly said as she finally came downstairs.

"You know, you're supposed to wait for your birthday dinner before eating your birthday cake," Mindy said without looking up from the white cotton balls she was trying to glue together into the shape of a snowman.

Kelly was about to tell her mother that someone else was guilty of gobbling up a third of the cake, but she was sure her mother wouldn't believe her.

"Sorry, I just couldn't resist. It looked so good," Kelly said.

A broad smile appeared on Mindy's face as Kelly's compliment sank in. "Just try to utilize more self-control in the future," Mindy answered happily. "I made banana bread. It's still warm," she added.

Kelly grabbed a slice of banana bread and a glass of milk before sitting next to her mother on the living room couch. On TV a blond female newscaster wearing too much makeup was standing in a hospital ward, holding the microphone too close to her face.

"The epidemic of chronic fatigue syndrome sweeping the D.C. area has many doctors baffled. I'm here today with doctor Pierre Montés. Doctor, what's going on?" She extended the microphone to a scrawny middle-aged man with thick glasses and green scrubs.

"Well, Melanie, many more people than usual are reporting nebulous symptoms like headaches, tiredness, and a general lack of energy. This might not sound serious, but some affected patients are missing weeks of work because they just can't get out of bed."

"Thank you doctor. We'll have more after the break. Melanie Johnson, morning news." Melanie flashed a plastic smile and winked at the camera.

Mindy shook her head. "That's what happens when you work too much. Bosses these days. It's really inexcusable the hours some people work."

Tell me about it, Kelly thought as she put down her now-empty plate and picked up some cotton balls of her own. But she knew better than to voice her thoughts out loud.

That evening Kelly was busy gluing glittery designs to Styrofoam spheres when the doorbell rang. It was Kelly's best and pretty much only friend Stephanie, her face freshly sunburnt from a family vacation to Orlando.

"I come with gifts," Stephanie said. She was carrying three boxes wrapped in floral wrapping paper. Kelly and Stephanie immediately retreated up the stairs to Kelly's room. As Stephanie placed the birthday presents on the bed, Kelly felt an intense urge to tell her friend about last night. But she had decided earlier it was best to keep it to herself for now. Stephanie would never believe anything as outrageous as fairies existing unless she were confronted with irrefutable evidence, what Stephanie liked to call "the smoking guns".

"Open them," Stephanie said.

The first present was a sweatshirt that said *Orlando*, with a graphic of the beach and trees on it. Then came a box of chocolates shaped like seashells. Kelly opened the third box.

"Wow, its beautiful." It was a snow globe, but it wasn't a tacky one like most snow globes. This snow globe was beautiful. It was about the size of Kelly's palm and contained a very realistic and detailed beach scene. There were little huts with thatched roofs and palm trees that looked as though they were actually swaying in a gentle breeze. Instead of snowflakes there were light golden flecks that floated down and about the globe after it was shaken.

"I thought you'd like it. I bought it for $1.50 from an old lady selling trinkets. Most of the stuff she was selling was junk, like plastic key chains that said 'Florida'. But this caught my eye."

"Thanks," Kelly said. She hugged Stephanie. "So, overall was the trip as boring as you thought it was going to be?"

"It wasn't a complete waste. I managed to escape my parents for almost an entire day, and you'll never guess what I did." Stephanie's eyes sparkled mischievously.

"What?"

Stephanie turned around and lifted the back of her T-shirt to expose the base of her spine, revealing a freshly inked tattoo.

17

Kelly leaned closer to get a better look. Her stomach lurched when she saw that Stephanie's tattoo portrayed a pink Tinkerbellesque fairy, sound asleep atop a purple flower.

"What is it?" Stephanie asked. "Don't you like it?"

"Yes, I do, it's really pretty," Kelly said quickly.

"You don't sound too enthusiastic." Stephanie returned her T-shirt to its normal position and turned back around. Kelly shifted under Stephanie's piercing gaze.

"Are you okay? Did something happen when I was gone?"

Kelly should have known that it wouldn't take long for Stephanie to suspect something. "Nope, same old same old," she lied.

"Are you sure?"

"Girls?" Mindy was at the door. "Dinner's ready."

Kelly was glad when Stephanie didn't ask any more questions on the way downstairs. Instead she just promised that later she'd tell Kelly more about getting her tattoo. For dinner Mindy had made Kelly's favorite: macaroni and cheese, green beans with garlic, fresh rolls, and mashed sweet potatoes with marshmallows on top. The damaged cake was incredible, and between the three of them they easily finished off what the fairy had left. After dinner Stephanie humored Mindy by helping to make ornaments while she told a very tame version of her trip. Before Kelly and Stephanie got another chance to speak alone, Stephanie's dad arrived to take her home.

"It was so nice to see you, dear," Mindy said as she held the door open for Stephanie.

"It was nice to see you too, Mrs. Brennan. And Kelly, I'll tell you more of my fairy story next time I see you," she said with a wink.

Wait until you hear mine, Kelly thought.

A tingling along her spine accompanied the thrill of the crisp wind on her face. She darted through the air, zipping in and out between tree branches. She heard a scream behind her, followed shortly by a sickening thud. She turned around and started to scan the forest floor, hoping to see who had fallen.

Kelly opened her eyes and blinked several times, not sure what she was seeing at first. Three days had passed since her birthday with no signs of the fairy, so she wasn't expecting to wake up in the middle of the night to find him perched cross-legged on top of her chest, staring at her. And he wasn't alone. There were two female fairies hovering in the air behind him. The fairy on his left was extremely thin, with a large, flat nose identical to his own and blazing curly red hair. She had a small heart-shaped mouth, blue eyes, and tan wings that were several shades lighter than the male fairy's brown wings, although presently Kelly couldn't see his wings very well. He had folded them down on his back and Kelly could only see two little points sticking up one over each shoulder. The other female fairy was a bit smaller and also had red hair and blue eyes, but her wings were pale yellow and glistened as if they were wet. Both female fairies wore flowing blue dresses and carried little cloth shoulder bags, details Kelly was able to make out clearly because the fairy with yellow wings was holding a tiny lantern that gave off a soft, pale light.

The male fairy spoke first. "The other night I didn't properly introduce myself. I'm Bubbles. This is Carmina." He gestured to the tiny fairy with yellow wings. She curtsied with a graceful motion while still hovering in the air. "And this is my sister, Beatrix." He gestured to the fairy with tan wings. Instead of curtsying, Beatrix did a somersault in the air and let out a fast string of excited words.

"Hwayuniceemetwuznampreetypreety!"

"Sorry?" Kelly responded.

"She said how are you, nice to meet you, what's your name, and she thinks you are pretty," Carmina answered. Carmina had a deep voice that didn't quite match her tiny frame.

"Oh." Kelly smiled nervously. "I'm Kelly." The fairies were silent for a moment. "Please tell me you haven't been watching me like this every night," Kelly continued, sitting up. Bubbles fell backwards and rolled off her stomach. Beatrix giggled.

19

"Izeitruwabubblesayorahafree?" Beatrix blurted out as she flew around Bubbles and Carmina in a blur of speed, ending up back at her starting place simultaneously as she finished her sentence.

Carmina saw that Kelly hadn't understood. "She wants to know if it's true, if you really are a half-fairy."

"A half-fairy?" Kelly asked.

"Meaning half-human, half-fairy," Bubbles said.

"I don't think so," Kelly said. "I never even knew fairies existed until three days ago."

"There's only one way to know for sure," Bubbles said seriously. "Beatrix?"

Beatrix giggled again and reached into her purse. She produced a tiny glass jar with a little cork in the top. The jar was filled with a fine silver powder, as fine as baby powder but with a metallic sheen. It sparkled in the light from Carmina's lantern. Beatrix popped off the cork and reached inside the jar. She collected a tiny pinch of the powder and zoomed towards Kelly's face.

"Hey, what are you doing?" Kelly asked.

Beatrix paused, her hand poised with the pinch of powder directly over Kelly's nose.

"We gonna see if yura half-free," Beatrix responded, attempting to speak more slowly for Kelly's benefit. Still she spoke barely slowly enough for Kelly to just catch what she had said.

"I don't know if that's such a good idea." Kelly eyed the powder suspiciously. She remembered what had happened to the grape when Bubbles had pointed his wooden stick at it, and she wasn't looking forward to anything similar happening with this mysterious silver powder.

"Don't worry, it's just fairy dust," Carmina said. "You see, if you are human all it will do is temporarily shrink you to fairy size. But if you are a half-fairy it will temporarily convert you to your fairy form."

"My fairy form? You mean I'd be able to fly?"

"Yes," Bubbles answered.

Beatrix let out another string of unintelligible syllables and Kelly could tell that she was impatient.

"All right, do it," Kelly said. She closed her eyes.

She felt a light tickling sensation on her nose as the fairy dust made contact with her skin. Nothing happened. She opened her eyes.

"It didn't work," she said.

"It always works," Bubbles said indignantly. "That is the highest quality fairy dust. Cost me fifty-five glitterons. It just takes a minute."

Then Kelly felt it – her toes started to tingle, a prickly tingling as if they were falling asleep. Then her fingers started to tingle in the same way. Immediately after her fingers started to tingle, the tingling spread both from her feet up to her hips and from her fingers up to her head, then down from her head to her torso. When the tingling halves of her body met at the waist, the tingling got stronger and stronger and a pressure started to build in the center of her body behind her belly button. The pressure built up until Kelly felt she might in fact explode like the grape, but then instead she felt a swirling feeling inside like she had just passed over a bump in a roller coaster and then – the sensations stopped. She felt normal again. But she was smaller. She realized that she was now sitting right on the edge of her pillow and Bubbles, Beatrix and Carmina were standing in front of her – all about the same size as she was.

"She's definitely smaller," Bubbles said.

"Look at her ears," Carmina said. Kelly reached up and felt her ears. While as a human she had unusually pointy ears, now they had become definitively pointed. They pointed at the top into a severe point. Kelly looked closer at the fairies' ears and realized that they were also all pointed.

"I knew it, I knew it. She is one. Come on now, unfurl your wings," Bubbles demanded.

"My wings?" Kelly reached back over her shoulder and felt a knobby joint sticking out. Her wings were presently folded flat against her back. "How do I do that?"

21

"Roll your shoulders forward as far as you can, then jerk them back in one sharp motion, as if you are trying to make your shoulder blades touch," Carmina instructed.

Kelly concentrated. She rolled her shoulders forward and then back. She heard a soft swoosh of air behind her ears and knew she had been successful. Bubbles, Carmina, and Beatrix were all standing with their mouths wide open in surprise.

"Ooooooh," Beatrix squealed.

"What is it?" Kelly asked. "What's the matter?"

"Nothing's the matter. We'll show you," Carmina said. Carmina and Beatrix zoomed up to Kelly's bedside table, on which rested a small handheld mirror. One on either side, they picked it up and flew it over to the bed. They held it in front of Kelly. Kelly walked forward to examine herself. She immediately saw why the fairies had reacted in such a way to her wings. They were light purple and had a network of sparkling silver lines running through them — like the veins of a leaf. The silver lines sparkled just like the fairy dust inside the jar. Her wings were beautiful. Kelly squinted into the mirror and could see that her eyes looked an even brighter green than they had been before and her skin had taken on a sheen as if moonlight were bouncing off of it.

"With wings like that, you must have really strong magic," Beatrix whispered. In fairy form Kelly had no problem understanding Beatrix's lightning-speed speech.

"Why do you say that?" Kelly asked.

"The color of a fairy's wings tells a lot about their powers. Purple is already a strong color. On top of that you have silver. That's really rare," Carmina said.

"Balderdash," Bubbles huffed. "There are plenty of powerful fairies without flashy wings."

Carmina rolled her eyes. "Of course, any fairy can develop their powers. But innate ability is reflected in the wings."

Bubbles crossed his arms and sulked. Beatrix bounded once again into the air. "Fly! Fly!" She clapped her hands in anticipation and started to fly circles around them again. Her curly hair bounced in time with the beating of her wings.

"How do I do that?" Kelly couldn't feel much sensation in her wings. She hardly would have known they were there save for the slight tug she felt along each shoulder blade. She had absolutely no clue how to move them.

"What do you mean how? You just fly. Like this, see?" Bubbles shot up into the air and chased Beatrix, who started to fly with even more speed.

"Settle down you two," Carmina chided. "We can't remember because we were so young, but it took each of us almost two full years before we could fly."

Beatrix and Bubbles stopped zooming around in circles and returned to respectfully hovering in the air.

"That's better. Now Kelly, you know the muscles between your shoulder blades? You have to tighten them and then release them and your wings will flap."

Kelly tried hard to isolate the muscles between her shoulder blades. "I can't feel if I'm doing it right," she said.

"Let me see." Carmina came over and put her palm between Kelly's shoulder blades. "Feel that? These are the muscles. But wow, they are usually much more developed. I can barely feel yours at all. You are going to have to practice to build up the muscle. I doubt they'll be able to get you too far in their present state."

"Let me try again." Kelly was eager to fly. She concentrated and with great effort squeezed the muscles between her shoulder blades. Her wings jerked in response and she rose up about what felt like half a foot, but what was really more like a centimeter in her present size, and quickly came back to the ground.

"That all you got?" Bubbles asked.

"You're just jealous her wings are prettier than yours are!" Beatrix taunted.

"Am not!"

"Are too!"

"Try again. This time you have to repeat the motion, you can't just do it once," Carmina encouraged.

Kelly tried again. She managed to squeeze her back muscles three times, but too slowly to actually stay aloft. Instead she rose up slightly and came back to the ground between each repetition. Flying was more difficult than she had thought. The muscles between her shoulder blades were already starting to get sore.

"You just have to practice. It's perfectly understandable considering you've never had to use those muscles before. Soon it will become automatic, like walking," Carmina said.

"I hope so," Kelly said. "How do I fold my wings back when I'm not flying?"

"You reverse the motion of unfurling them. Instead of rolling your shoulders forward and then snapping them backwards, you roll them backwards and then snap them forwards."

Kelly did this motion and heard a soft clap as her wings folded behind her back again.

"Once you can fly then we can go exploring," Beatrix said. "We can go anywhere we want because no one can see us if we don't want them too." Beatrix snapped her fingers and became transparent.

"I can still see you," Kelly said. Beatrix snapped herself back into solidity.

"Yes, but humans can't," Bubbles said. Kelly still hadn't quite absorbed the fact she wasn't all human.

"So if I snap my fingers I'll be invisible to humans?" Kelly asked.

"Unfortunately not. Half-fairies can't make themselves completely invisible to humans. You would appear to them as we appear to you in our invisible forms. They could still see you, but also see through you," Carmina answered.

"I didn't know that," Beatrix said.

"I did," Bubbles said. Beatrix stuck her tongue out at him. "Half-fairies can only be half-invisible."

"Like a ghost," Kelly said.

"Sorry?" Bubbles raised his eyebrows.

"Never mind. So if I snap my fingers I'll be half-invisible to humans?"

"Just snapping your fingers doesn't do it, it just helps," Bubbles said. "You have to imagine that you are becoming invisible."

Kelly snapped her fingers. She was still completely visible. She snapped her fingers again.

"You have to imagine harder," Bubbles said.

Kelly imagined with all of her might and snapped her fingers. This time it worked. She looked down at her hands and could see through them.

"Cool." Just at that moment Kelly started to feel a tingling sensation in her toes, followed a second later by a tingling in her fingers. "I think the fairy dust is starting to wear off."

"You sure about that being the highest quality dust Bubbles?" Carmina asked.

"Of course I am."

"But it can't have been more than fifteen minutes ago we dusted her," Beatrix said.

"Then she must be mistaken about it wearing off," Bubbles retorted. But Kelly felt the tingling spread simultaneously from her toes upward and from her fingertips to her torso, until again the two traveling streams of tingles met behind her belly button. Again pressure started to build at that point until it was almost unbearable and then the swirling feeling came. Then just as soon as they had come the sensations vanished and Kelly found herself once again human-sized on her bed with Carmina, Beatrix, and Bubbles hovering a few feet away.

Beatrix let out a burst of unintelligible words to Bubbles, who looked displeased. Once again in human form, Kelly could no longer understand Beatrix's rapid speech. She guessed Beatrix was commenting about the fairy dust because she was holding up the jar and shaking it at Bubbles while she spoke.

"Can I have more fairy dust?" Kelly asked. Beatrix made to uncork the jar but Bubbles snatched it away from her.

"We shouldn't waste it. It's very valuable." Bubbles hugged the jar to his chest.

"It is late, Thomas will start to worry about me," Carmina said. "Thomas is my husband," she added for Kelly's benefit. "Besides, now that you know what it is like to be in fairy form you should be able to transform yourself without the fairy dust."

"Without it?" Kelly asked.

25

"Half-fairies can transform from fairy form to human form whenever they want, without fairy dust."

"But how?"

Carmina looked puzzled. So did Bubbles and Beatrix. Bubbles shrugged. Finally Bubbles said he didn't know. After all, none of them had ever met a half-fairy.

"You will figure it out I'm sure," Carmina said. "It can't be that hard."

Kelly wasn't convinced, but the fairies were getting ready to leave. "We'll come back and visit you tomorrow night. Before then keep exercising your back muscles, and try to figure out how to transform yourself," Carmina said.

After they had gone Kelly lay awake for a long time. She had felt elated when she had been in fairy form and when Carmina, Beatrix, and Bubbles had been there. But now that they were gone the feeling of elation was replaced with a more uncomfortable one. If she was half-fairy that meant one of her parents was a fairy. She had always been told that her father had died in a fire before she was born, and that all photographs of him had been destroyed by the flames. She had learned almost nothing more about him because her mother always changed the subject quickly when he came up in conversation, saying it was too painful to talk about him because he was gone. Now she knew her father must have been a fairy. Was it possible Mindy had known about fairies all of this time? What reason could she have for keeping the truth from Kelly?

Chapter 2
The Miasmonians

When Kelly finally made it down to the kitchen at 10:30 a.m. the next morning, she found her mother had left a note on the counter. The note explained she had gone shopping and wouldn't be back until one or two in the afternoon. After eating breakfast Kelly sighed when she laid eyes on the fresh piles of cotton balls, Styrofoam spheres, and sequins alongside the extra large bottles of craft glue in the living room. Clearly Mindy wanted her daughter to keep up the ornament production while she was gone. Kelly called Stephanie but she couldn't come over because her parents were making her help with yard work. Stephanie joked that school was better than summer labor. Kelly had to agree. But at least with Mindy gone she could practice trying to turn herself into her fairy form. When Kelly finally heard her mother's car drive into the garage, she had made exactly zero new ornaments and the thumb and index fingers on both of her hands were almost raw from the hundreds of times she had snapped them while simultaneously imagining she was changing into fairy form. Sadly, it appeared that while imagining along with finger snapping might be enough to make a fairy invisible to humans, it was not enough to transform a half-fairy into fairy form.

"Help me with these, will you?" Mindy called to Kelly as she came in from the garage, which was right off the kitchen. Mindy was carrying three enormous paper grocery bags that completely blocked her face. Kelly was amazed how her mother managed to navigate without falling down. As they unloaded the groceries, Kelly examined her mother's face. Mindy was thirty-eight years old but didn't look a day over thirty. She was short, now about three inches shorter than Kelly, and she had curly brown hair that reached her shoulders. She had big, brown, deer-like eyes and a round face that gave an innocent, cherubic look. Kelly had always envisioned her mother as someone incapable of guile and deceit. As she handed Mindy a jar of peanut butter from one of the bags, she thought that that moment was as good as any other to try to get some information about her father.

"Did my father like peanut butter?"

"What?" Mindy laughed nervously.

"Just, seeing that jar of peanut butter made me wonder if my father liked peanut butter. Is there something wrong with that?"

"No, of course not. It's just you haven't asked about your father in years." Mindy put the peanut butter into a cabinet and proceeded to sort some frozen dinners from another bag. Kelly waited.

"You didn't answer my question," she said.

Mindy opened the freezer, appearing distracted. "He liked it all right."

"Did he like ice cream?"

"Sure." Mindy was now pushing a frozen dinner violently, trying to squeeze it into a space that was too small.

"What was his favorite flavor?"

"I don't remember."

"Do you remember what his favorite food was?"

Mindy had gotten frustrated with the frozen dinner, and instead of continuing to force it into the freezer she flung it into the refrigerator section. "I don't know. He liked all sorts of things." Mindy had started to rub her head like she had a headache.

"Did my father really die in a fire?" Kelly blurted out.

"Excuse me?" Mindy had an expression of supreme surprise on her face.

"You heard me. I also want to know if he was really a surgeon like you said he was."

Mindy's face got very red and she clenched her fists at her sides. For a moment Kelly thought her mother was about to shout at her, but when Mindy finally did speak she spoke in a quiet, steely tone. "I can't believe I just heard that come out of your mouth."

"Why? It's perfectly natural for someone to want to know the truth."

Mindy put up a hand to silence her daughter. "This conversation is over." She promptly turned and stiffly exited the room.

The exchange hadn't gone as well as Kelly had hoped, but she knew her mother had to be lying and she would keep asking about her father until she got some answers. She didn't feel like making any Christmas tree ornaments at the moment so instead she went out for a walk. It was a hot and humid day and as cars drove by the exhaust fumes hung in the air. Kelly's neighborhood was just a few blocks away from a main road with lots of shops and restaurants that were frequented by locals and tourists alike. As she walked by all of the stores she concentrated on the muscles between her shoulder blades, trying to contract and release them over and over again. There weren't that many people about because it was a Tuesday and most of the adults were working. After about half an hour she arrived at her favorite café on the street, ordered a lemonade and sat by the window for a rest. She reached back to massage the muscles between her shoulder blades. She could barely reach them with the tips of her fingers.

Something outside the café caught her eye. A man was sitting hunched over on the bench beside the window. Kelly thought the man might be homeless, since he was wearing a beaten up trench coat, his hair was decidedly greasy, and he was resting one arm protectively over a half-full black garbage bag. The sight of the homeless man was not particularly peculiar. Instead it was what was with the homeless man that was odd. Kelly could see the ghost-like form of a fairy circling the man's head. But this fairy didn't look happy like Bubbles, Beatrix, or Carmina. He was scrawny and his pasty skin contrasted sharply with his dark brown wings. He wore drab pants and a shirt with one of the sleeves torn off. The fairy was holding a tiny jar in one hand and a twisted stick in the other, and as he circled the man's head he kept poking the stick in the man's direction and then moving the tip of the stick over the top of the jar. He repeated this motion again and again. First he pointed the stick at the man's head and then he dragged it back over the top of the jar. After a few moments Kelly saw that the jar was filling up with a faint mist. She squinted and thought she could just make out a tiny hint of the mist drifting away from the man's head when the fairy pointed his stick at it. What was the fairy doing? Was he hurting the man? Kelly debated whether she should get up and do something. The man didn't look like he was suffering from the fairy's actions, however, and she didn't feel like acting like a crazy person by storming out of the café and shouting at a fairy no one else could see.

It didn't take the fairy long to realize he was being watched. He stopped circling the man's head and looked around suspiciously. He pulled a cork out of his pocket and sealed the jar. His eyes met Kelly's. He kept eye contact with her and flew a little to the left, then a little to the right. Kelly kept looking at him. When he realized that her eyes kept following him, which meant she could see him, he hastily pocketed his stick and zoomed off into the distance.

Kelly lay awake that night waiting for the fairies to arrive. Mindy had been in her room since Kelly got back home and for all Kelly knew her mother hadn't left it since their argument. Kelly had only eaten a ham and cheese sandwich for dinner. After several hours of staring at the ceiling she heard a knock on her window. She opened it and in flew Bubbles, Beatrix, and Carmina. They were disappointed that she hadn't figured out how to transform herself yet, but after a little coaxing from Beatrix Bubbles allowed them to use another pinch of his precious fairy dust. Once in fairy form Kelly managed to hover in the air for a whole five seconds by contracting the muscles between her shoulder blades as hard and as fast as she could. But she could only manage about ten repetitions before her muscles gave out.

"That was excellent," Carmina said, but Kelly was still disappointed.

"You'll be flying like us in no time," Beatrix said.

Kelly described the fairy she had seen earlier and how he had been filling his jar with mist that seemed to be coming from the old homeless man's head. The fairies' faces all became quite somber at the telling.

"Had to be one of them Miasmonians," Bubbles said.

Beatrix shivered. "Unnatural they are."

"Miasmonians?"

"Followers of Miasmos," Carmina said.

"Who's Miasmos?"

"He's *unnatural*," Beatrix said.

Kelly looked at them blankly. "Miasmos is a fairy," Carmina explained. "He lives deep underground in the metro system with his followers. No fairy in their right mind would want to live so far underground, but his band keeps growing in number."

"Rumor has it he's practicing perversions of magic. They say he's stealing energy from fairies and even humans," Beatrix said, brushing a stray piece of bright red hair behind her ear. "And the last few months some fairies have gone missing and no one knows what happened to them." Beatrix started to cry and Carmina patted her on the arm.

"The gent she fancied was one of them that disappeared, but I think he just ran off with another lady," Bubbles whispered to Kelly.

"He did not run off! He loves me." Beatrix apparently had very sharp hearing. She proceeded to break down into full-fledged sobs.

"Why doesn't somebody stop him?" Kelly asked.

"Because nobody cares about us free fairies," Beatrix sniffled.

"Free fairies?"

"Fairies that aren't part of a fairy band," Carmina answered. She went on to explain how fairies traditionally lived in fairy groups called bands. She said that around the world there were hundreds of small fairy bands that ranged from 200 or 300 in number. Then there were a smaller number of large fairy bands. The closest large fairy band was right in the D.C. city limits, the Glendenians, who had around 4,000 members. Carmina wasn't sure how many other large bands there were but she guessed there were close to a million fairies in the US alone, although at least half of them had retreated to national parks and other sparsely populated regions of wilderness in order to avoid all contact with humans. While most fairies preferred the structure and camaraderie of a fairy band, there were those who had chosen to leave their bands for one reason or the other, and those who had been banished. These free fairies and their children lived alone or in small family groups, living off of nature or scrounging from humans. Bubbles, Beatrix, and Carmina were all children of free fairies and had never lived in a fairy band. They, like other free fairies, had limited dealings with banded fairies but sometimes did interact with them to buy things like fairy dust or other items that were hard for free fairies to come by on their own.

"Free fairies enjoy the ability to do what they want to do, but they also lack the protection provided by a band. A band like the Glendenians is unlikely to get involved in issues affecting free fairies, unless they see a threat to the band," Carmina concluded.

"And up to this point the Glendenians don't see the Miasmonians as a threat because the Miasmonians haven't made any attacks on the Glendenians," Bubbles interjected.

"And they don't believe us," Beatrix said. "They think we're making up stories."

"But don't they see the Miasmonians stealing energy from humans when they go out?" Kelly asked.

"No. They are very sneaky and generally hide when they sense other fairies about. The reason you must have seen one is because it thought you were human so didn't bother to hide," Bubbles said. "If you'd been in fairy form it most likely would have avoided you."

"Unless it wanted to kidnap you," Beatrix said.

"There's no proof anyone's been kidnapped," Bubbles said. Beatrix's face scrunched up immediately and she lunged for Bubbles. Bubbles jumped into the air and soon there was a blur of wings and limbs as Beatrix flew up and tackled him. After the initial impact they fell down to the floor in a clump with Beatrix on top. Carmina and Kelly ran to the edge of the bed and looked down at them. Beatrix was pinning Bubbles down.

"Take it back, take it back!" she shouted at him.

Bubbles just glared at her. Beatrix reached into Bubbles's cloth bag and pulled out the thin wooden stick he had used to explode the grape the night Kelly and he had met. Beatrix pointed one end of the stick at Bubbles's face. "I said, take it back."

"All right, all right. I take it back."

Beatrix got off of Bubbles but she kept his stick. Holding it in her hand she flew back up to the bed to join Kelly and Carmina.

"Give me back my wand," Bubbles called up from where he was still sprawled out on the floor. Beatrix ignored him.

"Can I see it?" Kelly asked. Beatrix handed the wand to Kelly.

"It looks like a toothpick," Kelly said.

"It is a toothpick," Carmina said. "He stole it from the deli down the street."

"But it's a magic toothpick?"

Carmina laughed. "Not in itself. But using a wand, like a toothpick or sticks or other pointed objects, can help channel and direct fairy powers."

"Bubbles has become a little too reliant on his though. He thinks he can't do any magic without it except for making himself invisible," Beatrix said.

"I want my wand," Bubbles wailed. They ignored him and Kelly tried to fly again. She managed another five seconds in the air before the fairy dust wore off.

The next morning when Kelly came down to the kitchen for breakfast she found a perfectly visible Bubbles sound asleep on top of the kitchen counter. She poked him with her finger. He let out a loud snore and rolled over. She poked him harder. He jolted awake.

"That hurt," he complained.

"What are you doing here?"

"Beatrix and I are still fighting. I didn't want to sleep at home."

"You should be more careful about where you sleep. My mother could walk in here any minute and see you."

Bubbles realized he wasn't currently invisible to humans. "That's easy to fix." He snapped his fingers and became transparent. "What's for breakfast?" he asked, hovering behind Kelly's shoulder as she poured herself some cereal. She sliced a banana and handed Bubbles a piece. After breakfast Bubbles accompanied Kelly to the living room where the pile of supplies for Christmas tree ornaments beckoned. Kelly plopped down on the sofa and started to work on the ornaments. Bubbles was attracted by the container of green glitter on the table. He reached his hand into the container and pulled out a fistful of glitter. He threw it into the air and it fell down to the ground like confetti.

"Don't touch that," Kelly said. Bubbles giggled and reached for another handful. Kelly snatched the container out of his grasp and set it on the far side of the table.

"I mean it."

"Fine." Bubbles flew over to the remote control for the TV and turned it on.

Melanie Johnson's overly made-up face grinned from the screen. "Yesterday was an interesting day in Washington. Senator Greg Allen, until recently considered the democratic frontrunner for the US presidential nomination, engaged in a war of words with his young challenger, thirty-six-year-old entrepreneur Marcos Witherings. Senator Allen was unable to maintain his reserve in the face of sharp attacks from Witherings, and the latest opinion polls show that Marcos Witherings now has a five-point lead among democrats."

As Melanie's voice continued to speak about the details of the exchange between the two men, a visual of the men talking to each other came on the screen. The visual went to a close-up of the man Kelly knew had to be Marcos Witherings. He was much younger than the other man and he was quite handsome. He had dark black hair that couldn't possibly get any blacker and he was very tall. His eyes were a cool grey, almost silver. A little on the skinny side, he still held himself in a way that suggested great strength in his muscles.

"Look!" Bubbles exclaimed. Kelly immediately saw what Bubbles was reacting to. Two fairies had just entered the frame and taken up positions in the air on either side of the young businessman. The fairies were the strangest looking fairies Kelly had ever seen, but admittedly she had only ever seen four fairies. They looked like moving gargoyles. Their skin and wings were a stony grey color, and the greyness of their bodies was enhanced by the fact that they were in their ghostly transparent forms so that none of the surrounding humans could see them.

"Ugly buggers," Bubbles said.

"Do a lot of fairies look like that?" Kelly asked. Bubbles shrugged.

"What do you think they're doing there?" she asked.

"Haven't the faintest."

"Who are you talking to?" Mindy's voice startled both Kelly and Bubbles. Kelly looked over her shoulder to see her mother standing in the doorway leading from the kitchen to the living room.

"I didn't say anything, you must have heard the TV."

"Oh," Mindy said. Kelly turned back to the table and saw that Bubbles had started to creep towards the container of glitter. She gave him a warning look as her mother sat down next to her.

"Kelly, I feel badly about our argument yesterday," Mindy said.

"If you're expecting an apology you're going to be disappointed," Kelly said. Her mother looked hurt at these words and Kelly almost felt bad. Just almost. Mindy took a deep breath.

"It's really me who should be apologizing. You were right." Mindy paused. Bubbles had flown up behind Mindy and started making silly faces at Kelly over her mother's shoulder. Kelly did her best to ignore him.

"Go on," Kelly said.

"I haven't been honest with you about your father. But you have to understand I was trying to protect you." Mindy looked like she was about to cry. Bubbles found this statement intriguing. He stopped making funny faces and listened intently.

"It's okay mom. I won't think less of you whatever it is. I just need to know the truth."

"All right." Mindy smoothed out the edge of the robe she was wearing. "I thought it would be easier for you to believe that your father was dead, that he had been a good man but that he had died. And I wanted to believe it too. I didn't want to face the truth."

"What?" Kelly asked, feeling nervous.

"I don't know who your father was."

That was not the answer Kelly had been expecting. "How can you not know?"

"I went to the doctor for a routine checkup to get my teacher's license and he told me I was pregnant. I had him do the test again because I thought it was a mistake. I wasn't married; I didn't even have a boyfriend. I didn't know how it had happened." Mindy paused again and looked like she didn't want to go on. Kelly moved closer to Mindy and patted her shoulder reassuringly.

"Please understand. I felt ashamed, and embarrassed. And I didn't want you to have to deal with that. Not being able to say anything when people asked you about your father. So I moved to a new town where no one knew me and I told everyone that my husband had died in a fire. When you were born that's what I told you too. I'm sorry. I hope some day you can forgive me."

Kelly searched her mother's face for any signs of deceit but only saw remorse and sadness. She decided to believe her mother.

"It's okay mom," she said. They hugged. Kelly looked around for Bubbles but realized he was no longer in the room.

"So what are you watching?" Mindy asked Kelly, indicating the TV.

"Nothing."

"Mind if I change the channel?"

"Not at all."

If Kelly hadn't been so preoccupied with thoughts about her father, she soon would have regretted letting her mother pick the channel because Mindy selected a documentary program on the artistic process. It was an incredibly boring series of talking heads in front of garish plastic sculptures and abstract paintings. But Kelly wasn't paying any attention to the TV. She was thinking about the conversation she'd just had with her mother. Why couldn't Mindy remember who Kelly's father was? Could she have been drunk or under some sort of a spell? Kelly didn't want to believe that. She knew there had to be a reasonable explanation. And she felt a strange feeling of butterflies in her stomach at another prospect – that her father could still be alive. If he was, where was he? Kelly suddenly missed her father more than she ever had before because now he wasn't a ghost; he was real. Knowing that her real, living father could be out there somewhere was almost more painful than believing he was dead. There was no way a dead person could be with his family. But a living person had a choice. Why hadn't her father ever come to see her? Did he even know she existed? In spite of these uncertainties Kelly felt a twinge of hope. Meeting her father was no longer an impossible fantasy. Instead it was a real possibility – if only she knew how to find him.

Kelly's attention was suddenly drawn back to the TV by the words of one of the artists speaking about his work. The artist was a potter who had just been asked by the interviewer how he was able to get the exact same strange shape of pottery on the pottery wheel over and over again. The artist said he just remembered how it had felt the first time and then he tried to find that feeling again. Something clicked in Kelly's mind when she heard these words. That was the key. Until that moment she had been merely visualizing, imagining the transformation into fairy form. Perhaps instead she had to focus on the feeling, the physical sensation – how it felt to be transformed into a fairy. Kelly raced up to her room, leaving a bewildered Mindy behind.

She sat on her bed and closed her eyes, putting all of her attention into trying to recreate the feeling of transformation. She focused on her toes and tried to imagine they were tingling. After about ten minutes she felt a tingling in her toes. Then she tried to get her fingers to tingle too. It was working. She felt a surge of anticipation. But after almost an hour she had only succeeded in getting the tingling to travel from her feet up to her knees and from her fingertips up to her elbows. At the knees and elbows the tingling got stuck. She wasn't discouraged though because she was sure this was indeed the way to transform herself into fairy form. Like flying, it must just take some practice to perfect.

A few minutes later the phone rang. It was Stephanie.

"Where have you been? I've been lonely," Stephanie began.

"Sorry, my mom's keeping me busy with making ornaments."

"Is that all? You sound different. Distracted."

"I don't think so," Kelly said. She wasn't sure she was ready to tell Stephanie about being a half-fairy.

"Come on, I know you. Something's going on."

"All right. Ask your parents if you can come spend the night tonight and I'll tell you." The fairies had said they would be back again that night. Kelly hoped they wouldn't mind if Stephanie was there too.

That afternoon when the doorbell rang Kelly was expecting to see Stephanie with her sleeping bag. Instead she found herself face to face with two men in suits and dark sunglasses. Both of the men had huge chests and arms. Kelly wondered if they were on steroids. One of the men had a twisted nose that looked as though it had been broken many times. The other man had a delicate, almost girlish face that contrasted comically with his massive frame.

"Kelly Brennan?" the man with the twisted nose asked.

"Who's asking?" Kelly answered, unnerved by the men's sudden appearance and impassive expressions.

"I'm Agent Crisp, this is Agent Grimes. We're Homeland Security." Both men flashed their badges.

Mindy had heard the doorbell as well and arrived just in time to hear Crisp say Homeland Security.

"How may we help you gentlemen?" Mindy asked.

"I'm afraid your daughter's going to have to come with us," Crisp said. Kelly felt her mouth go dry and her heart start to beat faster.

"There must be some mistake," Mindy said.

"We don't make mistakes Ma'am," Crisp answered coolly. Grimes stood like a statue beside him. Kelly could tell he was staring at her from behind his sunglasses even though she couldn't see his eyes.

"What's she accused of?" Mindy demanded, gripping Kelly protectively by the arm.

"I'm not at liberty to discuss that Ma'am."

"Not at liberty to discuss it? You want me to let you take my fourteen-year-old daughter away with you and you can't tell me why?"

"We're not asking for your permission."

Grimes stepped forward through the doorway towards Kelly. Mindy moved to stand in between him and her daughter. Kelly considered making a break for the back door. She started to take small steps backwards.

"Ma'am, I need you to step aside," Grimes said to Mindy.

"You're not taking my daughter anywhere until I verify you're who you say you are and you tell me exactly what's going on."

"Ma'am, I'm going to ask you one more time to step aside." Grimes's voice had taken on a clearly menacing tone.

"I will not."

"Then you leave me no choice," Grimes said. In a blur of motion he reached out and hit Mindy in the face. She fell to the ground.

Kelly screamed as she saw her mother fall down unconscious. Grimes had knocked Mindy out with one blow. He stepped over Mindy's limp form and headed for Kelly. Kelly turned and ran for the back door. She heard heavy footsteps behind her. She reached the back door and had just clasped her hand around the doorknob when she felt strong arms grab her from behind, pinning her arms to her sides. She screamed and kicked but Grimes

39

didn't let go. A few seconds later Crisp appeared, and while Grimes continued to hold her Crisp pulled a tiny bottle and a little square cloth out of his pocket. He placed a few drops of liquid onto the cloth and pressed the cloth to Kelly's nose. Kelly knew it must be some sort of drug to make her go to sleep. She held her breath and after a short time closed her eyes and went limp, pretending to pass out. Crisp must have suspected she was pretending because he kept the cloth pressed to her nose even after she had gone limp. She held her breath until her lungs started to burn – but finally she had to take a breath. She was aware of a prickling in her nose and a smell similar to rubbing alcohol before she was plunged into unconsciousness.

Chapter 3
The Offer

    The first thing Kelly became aware of was the smell. It smelled like stale dust and a hint of mildew. She felt groggy and her head was pounding. She opened her eyes. The flickering fluorescent light above her buzzed softly. She realized she was lying on a small cot. She looked to her left and saw a wall of cement blocks. In front of her, past her feet, was a large metal door. The door had a small grate near the top that someone could look through and what looked like a wide mail slot near the bottom – maybe for passing in food trays. The room was perhaps ten feet by ten feet. There was a curtain in the far corner to Kelly's right. It was pulled to the side and behind it the corner of a toilet was visible.
    Kelly sat up slowly as to not jar her head too much. She remembered how Mindy had been knocked out. It made her feel sick. She hoped her mother was all right. Kelly moved to the door and peeked out through the grate near the top. All she could see was a wall of cement blocks about six feet away – the other side of a hallway.
    "Hello?" she called through the grate. No answer. She called again. Nothing. Frustrated, she sat back down on the cot. She tried to recall all of the details from the previous night. At least she thought it had been the previous night. She had no idea how long she had been drugged and her cell had no windows. The only illumination was provided by the buzzing fluorescent light, so it could have even been the dead of night for all she knew.

She remembered how Crisp had held the cloth over her nose until she had passed out. She cringed at the memory. Their actions didn't match her idea of how government agents should act, unless maybe they were dealing with highly dangerous criminals. But she wasn't dangerous. Had they somehow found out she had been talking to fairies? Did they know she was a half-fairy? Did they even know about fairies? Were they even really from Homeland Security? Kelly's mind was swimming under the weight of all of these questions. She felt a wave of anger and indignation sweeping up inside of her. She went back to the door and started banging on it with her fist.

"I need to speak with someone right now!" she shouted. She stopped banging on the door for a minute to listen but she heard only silence from the hallway. She kept pounding on the door with her fists until bruises started to form on the edges of her hands. After that she started kicking. Finally she heard footsteps in the hallway and was soon confronted with Crisp's eyes and twisted nose looking down on her through the grate.

"What's all this ruckus?" he asked.

"Um, I want to know why I'm being kept here," Kelly stammered.

"You'll find out soon enough," he answered and started to move away from the door.

"Wait – you can't just keep me here without telling me why," Kelly yelled through the grate. Crisp's eyes and crooked nose appeared again.

"Young lady, you aren't exactly in the position to tell us what we can and can't do now, are you?"

Kelly didn't answer.

"That's what I thought. Now I don't want to hear as much as a peep from this cell, or you're going to be punished. Do you understand me?" Judging from how easily Crisp's buddy Grimes had thrown her mother violently to the ground, Kelly had no doubt that he was making a very real threat. She decided it was best not to press him for any more information at the moment.

"Do you understand?" Crisp repeated. Kelly nodded. "Good," he said. Then his face disappeared from view and Kelly heard his footsteps echoing back down the hallway.

Kelly examined the bars of the grate more closely. There were four bars, each about two inches apart. Maybe if she were in fairy form – but no, there really wasn't enough space between the bars. She bent down to examine the oversized mail slot. It was a rectangular hole in the metal, with a metal flap hanging over it from the other side. It was one foot wide and three inches high. *That's more like it*, Kelly thought. She pushed the metal flap with her finger, hoping it wasn't locked from the other side. It wasn't. It swung out easily under the pressure of her finger. This slot was big enough. If only she could successfully get into fairy form she would have a chance of escape.

After several hours of practice Kelly still couldn't get the tingling sensations to go past her elbows or above her knees. She was growing increasingly frustrated and frightened. She had no idea what was in store for her and her imagination was crafting more threatening scenarios by the minute. Maybe the government knew she was a half-fairy and wanted to study her like a lab rat. Maybe they were going to pump her full of needles and noxious drug cocktails. She had never felt more alone or helpless and she didn't like the feeling one bit.

At some point during her transformation attempts someone had pushed a plastic bag containing a peanut butter and jelly sandwich and a juice box through the slot in the door. Kelly had initially ignored the food in favor of practicing, but hunger pains were now nagging at her. She gave in and started to eat the sandwich. As she ate her mind drifted to the last time she and her mother had made peanut butter and jelly sandwiches. It had been almost three weeks ago, before she had discovered that she was a half-fairy. She almost wished she had never found out, but only for a split second. Discovering she was a half-fairy was the most amazing thing that had happened in her life so far. She only wished that it hadn't led to this. She was sure her being kidnapped had something to do with fairies. But what, she had no idea. She could only imagine how her mother must be feeling now – how worried she must be. Then Kelly thought about Stephanie. Had she arrived to spend the night to find Kelly's mother still unconscious on the floor? Kelly shivered. She finished her sandwich and started to practice flexing her back muscles. If she did finally figure out how to transform herself into fairy form it would be helpful to be able to fly.

She was somewhere dark and damp. The air around her was cool. She could hardly see more than a few feet in front of her as she flew cautiously down an arched tunnel made of old bricks. A faint blue light filled the archway at the end of the passageway in the distance. She approached the light, drawn to it like a magnet. Something in the back of her mind was telling her no – telling her to turn back, but she couldn't. She kept moving towards the light. As she moved closer she realized she was passing through a thin, cold fog that was tinted the same blue color as the light at the end of the passageway. The fog got thicker and thicker as she approached the light. She was almost there – she could feel it – but then she felt a searing pain on her right wing and she was falling down and down and down. Finally she smacked into the ground. Little black dots appeared around the edge of her vision and started to creep inward. Before everything went black she saw two pairs of eyes above her, glowing eerily in the darkness. One pair of eyes was a silvery grey color, like stone. The other pair was a piercing blue, like the light in the hallway. A piercing blue that held a cold like ice.

Kelly awoke at the sound of something clanging through the slot in the door. This time it was canned peaches and canned soup. She had to struggle to keep from gagging at the room-temperature vegetable chunks in the soup, but she knew she had to eat. She would need all her strength when she tried to escape. The next several days passed in much the same way as the first. She spent all of her time trying to transform and exercising her back muscles, punctuated by eating the packaged food sent through the door slot and taking fitful naps. She wasn't sure how long she had been held so far, but she thought it was maybe three or four days, judging by how many meals she had received. She wasn't making as much progress with the transformation as she had hoped. While she had succeeded in getting the tingles to move from her elbows up to her head and then down to her bellybutton, she was still unable to get the tingles to progress from her knees up to her waist. She was lying flat on the floor, a new position of the several she had tried, when she heard footsteps approach and stop outside her door. She didn't move at first, thinking it was merely another food delivery, but then there was a loud clang as the door was unlocked and opened. Kelly jumped to her feet.

"Follow me," Crisp said, "and you best behave."

Kelly reluctantly followed him down the hallway, up some stairs, and down a few more hallways. She tried to take mental notes of all the different turns they made but she soon lost track. Although they were in a large building, she saw or heard no signs of anyone else's presence. "Where are we going?" Kelly asked. Crisp didn't answer. After a few more stairways and a few more cement-block hallways they reached a large metal door. Crisp knocked on the door – three fast knocks followed by four slower knocks. The door opened and Kelly saw Grimes on the other side. He motioned for Kelly to enter, then instead of staying inside with her he went outside to join Crisp, closing the door behind Kelly. She looked around the room. It was a square room, cement like everywhere else in the place, but it was about three times as large as Kelly's cell. A large rectangular wooden table sat in the center of the room. There were also two wooden chairs, one on either side of the table. The room reminded Kelly of interrogation rooms she had seen on TV police dramas. She walked over to the table, sat in the chair facing the door, and waited. She had a feeling someone must be coming to ask her some questions.

She didn't have to wait long. A few minutes later the door opened once again and in walked a man Kelly instantly recognized. But she hadn't ever met him before. Rather, she had seen him on TV – seen him making his opponent, a respected senator, look like a fool. The man was Marcos Witherings, the frontrunner for the democratic presidential nomination. He was dressed exactly as he had been on television, in a sharp black suit and a silver tie, and he was accompanied once again by the transparent forms of two gargoyle-like fairies.

Marcos Witherings sat down in the chair across from Kelly and placed his hands, fingers interlaced, on the table. His face gave away no expression and he merely scrutinized her with his cold grey eyes. Kelly shifted nervously in her seat. After a few moments one of the gargoyle-like fairies, the one who had been hovering by Marcos Witherings's right ear, darted towards Kelly and flew right at her face. Kelly ducked just in time to avoid a collision and the fairy flew past her. The fairy circled back and was about to fly at her face again when Marcos Witherings finally spoke.

"Murk, heel," he commanded. His voice was deep but raspy at the same time, as if he had smoked for many years. Kelly would have expected such a voice to come from a wizened old man, not a young man in his prime. The fairy immediately darted back to resume his position beside his master's right ear. Meanwhile a slight smile had appeared on Witherings's face.

"So it is true then, you are a fadaman. Otherwise you wouldn't be able to see Murk or Lurk," Witherings's voice rasped. The fairy on Witherings's left, who had remained motionless since Witherings had sat down, perked up at the sound of his name and flew to sit on Witherings's shoulder. Witherings lifted a hand absent-mindedly and patted the fairy's knee. Kelly waited for him to say something else. Again he was quiet for a long time and Kelly grew increasingly uncomfortable because she couldn't tell what he was thinking. Just as Kelly finally got up the nerve and was going to ask him why she had been kidnapped, he spoke again.

"I suppose you're wondering why you are here," he said. "You see, you and I, we're special. There are very few of our kind, the fadamen – half-human, half-fairy." Kelly felt her mouth drop open with surprise. One of the frontrunners for the US presidential election was a half-fairy? "What, you didn't notice my unusually pointed ears?" he asked. Kelly shook her head.

"There are very few of our kind because fairies know, and when humans used to know about fairies they knew as well, that fadamen are dangerous beings. Dangerous because we have the strengths of both species and few of the weaknesses. We have the thick skin of humans yet we possess ancient magic in great quantities. Thus very few would take the risk of bringing a fadaman into the world. Yet, here we are..." Witherings's voice drifted off and he got a faraway look in his eyes. Murk, the fairy who had flown at Kelly's face before, had grown tired of hovering in the air and perched himself on Marcos Witherings's right shoulder. Both fairies were staring at Kelly curiously. It was unnerving.

"You-er-were going to tell me why I'm here?" Kelly asked. Witherings gave a start, sending the two gargoyle-like fairies up into the air again.

"Oh yes. You are here because my father Miasmos and I want to make you an offer. We want you to join us."

"Join you in what?"

Witherings looked like he couldn't believe his ears. "World domination of course. Power, riches, pleasures beyond your wildest dreams, et cetera. What else could it be?"

This guy is completely insane, Kelly thought. "If you help us," Witherings continued, "you can enjoy all of those things."

"And if I don't help you?"

"Then you will stay here until you decide you would like to enjoy them," Witherings answered coolly.

"I see," Kelly said. This wasn't looking good.

"Now, let's see your fairy form."

Kelly felt her cheeks growing hot. "I haven't been able to transform without fairy dust yet."

Witherings raised his eyebrows. "Is that so? Lurk, dust her please would you?"

Lurk excitedly reached into the tattered grey knapsack that was strung over his shoulder and pulled out a jar of fairy dust. He grabbed a handful and sprinkled it on Kelly's nose. Kelly knew immediately that this fairy dust was stronger than Bubbles's fairy dust had been. The tingling in her toes and fingers started out much more intensely and progressed through her body much more rapidly. In less than a second the tingling had reached the spot behind her belly button and pressure had started to build there. Again just as she felt like her belly was about to burst, the pressure suddenly gave way to a swirling feeling. A second later she was standing on the seat of her chair instead of sitting in it, the table top was about a forearm's length above the top of her head, and all of her clothes had magically shrunk and opened up a space for her wings to come out of as they had before. Just after the transformation was complete, a fairy clad in a miniature black suit and silver tie swooped down do join her. In fairy form Marcos Witherings was strangely bulky. It was as though being in human form somehow stretched and thinned him out. As Kelly looked at him now his limbs were much thicker – he looked like a body builder. His wings were a metallic silver that resembled the silver threads in Kelly's wings, but in his case the entire area of his wings shone like fairy dust. Murk and Lurk arrived at her chair and stood behind Witherings, peering around him to get a better look at Kelly.

"Let's see them," he said, flapping his wings a few times. Kelly didn't wish to comply but she didn't see what else she could do at the moment. She rolled her shoulders as far forward as she could and then snapped them back in one swift motion.

"Interesting, very interesting," he said, reaching out a hand to feel the tip of her left wing. It tickled slightly when he touched it.

"Now, let's see some magic," he said. Kelly stared at him blankly.

"Set this on fire." He took off his tie and placed it on the seat of the chair between them.

"I don't know how," she said.

"Don't play dumb with me."

"I'm not."

"All right, if that's how you want to be." Witherings pulled a thin crystal rod out of his jacket pocket. He pointed it at Kelly. "I'll make you show your magic." With a flick of his wrist an electric current blasted from the glass rod and shot through the air towards Kelly. Before she could get out of the way she felt a searing pain as the sparks hit her shoulder.

"Ow!" She looked down at her shoulder and saw that the current had burnt a hole in her shirt and the skin inside the hole had reddened slightly.

Witherings flicked his wrist again and another bolt of electricity flew from his wand and hit her other shoulder. This time the pain was even more intense and when she looked down she saw that the electricity had actually burnt her skin instead of just reddening it.

"Are you going to keep pretending you can't defend yourself until you don't have any skin left?" With another flick of his wrist Witherings shot another bolt. This time it hit Kelly's right knee. She fell down clutching her knee. Witherings smirked and lifted his wand again but just then there was a knock on the door. Witherings paused for a moment, thinking, then flicked his wand in Kelly's direction. Kelly winced, expecting another searing jolt, but instead she felt the familiar tingling start in her toes and then in her fingers. A few seconds later she was back in human form. So was Witherings. He put the now foot-long glass rod back into his jacket pocket.

"We'll continue this discussion later," he said. He turned and left the room, Murk and Lurk flying dutifully behind him.

Kelly limped on the way back to her cell behind Crisp, who hadn't even glanced a second time at the holes in her shirt and pants when he had come to take her back to her cell. Both of Kelly's shoulders ached and her knee was pounding with every step. When she got back to her cell she threw herself down on the bed and fell asleep almost instantly, too exhausted to contemplate her plight any further.

Chapter 4
Transformation

Kelly thought she felt something brush her face. Still half-asleep, she lifted her hand to scratch her cheek. She felt it again. She scratched her cheek a second time and rolled over onto her more tender shoulder. This movement caused a sharp pain and she sat up, now fully awake.

"About time," she heard a familiar voice say. She looked up to see Bubbles hovering above her.

"What are you doing? How did you get in here?"

"Through there." Bubbles pointed to the slot near the bottom of the door. "Bit of a squeeze though, wasn't designed for fairies. But no time for talk, no time. I've come to help you escape."

"How did you find me?" Kelly asked.

"Fairy senses. See when you disappeared a few days ago we got nothing. But today I felt you were in great danger, sensed it I did. So we followed my fairy senses and they brought us right here. Well, they brought me right here. Carmina and Beatrix are waiting on the roof. But come on, we must hurry. They might be back any moment." Bubbles fumbled in his bag and pulled out his jar of fairy dust. He hesitated for a moment before pouring almost half of the jar's contents onto Kelly's head. "That should last long enough to get us out of here," he said. Once in fairy form Kelly snapped her fingers and imagined being invisible. She knew she would only be half-invisible to humans, but something was better than nothing. They approached the door. The slot was just above Kelly's head as she stood under it. She reached up and laboriously pulled herself upwards, whilst Bubbles kept whispering *Hurry up, hurry, hurry up.* She managed to pull herself through the slot and into the hallway. Bubbles soon joined her and took the lead.

Kelly ran down the hallway, following Bubbles as he flew along in front of her. She wanted to save flying unless it was absolutely necessary, since she didn't think she would be able to go very fast or sustain it for long. They hurried as quietly as they could through the maze of cement hallways and corridors, up several different stairways. Kelly was amazed Bubbles could remember which way he had come. Suddenly Bubbles came to a stop beside a large air vent, which was about a foot and a half by a foot and a half. He tugged on the vent. It wouldn't budge.

"Are you sure this is the right vent?" Kelly whispered.

"Of course," he answered indignantly. He gave the vent another tug, this time so strong that when it came loose he was flung backwards by his own force. He slammed into the far wall of the corridor and dropped the vent, which clattered to the ground with a spectacularly loud clank that echoed down the empty hall. Kelly heard muffled voices from below and then heavy footfalls on the stairway leading up to their floor.

"Come on." Kelly pulled Bubbles to his feet and pushed him into the air duct. She looked up and was filled with a sense of dread. The air duct was round and about two feet in diameter. It was at least three stories high. Considering Kelly was now only about a foot tall, this distance was overwhelming. When she spread her arms out they failed to reach both sides of the cylinder. There was no way she was going to support herself on the walls and pull herself up. Bubbles, who was already in the air above her, seemed to be reading her mind.

"Grab my ankles and try to flap your wings at least a little bit because I don't know if I can carry you all the way up," he said. Kelly hastily complied. She clenched and unclenched the muscles between her shoulder blades as strongly and as fast as she could. They had only just managed to rise a couple of feet up when there was a loud thud from the bottom of the duct. Kelly chanced a look down and saw Crisp's face poking into the vent. It looked at first like he was going to retract his head without having seen them, but just as he was starting to pull back he stopped and squinted. He had seen Kelly's half-invisible form. He quickly pulled his head out of the duct and Kelly heard his steps pounding away as he ran down the hall for help. They quickened their pace, but Kelly couldn't make her wings beat much faster because her back muscles were already starting to cramp. A few seconds later there was a bigger problem. With still about a third of the way to go, Kelly felt the telltale tingling start in her fingers and toes.

"I need more fairy dust!"

Bubbles fumbled with his bag and pulled out the jar. The tingles had already united at Kelly's waist and the pressure was building.

"Hurry!"

Bubbles was having trouble opening the jar. He finally managed to uncork it – but it was too late. Just as he was reaching into the jar to retrieve a handful of dust, Kelly felt the change occur. She quickly pressed her legs and hands to the inside of the walls to prevent herself from falling down the duct. Somehow during this maneuver she knocked the jar of fairy dust out of Bubbles's hands. They both looked down at the fine, silvery powder wafting softly about in all directions. Bubbles scrambled to try to catch pieces of it as it fell, but Kelly knew he would never be able to collect enough before Crisp came back with support. Kelly closed her eyes and concentrated on the feelings in her fingers and toes. Maybe it was because she had so recently been in fairy form, or maybe all of her practicing had finally paid off, but this time she felt the intense tingles pass swiftly through her body. They were no longer blocked at the knee. She felt the pressure building behind her belly button and then she was falling down the duct, no longer supported by her limbs on the walls. So surprised she had actually succeeded in transforming herself, she hadn't thought to unfurl her wings and start beating them again. Luckily Bubbles caught her.

"Why couldn't you have transformed yourself before? Now I wasted all of that fairy dust for nothing." Bubbles pouted.

"Sorry Bubbles, but let's just concentrate on getting out of here, okay?" They began their ascent again. When they were near the end of the duct, at the point where it opened to the roof and bent sideways so that rain couldn't enter, Bubbles lifted a hand to signal for Kelly to stay and wait. He disappeared from view and a few seconds later reappeared, accompanied by Beatrix and Carmina. Beatrix waved energetically with a wide smile. Carmina jabbed Beatrix with her elbow, a stern expression on her face.

"There's two men out there," Carmina whispered. "Beatrix and I will go back out in a minute and distract them. Bubbles will stay at the grate and signal you when it's clear. Once you get out of the duct, fly up out of their reach and then we'll meet you," she instructed.

Kelly nodded. Beatrix patted her on the shoulder reassuringly. Kelly winced because her shoulder was still sore from when Witherings had zapped it.

"Sorry," Beatrix whispered.

"Let's go." With those words Carmina zoomed up and disappeared from view. Beatrix followed. A moment later Kelly heard the ensuing chaos from the roof.

"Get it off! Get it off!" a man yelled. Kelly recognized his voice as Crisp's.

"Get what off? There's nothing there," Grimes said.

"Ahhhhhh!" Kelly couldn't tell which one of the men had screamed, but whichever one it was, he was quite disturbed. Bubbles reappeared and waved to Kelly. She flew up to the grate and saw that a hole had been cut out of it. She peered through the hole to see that Crisp was running in circles and his backside was on fire. Grimes had taken off his jacket and was chasing Crisp with the aim of stifling the flames with it. Crisp was not thinking rationally, however, and kept running from Grimes. Neither of them had their eyes on the opening of the air duct. Beatrix and Carmina were flying around the men and giggling gleefully. The men couldn't hear their laughter.

Kelly flew through the hole and out into the open air. She pumped her wings hard and fast until she was at least ten feet above Grimes and Crisp. Beatrix, Carmina, and Bubbles flew up to join her. No longer with fairy influence so close by, Grimes finally succeeded in putting out the flames on Crisp. Crisp panted and tried to twist himself so that he could see his backside. He wasn't quite flexible enough to achieve this goal.

"How much more do I have to keep flying? I don't think I can keep it up much longer," Kelly said.

"We'll carry you," Carmina said.

Carmina and Bubbles each grabbed a hold of her under her armpits, while Beatrix flew underneath sustaining her feet. They flew away from the roof and over the street. Kelly recognized that they were still in the city and only about three miles away from her house. Turning to look over her shoulder, she saw that the building she had been held in didn't look any different from the surrounding buildings. If she hadn't known any better she would have thought it was an office building. It was true that the building's few windows were tinted like two-way mirrors, but she had seen many buildings with windows like that.

"Where are we going?" Kelly asked.

"Back to my house," Bubbles said.

"We can't go back there, don't you think they'll look for her there? You do live in the tree in her backyard," Carmina said.

"You live in the tree in my backyard?" Kelly asked. Bubbles nodded.

"We could go to your house," Beatrix said to Carmina.

"Okay," Carmina said.

During the flight, which took about twenty minutes, Beatrix incessantly asked questions. The fairies were quite angered by how Kelly had been captured and by how Grimes had punched Kelly's mother in the face. When Beatrix found out she had set Crisp's pants on fire, not Grimes's, she said she was irritated with herself. Kelly assured her that both of the men had deserved it. The fairies were even more indignant when Kelly told them about her meeting with Marcos Witherings.

"How dare he, if I get my hands on him I'll squash him like a pancake!" Bubbles said.

"No, you'd run and hide like a big baby," Beatrix said.

"Would not!" Bubbles shouted.

"Would too!"

"Cut it out you two," Carmina chided.

They started to descend from the air and Kelly recognized they were heading straight for Stephanie's house. "Hey, my best friend lives here," Kelly said.

"We know. I've lived here for a long time. One day I followed the Stephanie girl around because I was bored and she went to your house. You two were playing in the yard and that's how I met Beatrix and Bubbles," Carmina explained.

They set down on a branch of the large, old tree in Stephanie's backyard. There was a tree house in the tree, but Stephanie's mother had forbidden them to play in it ever since Stephanie had fallen from it and broken her wrist. Stephanie's mother had removed the ladder so there was no way for them to get up to the tree house even if they had wanted to.

Carmina pushed aside a piece of wood that had been blocking the tree house's doorway and Kelly followed the fairies inside. Carmina had clearly taken advantage of the vacant space. The interior looked just like a miniature human home. They were standing in the living room, which was the front half of the tree house. A wall had been put up to separate the front half from the back half and there were three doorways in the wall. All of the doorways were covered with cloth curtains.

Inside the living room there was a small table with six chairs around it, and Kelly thought they looked like they had come from a set for dolls. There was a sofa, an armchair, and a bookshelf with tiny books. The corner of the room held a small stove, refrigerator, and some cabinets. There was even a lamp that provided the room with a homey light. Kelly couldn't see any wires and wondered where the electricity was coming from.

"Do you like it?" Carmina asked.

"It's amazing," Kelly answered truthfully. She hadn't really known what to expect, but she hadn't been expecting everything to be so similar to a human house.

Just then a male fairy walked into the room from the far left doorway in the dividing wall. "This is my husband, Thomas," Carmina said. Thomas was a little taller than Carmina and very thin. His long brown hair was braided down his back and like Carmina he had blue eyes. He unfurled his wings, which were dull brown with a strangely fibrous texture, then reached out and shook Kelly's hand politely. He then folded his wings back down, retrieved a book from the bookshelf, and disappeared back behind the doorway from which he had come.

"He's shy," Carmina said.

Kelly wondered if fairies always showed their wings when they met someone new or if that was just a habit peculiar to Thomas.

"You sit down here on the sofa while I look for a salve for your burns," Carmina said. Kelly gratefully obliged, first folding her wings down on her back so they wouldn't take up too much room. Kelly felt tired and her back muscles, shoulders, and injured knee all ached. Beatrix joined Kelly on the sofa while Bubbles went straight for the refrigerator. He soon returned bearing a glass jar filled with a pale yellow liquid and three glasses. He poured some of the liquid into the glasses and handed one to Beatrix and one to Kelly. When Kelly's glass contacted her hand, its temperature surprised her.

"It's cold," she said.

"Of course, it was in the refrigerator," Bubbles answered.

"Where does the electricity come from?" Kelly asked.

"We use power cells, like batteries," Beatrix said.

"Try it." Bubbles indicated Kelly's glass.

Kelly raised the glass to her lips. First she smelt a flowery aroma, like a fresh flower. She tasted the liquid. It had a wonderful sweet taste – cool and light, yet she felt more energized just from a sip.

"It's called nectala. Kind of like beer, but better," Bubbles said.

"It doesn't taste much like beer," Kelly said. Mindy had let Kelly try a sip of beer a couple of months ago. She hadn't liked the bitter taste at all.

"Well, it has alcohol in it, and it's yellow," he replied.

"It has alcohol?"

"It's made from flower nectar and fermented corn, which contains some alcohol. If you drink more than a few glasses you might get tipsy," Beatrix said.

Moments later Carmina came back into the room with a small bottle of pink liquid. "Come on, this way," she said, motioning for Kelly to follow her. They passed through the third curtain of the dividing wall into a bathroom, complete with sink, toilet, and bathtub. Carmina started to draw a bath.

"The water is rainwater, stored inside the roots of the tree. We divert some of the water here. It's heated with the power from the main power cell for the house," Carmina explained. Carmina unscrewed the bottle of pink liquid and poured a capful into the bathtub. "You need to soak in this for half an hour. Then afterwards put one drop onto your hand and apply it directly to the burns."

"What is it?" Kelly asked.

"It's a healing tonic made from the nectar of a rare flower and charmed by powerful healers. Let me go find you some extra clothes."

Kelly felt much better after her bath. The healing tonic worked wonders on her burns. Her skin looked like it had been healing already for several days and it wasn't nearly as painful as it had been before. She put on the flowing pale green dress that Carmina had brought her. It fit perfectly. When she came out to the living room the fairies were all sitting at the table. They beckoned for her to join them and she sat down at the empty place between Bubbles and Beatrix. More nectala was served around and a steaming pot of an orange mush sat in the middle of the table. Carmina served heaping portions of the mush onto all of their plates. She then brought a bowl full of little off-white chunks over from the counter. She handed the bowl to Bubbles and he sprinkled some of the off-white pieces onto his mush. He passed the bowl to Kelly.

"They're pieces of cashew," he said in response to her apprehensive look.

"Oh." Kelly sprinkled a few on her plate and passed the bowl to Beatrix.

The mush had a texture similar to that of grits and a hearty, slightly sweet taste.

"Do you like it?" Carmina asked Kelly.

"Yes. What is it?"

"It has mashed up corn and carrots and a little bit of pumpkin," Carmina said. "Thomas made it."

"It's very good," Kelly said to Thomas. He blushed and stared down at his plate. After dinner, Carmina showed Kelly and Beatrix into the middle room, which was the guest room. Kelly and Beatrix would sleep there and Bubbles would sleep on the couch in the living room. Kelly lay down but couldn't fall asleep. What was she going to do now that she had escaped? She couldn't go home because surely they would be looking for her, but she couldn't just hide out here forever. She knew the fairies would probably be against it, but tomorrow she would go and speak to Stephanie. Stephanie might have an idea about what to do. Besides, there was no excuse not to visit Stephanie – considering Kelly was already in her friend's back yard. Kelly just hoped that Witherings's thugs wouldn't come looking for her at Stephanie's house. Feeling a little bit better at the prospect of seeing her best friend, Kelly drifted off into a dreamless sleep.

Chapter 5
A New Plan

The next morning Kelly awoke to the smell of something sweet being baked. Beatrix had already left the room. Kelly went out to the living room to find Thomas reaching into the oven to pull out a large loaf of orange bread. Kelly thought perhaps it had been made with the leftovers from the night before, and she also smelt a hint of banana. Bubbles was still asleep on the couch and snoring blissfully. Carmina and Beatrix were nowhere to be seen.

"Good morning," Thomas said. These were the first words Thomas had directed to Kelly. He seemed to be feeling a little more comfortable with her presence.

"Good morning," she answered. He motioned for her to sit down and served her a large piece of the freshly baked bread, along with some orange juice.

"Where are Beatrix and Carmina?" Kelly asked.

"They went to gather some things for lunch."

Kelly tasted the bread. "It's very good," she said. Thomas smiled quietly.

"I have a meeting to go to," Thomas said. "If Bubbles wakes up, make sure he leaves some bread for Carmina and Beatrix."

After Thomas left and Kelly finished her breakfast, she glanced furtively at Bubbles. He was still sound asleep and showing no signs of waking up anytime soon. Now was a perfect time to go and see Stephanie. Remembering what Thomas had said about the bread, Kelly cut a few pieces, wrapped them in a towel, and hid them inside one of the cabinets. This way if Bubbles ate all of the bread from the counter there would still be some left for Carmina and Beatrix. After stashing the pieces of bread away Kelly tiptoed to the door of the tree house.

Looking outside Kelly saw no sign of any fairies. There weren't any signs of movement coming from Stephanie's house either. That meant Stephanie and her parents were probably still sleeping. Kelly snapped her fingers to make herself half-invisible and flew down to the house. She flew around the house's perimeter, looking for a way to enter, but all of the doors and windows were securely locked. Snapping her fingers while imagining they were opening didn't work, and she didn't have any other ideas. Finally she decided she would ring the doorbell and try to sneak inside without being seen when the door was opened. Kelly rang the doorbell and quickly flew up to the top of the doorframe. After a few moments Stephanie's father, dressed in a bathrobe, opened the door. He leaned forward and looked about curiously but saw no one.

"Darn kids," he muttered. Then he noticed that the paper had been left on his doorstep and he bent to pick it up. As he bent down Kelly took the opportunity to fly through the door and rushed up the stairs towards Stephanie's room, staying close to the ceiling at all times. She was happy to discover that her back muscles were getting much stronger and they didn't feel that tired as she arrived at the door to Stephanie's room. The door was slightly ajar so Kelly walked right in. She saw Stephanie's blond hair poking out from beneath her bed covers. She decided it might be best to appear first in human form so Stephanie wouldn't be too surprised. Kelly envisioned the tingling sensations in her toes and fingers and again the sensations traveled quickly and easily through her body. Once Kelly had succeeded in transforming herself in the air duct, her body seemed to remember what to do and the change was now effortless.

Once in human form, Kelly quietly shut Stephanie's door and tiptoed to her bedside. She shook Stephanie to wake her up. Stephanie moaned and rolled over.

"Just a few more minutes Mom," Stephanie said.

"It's not your mother."

Stephanie sat upright with a start and stared at Kelly in disbelief. Kelly put her finger to her mouth to warn Stephanie to be quiet.

"Kelly? What are you doing here? How did you get here? I've been so worried, I was afraid you might be dead!" Stephanie reached out and hugged Kelly. "When I got to your house to spend the night your mother had a black eye and was crying and talking nonsense. It took her almost half an hour to get out that you'd been taken into custody by Homeland Security."

"How's my mother now?"

"She's calmed down a bit but not much. I went with her yesterday to Homeland Security Headquarters for the third time, but they just said they had no record of arresting you, and she threw such a fit they almost arrested her. She called them fascist pigs and threatened to go to the media. Later she actually called the news station but they declined to run the story because they said they needed evidence."

"I don't think the men who kidnapped me were really from Homeland Security."

"What? Then who were they?" Stephanie asked. "And what did they want with you?"

"What I'm about to tell you is going to sound crazy, but it's true," Kelly said.

"I'm all ears."

Stephanie listened intently as Kelly told the story from the beginning, starting with how she had found out she was a half-fairy. When Kelly got to the point of Bubbles exploding the grape on the floor of her kitchen, Kelly could tell from Stephanie's incredulous expression that she didn't believe her.

"You don't believe me do you," Kelly said.

"It is just a little unexpected," Stephanie admitted.

"All right, I'll show you. But you have to promise not to scream or anything because I don't want your parents to know I'm here, okay?"

Stephanie nodded. Kelly transformed herself into her fairy form, unfurled her wings, and flew around the room in a circle. Then she came back to her starting position and transformed back into human form. Stephanie sat with her mouth open in shock the entire time.

"Do you believe me now?" Kelly asked.

"So after he exploded the grape, then what happened?"

When Kelly had finished explaining everything up to the point of coming to the tree house in Stephanie's backyard, Stephanie got up and started to pace the room.

"This is bad," she finally said. "You can't go home, that's certain. You can't stay here for long either, because it's only a matter of time before they find out we're friends. You can't go anywhere in your human form because they probably have law enforcement looking for you, probably told them you were a criminal. Even worse is if these fairy senses you mentioned really exist, then we can't even be sure they don't already know exactly where you are. I mean, if Witherings is a powerful fadman—"

"Fadaman," Kelly corrected.

"Fadaman, sorry. If he is a powerful fadaman, he might be able to sense where you are. You have to wonder how he found out about you in the first place, right?"

Kelly hadn't thought about that. How had they known where she was?

"You have to go to the fairy police," Stephanie said.

"There aren't any fairy police."

"Are you sure? They have to have some way of keeping order. In any case you have to go where there are a lot of fairies, and powerful ones at that, so they can for one thing protect you. They might also be able to get rid of Witherings and his father, what's his name again?"

"Miasmos."

"Right. So they can get rid of Witherings and Miasmos so that you can come back to your normal life. That is, if you want to come back."

"What do you mean if I want to come back? Why wouldn't I want to come back?"

"I don't know, being a half-fairy must be kind of cool, being able to fly and do magic."

"Of course it's cool, but I like my human life and I'm not going to give it up any time soon."

Stephanie smiled. "That's good to hear, otherwise I'd have to find a new best friend."

A movement from the window caught Kelly's attention. Beatrix, Carmina, and Bubbles were all outside the window in their invisible-to-humans forms.

"We have company," Kelly said as she got up to open the window for the fairies. They flew in looking displeased. "You can show yourselves," Kelly said. The fairies popped into visibility one by one.

"What are you doing? I almost had a heart attack when I got back and you weren't there," Carmina said.

"For all we knew you'd been kidnapped again," Bubbles said.

"Welifuntinslepingwedvenonwershwuz!" Beatrix shouted at Bubbles and started to chase him around the room.

"She said that if he hadn't been sleeping then we would have known where you were," Carmina translated.

"Oh," Kelly said, noticing Stephanie was standing awkwardly off to the side, watching the fairies. "This is my friend Stephanie. Stephanie, this is Carmina, and those two chasing each other are Bubbles and Beatrix. They're brother and sister."

"That doesn't surprise me," Stephanie said. "Nice to meet you," she said to Carmina. Carmina curtsied. Bubbles and Beatrix flew back to join them.

"Stephanie doesn't think it's safe for me to stay here. She thinks it's only a matter of time before they find me," Kelly said.

"Yes, Thomas thinks so as well. He has a cousin who lives in the mountains of West Virginia, and he thinks it's best if you go there and hide out for a while," Carmina said.

"And then what?" Kelly asked.

"We have a cousin too," Bubbles said. "He lives in Montana."

"Look, I appreciate the offers but I don't want to just run away and hide. It would never end. I have to do something. I think I should go to Glendenland."

Beatrix gasped and let out a string of unintelligible speech. Kelly could tell from her tone that she was not happy with the idea.

"She's right," Bubbles said. "They won't care. Besides, why would you ever want to go there? That place is horrible."

"You've never actually been there," Carmina said.

"Neither have you," Bubbles said.

"No, but Thomas has, so I think I have a better idea about what it's like than you do," Carmina retorted.

"If it wasn't horrible then why did he leave?" Bubbles asked.

"That's none of your business," Carmina replied coldly.

"Can you tell me how to get there?" Kelly asked.

"Yes, if you are sure you want to go there I can show you the way," Carmina said.

"But they won't listen to us," Bubbles said.

"To us?" Kelly asked.

"Well, if you're going I suppose I'll come too. You need a bodyguard," Bubbles mumbled.

Beatrix giggled. Kelly knew she was laughing at the idea of Bubbles being a bodyguard. But he hadn't done such a bad job of helping her escape from Witherings, and Kelly would be glad to have him along even if just for the company.

"I'll – come – to," Beatrix said, laboriously slowing down her speech. Containing her energy enough to speak slowly was so effortful for her that after uttering the sentence she raced around the room energetically three times.

"Does anyone have any fairy dust?" The fairies jumped at the sound of Stephanie's voice. They seemed to have forgotten she was there.

"Why would you want fairy dust for?" Bubbles asked suspiciously.

"I want to come too, why else?" Stephanie answered. "It would shrink me to fairy size, wouldn't it?"

"Out of the question," Bubbles said. "Glendenians hate humans."

"I'll take my chances," Stephanie said.

"It's impossible either way. We don't have any more fairy dust," Bubbles said.

"Liar!" Beatrix squealed. "Hezumhidunderizbed!"

Carmina laughed. "Is that true Bubbles? Do you have some hidden under the bed in your house?"

"No, I don't. But if I did, I wouldn't give it to *her*."

"Really? Even if I gave you these?" Stephanie asked, opening the top drawer of the desk by her window and pulling out a small plastic bag. Stephanie held the bag up in front of Bubbles. Kelly recognized the leftover sequins from Stephanie's Halloween costume. She had dressed up as a disco dancer from the seventies, sewing hundreds of flashy silver sequins onto an old miniskirt. Kelly grinned. She had told Stephanie how Bubbles had gone after the glitter for the Christmas tree ornaments. Bubbles's eyes widened in glee at the sight of the sequins. He lunged for the bag.

"Not so fast," Stephanie said, pulling the bag out of his reach and putting it into one of her pajama pockets. "What do you say?"

"All right," Bubbles answered begrudgingly.

At sunset Stephanie met Kelly, Bubbles, Beatrix, and Carmina by the tree. Stephanie handed Carmina a letter to be delivered to her parents after they had gone. Kelly had also written one for her mother, and instructed Carmina to leave it in Mindy's mailbox. The letter didn't mention anything about fairies, but it would let her mother know Kelly was okay and lying low for a while in a safe place. Thomas still hadn't returned from the meeting he had gone to, and Carmina said it was a good thing because she didn't think he would approve of their going to Glendenland. Kelly thought that it wouldn't have made much of a difference if he had been there since he was so timid. If he didn't approve it wasn't like he would do anything to stop them – he would probably just frown.

"Let's do it," Stephanie said eagerly. Stephanie had always been adventurous. She extended the bag of sequins to Bubbles and he took them, giving her a jar of fairy dust in exchange. The jar was too small for Stephanie to open in human form, so Kelly transformed into fairy form and took the fairy dust. She dusted a generous amount on Stephanie, doubtful that this dust would be any stronger than the other dust Bubbles had provided. She hoped it would last them until they reached Glendenland. Unlike Kelly, whose eyes, skin, and ears changed slightly in appearance in addition to her gaining wings when she was in fairy form, Stephanie under the influence of fairy dust was just a tiny version of her human self. Bubbles, Beatrix, and Kelly lifted Stephanie into the air and followed Carmina into the night.

"This is fun," Stephanie said as they flew through the air. "I wish I had wings too," she sighed.

The journey was not long. Kelly had expected that Glendenland would be very far away, but they had only flown for a little over half an hour when Carmina motioned for them to stop. Kelly guessed they had flown about two miles, and they had reached a small park beside a wide and deep area of the Potomac River. There was a walkway along the water that was lit by a series of old-fashioned street lamps. The others followed Carmina's lead and perched themselves in a nearby tree. Bubbles panted and wiped his brow. Kelly massaged her shoulders. Stephanie looked expectantly at Carmina, and Beatrix flew circles around all of them, still bursting with energy.

"This is where I'll leave you," Carmina said to the others. "Do you see that bench by the water?"

"Yes," Kelly answered.

"Beside it is a statue of a lion, do you see it?"

Kelly squinted and saw a hazy outline beside the bench. On first glance she had thought it was a large rock placed near the bench as another place to sit or for children to climb on. Now she realized that the rock had a feline shape and was in fact a sculpture of a seated lion. She nodded.

"The lion is one of the entrances to Glendenland. I've seen Glendenians go up to it and touch its nose. Then it opens its mouth and they fly inside," Carmina said.

"How do you know it's an entrance and the lion didn't just eat them?" Bubbles asked, looking worried.

"Because they come out again, silly," Carmina answered. "Don't worry, you'll be fine."

Carmina hugged each of them in turn. Beatrix sniffled and wiped a tear from her eye, which caused Bubbles to laugh.

"Why are you crying for? We'll be back at her house by morning after they turn us away, you'll see," he said. Beatrix stuck her tongue out at her brother.

"Do they always act like this?" Stephanie whispered to Kelly.

"I'm afraid so."

"Good luck," Carmina said. Then she flew away.

Once Carmina was out of sight, Beatrix, Bubbles, and Kelly picked Stephanie up and flew down to the lion statue. No people were around so Bubbles, Beatrix, and Kelly were all in their completely visible forms. When they reached the statue they stood in front of it uncertainly. The statue was about three feet tall, making it about two feet taller than they were. After a few moments of indecision, Kelly flew up to the lion's face. It looked serene – its eyes were closed and it looked almost like it was meditating. Tentatively, Kelly reached out and touched its nose. She was startled when the lion's nose twitched in response, and she involuntarily flew back a few inches when the lion's mouth started to open. She thought it might be opening to let them through but then she realized it was just a yawn. The lion proceeded to lick its lips and finally opened its stone eyes. Kelly felt an uneasy pressure under their emotionless gaze. The lion stared at her for a few seconds before speaking.

"State your business, fairy," it said with a robotic, impersonal voice.

"It can't tell you're a half-fairy? What kind of gatekeeper is he?" Bubbles exclaimed behind Kelly. She hadn't realized he had flown up after her.

"State your business, fairy," the lion repeated in the exact same manner as before.

"Um…" Kelly wasn't sure what to say. "Well, you see it's a long story actually, we were hoping maybe you could, I mean, maybe the Glendenians could help us, you see Marcos Witherings—"

"Statement too long, please simplify," the lion interrupted.

"You've got to be kidding," Bubbles said.

"Invalid business, please rephrase," the lion answered.

"I wasn't talking to you," Bubbles retorted.

"Invalid business, please rephrase."

Bubbles lunged forward as if he was going to attack the lion but Kelly held him back and motioned for him to be quiet.

"We want to talk to somebody to see if they can help us," Kelly said.

There was a pause. Then again the lion repeated: "Invalid business, please rephrase."

"We want to talk to somebody," Kelly said.

"Invalid business, please rephrase."

Kelly was starting to get frustrated. *Psssst* Kelly heard from below. She looked down and saw Stephanie motioning for her. Kelly set down on the ground.

"I have an idea," Stephanie whispered. "Let me talk to it." Kelly and Beatrix lifted Stephanie up to face the lion. It had gone back to sleep – apparently too much time had passed since they last engaged it in conversation. Kelly reached out and touched its nose again. It awoke.

"State your business, fairy," it said.

"Take us to your leader," Stephanie demanded in a loud, confident voice. Kelly tried hard not to laugh. What Stephanie

67

had just said had sounded completely ridiculous, especially since it was a phrase that was used in almost every B-rated science fiction movie Kelly had ever seen. *At this rate we'll never get inside*, Kelly thought. But seconds later she felt her mouth drop open in surprise at the lion's response to Stephanie's demand.

"Valid business, please wait," the lion said. Stephanie smiled smugly.

"It's about time," Bubbles muttered.

"Please enter and when you reach the entrance room proceed through the transport portal to your right. It has been set for the audience hall. Once there please wait for your audience with his Grace the honorable, noble, wise and benevolent Glenden Grand. Thank you, enjoy your visit," the lion's robotic voice concluded.

After the lion fell silent its mouth opened up wide until it was a little over a foot tall and at least eight inches wide. Kelly went in first, followed by Stephanie, Beatrix, and Bubbles in the rear. Passing into the lion's mouth, Kelly came upon a stone spiral stairway leading downwards. The stairway took them down through the body of the lion statue. She wasn't sure exactly how light was provided in the stairway, but it seemed to be coming from the ceiling itself, which glowed faintly. The bottom of the stairway opened up into a small square room, just big enough for all four of them to stand in side by side. All of the walls had door-sized archways in them. The archways in front of them and to the left were completely black inside – Kelly and the others couldn't see what lay beyond them. The archway on the right, however, was not black inside. Instead, it was bright blue. It looked like it was filled with the sky on a sunny, cloudless day.

"He said to the right," Stephanie said.

"Come on, let's go through before it deactivates," Kelly said.

"You first," Bubbles said to Kelly.

"All right." Kelly approached the door. As she got closer the space inside the doorway still looked the same sky blue. She took a deep breath and walked through it.

Chapter 6
Glendenland

Kelly had been expecting to feel at least some sensation or another as she walked through the doorway, but she hadn't felt anything at all. After she stepped through she found herself in a large, dome-shaped room. The room was empty save for a dark red curtain directly in front of her that hid about a third of the room. The floor looked like smooth, white marble. As Kelly reached down to touch the floor to see if it really was marble, Bubbles, Beatrix, and Stephanie appeared next to her in rapid succession. Bubbles was looking downright frightened and Beatrix was standing completely still and quiet, which was quite unusual for her.

"It's like we're inside a big bubble," Stephanie said excitedly. At those words Kelly took a closer look at the walls of the dome. They were a cloudy, opaque white. But they weren't rigid like normal walls. Instead they were moving slightly in and out in response to the water currents of the river above them. The movement was slight but it was there. Kelly looked away before it made her seasick.

"I guess we just wait until the leader gets here," Stephanie said, sounding bored. Kelly was in awe of how Stephanie wasn't the least bit nervous about meeting the fairy leader of Glendenland. Stephanie had always been fearless, even a bit reckless at times. At that moment she was approaching the red curtain and reaching out in preparation to look past it. Kelly grabbed Stephanie's shirt and pulled her away from the curtain.

"I have a feeling we'll see what's behind there soon enough," Kelly said. She was right. Less than a minute later the curtain parted in the middle and drew itself aside silently. It revealed a wide set of stairs, fifteen steps tall, leading to a platform. Three ornate thrones sat on the platform. The leftmost throne was made entirely of gold and an intricate design of ivy and flowers circled its entire surface. The throne in the middle was silver and completely smooth, devoid of designs. The third throne was gold like the first and had a large tulip blossom engraved on its backrest. The remaining surface of the third throne was smooth and polished like the middle throne. Behind the thrones hung a dark purple velvet drapery. As soon as the red curtain was fully drawn back, two imposing bald male fairies dressed in black marched out from behind the drapery and positioned themselves slightly behind and to the side of the thrones, one on either side. They were carrying bows and wore cases of arrows on their backs. Once in position they unfurled their wings, which were also a dark black color. They stood completely motionless.

"Bodyguards," Bubbles whispered to Kelly.

As soon as the bodyguards were in place a short and rotund fairy bearing a horn arrived. He blew a sequence of shrill high notes on the horn and then announced in a squeaky voice that they should all rise for his Grace the honorable, noble, wise and benevolent Glenden Grand. Of course they were all already standing because there were no chairs at the bottom of the stairs where they stood. Glenden was very tall for a fairy and his height was magnified by the fact that he was standing on the raised platform. His wings were a dazzling metallic gold with flecks of green in them. His skin was the color of smooth milk chocolate and though he was clearly still strong and agile, his chiseled facial features were beginning to look worn with time like the edges of rocks smoothed down by centuries of wind, and his very short black hair was touched with grey. He held himself with a quiet dignity. As Glenden sat down in the golden throne his piercing gaze caught Kelly's. His eyes were the same dazzling metallic gold as his wings. As soon as his gaze caught hers it quickly moved on to each of her companions and ended on

Stephanie. Kelly thought his eyes narrowed when they fell on her human friend. Stephanie was gawking at him.

Another fairy entered the room and Kelly knew he had to be Glenden's son even before the rotund fairy announced him as the brave and honest Venuto Grand. The fairy prince was tall and slim like his father but his skin was lighter, more like caramel than chocolate. His wings were a metallic, shiny copper and his eyes were the same golden color as his father's were. His face was round and had a bit of a boyish quality thanks to the dimple in his chin. Prince Venuto sat in the last throne, leaving the middle one empty. Kelly assumed it must be the throne of Glenden's wife. After his son sat down Glenden spoke.

"It has been some time since we've had unknown visitors to our realm," Glenden began. His voice was loud and deep. "And even longer since a fadaman or a human has been in our midst." He kept a straight face that made it impossible for Kelly to tell how he was feeling. Venuto was easier to read. He was sitting on the edge of his throne and gaping at them with intense interest.

"To what do we owe this new acquaintance?" Glenden asked.

Kelly stepped forward a bit from the others. "We were hoping maybe you could help us. You see, Marcos Witherings kidnapped me because he wants me to join him and his father. I escaped with the help of my friends, but now he's still after me." Kelly paused, looking at Glenden uncertainly.

"I am not familiar with this name Marcos Witherings," Glenden said.

"He's a fadaman like me. Miasmos is his father," Kelly answered. One of Glenden's eyebrows rose slightly at the mention of Miasmos.

"And who is your fairy parent?"

"I don't know," Kelly said. "I know my father was a fairy, but I don't know who he is."

"Your mother never told you his name?" Glenden asked.

"My mother doesn't remember his name, or anything else about him," Kelly stammered.

"Most curious," Glenden said. "Most curious indeed. But please, you were explaining why you are here."

Kelly continued to tell the details of her kidnap, meeting with Witherings, and subsequent escape. When she finished Glenden was quiet for a few moments while his son looked at him expectantly. The prince appeared anxious to hear Glenden's reply. Glenden sighed.

"I have felt the growing power of Miasmos for some time now. I was not aware of his son, however. Fadamen are difficult for full-blooded fairies to sense, especially when they know how to hide themselves. The news that Miasmos has a fadaman on his side is most distressing."

"So can they stay father?" Venuto asked eagerly.

"Yes, but the human must go," Glenden said.

"But father—"

"We can't risk having humans know about us and how we function. Do you want a swarm of humans to descend upon us?"

Stephanie giggled. Both Glenden and Venuto stared at her. "I'm sorry," Stephanie managed to say through her fit of laughter, "but in the first place, there is no such thing as a swarm of humans. Secondly, if I told anyone about this place they would put me in the loony bin."

"They'd put you in the what?" Venuto asked.

"In the mental hospital, where they put crazy people," Stephanie answered.

"She's right," Kelly said. "No one would believe her."

Glenden considered for a moment. "All right, she can stay, but under these conditions. The human will wear prosthetic wings and ears and will reveal to no one that she is not a real fairy. She will undergo a shrinking charm that will keep her fairy-sized until it is removed, and she will not infect any fairies with human ideology."

"Will I be able to fly with prosthetic wings?" Stephanie asked.

"Of course," Venuto chimed in, looking offended.

"Do you agree to the terms?" Glenden asked.

"Absolutely." Stephanie grinned.

"Then please come halfway up the stairs so I can apply the shrinking charm."

Stephanie complied. Once she was standing halfway up the stairs, Glenden stood up, waved his hand in her direction and sat back down. "It is done. You no longer need to use fairy dust to maintain fairy size."

"Thank you," Stephanie said politely and returned to the bottom of the stairs.

"Venuto will get the prosthetic wings and ears and show you to your quarters." Glenden turned to leave the room but then paused to say one more thing. "It would be best if the fadaman also didn't reveal she isn't a full-blooded fairy, at least for the time being." With those words Glenden left the room, followed by one of the bodyguards. Venuto beckoned the short, rotund fairy with the horn and whispered something to him. The rotund fairy then hurriedly exited the room. Venuto turned his attention to Kelly and flashed a wide smile.

"My father is always so serious, please don't be bothered," he said. "Now, we still haven't been properly introduced. I know you're Kelly, but I'm not sure of the names of anyone else."

"I'm Beatrix," Beatrix said, curtsying deeply and batting her eyelashes. "That is my brother, Bubbles." She pointed to Bubbles, who gave a very slight bow, his previous expression of fear now replaced with a surly scowl. Kelly could tell he was irritated they were being allowed to stay in Glendenland.

"And I'm Stephanie," Stephanie said.

Before any of them had a chance to say anything else the rotund fairy was back, carrying an awkward-looking jumble of metal wires and what appeared to be a brown blanket. Venuto took the jumble of wires from him and came down the stairs to join Kelly and the others. The rotund fairy followed with the brown blanket.

"Are those my wings?" Stephanie asked, a clear look of disappointment on her face. Venuto just smiled and pulled two of the wires in the middle of the jumble in opposite directions. In response to this motion the wires sprung out to form the skeleton of full-sized fairy wings. Stephanie sighed visibly in relief. However, she soon looked perplexed because the wings had no straps and it was unclear how they would be attached.

"How does she put them on?" Kelly asked Venuto.

"This model is designed for fairies with absolutely no wing functionality, so they attach directly into the back."

"You mean they go inside my back?" Stephanie's eyes widened.

"Partially," Venuto answered.

"Will it hurt?" Stephanie asked.

"No. The part that inserts is coated with pain dulling and anti-infection tonics. Lift up the back of her shirt please," Venuto asked Beatrix, who was standing closest to Stephanie.

"What is *that*," Bubbles said as soon as Beatrix had lifted Stephanie's shirt. Kelly realized his eyes were fixed on Stephanie's fairy tattoo. The other fairies looked at the tattoo curiously.

"I got it before I knew what fairies really looked like," Stephanie said simply.

"It's supposed to be a fairy? That's insulting!" Bubbles said.

"I'm sure she meant no offense," Venuto said with an unmistakable air of authority.

Bubbles's face grew red, but he didn't argue.

"Now, if you would hold absolutely still," Venuto instructed Stephanie. He held the prosthetic wings up at the appropriate place on her back.

"Ready?" he asked. Stephanie nodded.

Venuto pushed a button in the center of where the two wings of the skeleton met. There was a soft popping sound. Then Venuto simply removed his hands and the wing skeleton stayed in place.

"Wow, I didn't feel anything," Stephanie said, craning her neck to try to get a look at the wing skeleton over her shoulder.

"Flimsly?" The rotund fairy jumped at the sound of his name. He rushed forward and handed Venuto the brown blanket. Seeing the blanket up close, Kelly realized that it wasn't really a blanket at all. Rather, it was a stretchy fabric in the shape of wings. Venuto pulled the fabric over the wing skeleton and when he was finished Stephanie had dull brown wings. The wings had a strange fibrous texture that Kelly instantly recognized. She had seen that same texture before, on Thomas's wings. Could his wings be prosthetic as well?

"All right, let's see how they work," Venuto said.

Stephanie looked confused and Kelly explained how she had to contract the muscles between her shoulder blades in order to fly. To Kelly's amazement Stephanie floated effortlessly up into the air and raced exuberantly around the room several times.

"How come she can fly so easily?" Kelly asked.

"The prosthetic wings sense the electrical signals in the muscles and generate their own power to compensate for any muscle weakness," Venuto said.

"I see," Kelly said. She was realizing that fairies were not only adept at magic but they were also technologically advanced. Human medicine wasn't capable of creating perfectly functional prosthetic limbs.

"Put these on," Venuto said, offering two small rubbery triangles to Stephanie once she had touched back to the ground. They were the prosthetic ears Glenden had mentioned. Stephanie slipped the prosthetic ears onto the tops of her ears. If Kelly hadn't known any better she would have thought she was looking at a full-blooded fairy.

"You look just like one of us now," Beatrix said.

"Sorry?" Stephanie still couldn't understand Beatrix's rapid speech because although she was now fairy size, her sense of hearing wasn't any sharper.

"She said you look just like a fairy now," Kelly translated.

Venuto looked perplexed by this exchange.

"Beatrix talks too fast for Stephanie to understand. I can't understand her in human form either," Kelly explained to him.

"We can fix that," Venuto said. He waved his hand unceremoniously in Stephanie's direction.

"Now say something," he told Beatrix.

"Your new wings and ears are very pretty."

"Thank you," Stephanie answered, having clearly understood Beatrix's words.

"Now for living quarters. You two," Venuto said to Bubbles and Beatrix, "since you are free fairies will go stay in some of the quarters we have reserved for visiting fairies. Flimsly will show you the way."

"But we want to stay with them," Beatrix protested.

"You'll still get to see each other as much as you want, quarters are just where you sleep," Venuto said patiently.

"Oh," Beatrix said.

"My father will want to keep a closer eye on you two, so you'll stay in one of the guest quarters usually reserved for visiting fairy nobility," Venuto told Stephanie and Kelly. "I'll show you two there because it's close to my quarters."

"Also, it occurs to me that you should all have a cover story for why you are here in Glendenland, because my father wants to keep your true reasons a secret for now. Why don't we say that Kelly and Stephanie are distant free-fairy relatives of mine, which would explain why they are staying in the quarters for visiting nobility. Bubbles and Beatrix, you can be their free-fairy friends who live with them and therefore accompanied them here on the journey," Venuto said.

They all agreed that was a good plan. Then Bubbles and Beatrix followed Flimsly as he led them towards the curved wall to the left of the stairs. Flimsly proceeded to walk straight through the seemingly solid wall and disappear through to the other side. The wall wiggled a little bit like Jell-O in response to his walking through it. Beatrix and Bubbles exchanged quizzical looks but then followed him through the wall.

"This way." Venuto approached the wall on the right side of the base of the stairs. His bodyguard, who until that point had remained motionless at the top of the stairs, took up a position in the lead. As they got closer to the wall Kelly noticed that there was a faint semicircular shadow on the wall in the form of an archway. This shadow marked the intersection of two bubble-like rooms and therefore was darker, but only a small amount darker, than the rest of the wall. Kelly and Stephanie followed Venuto and his bodyguard through the wall. When Kelly walked through it she felt like she was walking through Jell-O. Everything became wet and squishy. But the sensation only lasted for a few seconds and when she came out on the other side of the wall she found she was still perfectly dry. They were now in a large hallway that curved as if it encircled a large bubble. Its walls were the same opaque whitish color as the walls of the audience hall. The ceiling of the hallway arched like a domed tunnel, and the floor was flat and resembled slate. As they walked down the hallway Kelly noticed many shadow archways on either side of them, points where other bubble rooms intersected with the hallway bubble. None of the archways had any identifying markers, though, and Kelly wondered how fairies kept track of where they were. After a few minutes of walking Venuto stopped in front of one of the shadow archways.

"These are your quarters," he said. "Since this is a private section, to enter you need to first place your hand against the center of the archway. After you hear the chimes, then you can walk through. The archway will remain unlocked until you place your hand in the middle of the other side of the archway and hear another set of chimes. Then the archway will be locked. To ask admittance to an archway that you aren't authorized to unlock, you put your hand up to the center of the archway in the same manner, and whoever is inside will hear the chimes." Venuto put his hand up to the archway and a second later they heard a soft musical cascade of chimes like wind chimes blowing in a gentle breeze. They stepped through the doorway and entered a cozy living room equipped with a sofa, table, and a few welcoming armchairs.

"Those three archways on the far side of the room lead to your bedrooms and the bathroom. There is no kitchen because the usual royal visitors are brought specially prepared food by their attendants, and never need to cook their own food. We do have a mess hall where fairies can go and eat, however, and that's where you will be taking the majority of your meals. Tomorrow you can see more of Glendenland but now you should get some rest," Venuto said.

Once Venuto left, Stephanie tried out each of the armchairs before finally plopping herself down on the sofa.

"Isn't this awesome?" she asked.

"I guess," Kelly said as she joined Stephanie on the sofa.

"You guess? We're in a city of underwater bubbles, we can fly and walk through the walls, and all you've got is 'I guess'?"

"I guess so," Kelly answered.

"You don't think this place is the least bit cool?"

"I'm just a little too preoccupied to fully appreciate it."

"Don't worry, you're safe here from Witherings," Stephanie said.

"He's not who I was thinking about."

"Who were you thinking about then, his henchmen?"

"No silly, I was thinking about my father."

"Oh. You don't think," Stephanie began, "never mind."

"I don't think what?"

"I was just thinking, you don't think Witherings's father could be your father too, do you?" Stephanie asked.

"I don't know," Kelly said. The truth was it had crossed her mind that Miasmos could be her father and she didn't like the idea at all. "I hope not," she added.

The next morning Kelly was awakened by the sound of the archway's chimes. She groggily staggered out of bed and into the living room. Stephanie was nowhere to be seen, no doubt still sound asleep. The chimes sounded again. Kelly approached the archway and placed her hand up to it. There was another chime to signal the door was unlocked, and no sooner had the chimes ended than Bubbles and Beatrix burst into the room. Kelly noticed that Bubbles had sewn the silver sequins Stephanie had traded him for his fairy dust all over the outside of his bag. The bag was now positively gaudy and Kelly decided not to mention it.

"Come on, it's time for breakfast!" Bubbles exclaimed.

After Kelly had woken Stephanie, Bubbles and Beatrix led them out of their quarters and back down the circular hallway they had traveled the night before. When they passed one of the many unmarked shadowy archway markers, Bubbles pointed to it and said it was the entrance to the audience hall where they had met with Glenden and Venuto.

"How can you tell? They all look the same," Stephanie said.

Bubbles looked surprised. "I don't know. We can just tell. Can't you?"

"No," Stephanie and Kelly said at the same time.

Bubbles shrugged. A few archways later the hallway opened up to a small domed room with three archways placed evenly around its circumference. In the middle of the room was an object similar to a teacher's podium. Bubbles approached it and stood looking intently at its surface. Kelly joined him and saw that the top of the podium consisted of what she assumed to be a map of Glendenland. The map included many unlabelled black circles and ovals, both large and small, and a series of winding pathways between them. There were also six red circles spaced out over the map's area.

"We're here," Beatrix said, pointing over Kelly's shoulder to one of the red circles. "In a transport bubble."

"Transport bubble?" Kelly asked.

"From here we can get to any of the other red circles on the map. First we select the one we want to go to, then walk through the archway that lights up," Bubbles said.

"How did you learn all of this so fast?" Kelly asked.

"Dimpleton gave us a tour last night," Beatrix said.

"Dimpleton?" Stephanie asked incredulously. Kelly understood Stephanie thought the name Dimpleton was ridiculous, but Beatrix interpreted her statement as a request for more information.

"Dimpleton's one of our neighbors," Beatrix said.

Stephanie laughed.

"What's funny?" Beatrix asked.

"I've got it," Bubbles interrupted. He placed his finger over one of the red circles on the map and pressed downwards. The shadow archway directly in front of them became filled with the same sky blue that had filled the doorway leading from the inside of the lion statue to the audience hall the night before. Bubbles eagerly sprinted through the sky blue archway and the others followed. They immediately entered another transport bubble identical to the one they had just been in. Bubbles strode purposely through one of the shadow archways in the wall of the new transport bubble with the others close behind.

When Kelly stepped through the archway her ears were met with the cacophony of sound that was hundreds of fairies talking, laughing, eating, and flying through the air. They had entered a large mess hall. Stephanie let out a low whistle. Most of the fairies in the mess hall had relatively plain wings in various shades of brown, tan, yellow, and orange. Amid the masses of wings in these main colors Kelly caught glimpses of purple and blue wings and here and there a few sparkles of copper or gold. She didn't see any fairies with silver in their wings, however. Fairies continually popped in and out of the room through the many shadow archways along the room's circumference, and some came in and out through various points in the ceiling. The fairies coming in from the ceiling all wore masks over their mouths and noses that resembled surgical masks. Once inside they took off the masks and stored them in their knapsacks. Kelly supposed the masks were some kind of underwater breathing device, as the top of the mess hall was in direct contact with the river above. Bubbles raced towards one side of the room and Kelly saw he was headed towards the serving line, which bore a striking resemblance to a human buffet. They each got a tray from the start of the line and proceeded to help themselves to the ample selection of food. There were pastries, breads, chunks of fruit, cups of grape pulp, pancakes, and what looked like round sausages.

"What are those?" Kelly asked, pointing to the sausages.

"Grasshopper cutlets," Bubbles answered, helping himself to seven.

"Gross," Stephanie said.

Bubbles looked at her in utter astonishment. "Grasshopper cutlets are most delicious. You must try them."

"I don't think so," Stephanie said.

"I insist," Bubbles said as he placed three of the cutlets on Stephanie's plate. Stephanie wrinkled her nose.

They sat near the end of an empty row of tables. But as soon as they had sat down three fairies carrying trays laden with food swooped down from the air and sat beside them.

"Dimpleton!" Beatrix shouted gleefully.

"Hey-O," bellowed a skinny blond fairy with sand-colored wings. "These are my brothers, Wimpleton and Pimpleton."

Stephanie struggled to keep her giggles under control at the name Pimpleton. Kelly poked Stephanie with her elbow.

Wimpleton and Pimpleton were also blond, but not as skinny as Dimpleton. They both had dark orange wings.

"Did you try the ant legs? They're quite good today," Dimpleton asked Bubbles, stuffing four of the twig-like appendages into his mouth. It seemed Dimpleton shared Bubbles's voracious appetite, although he clearly enjoyed an active metabolism Bubbles did not.

"I didn't see them!" Bubbles jumped up to get himself some ant legs.

"So Bubbles tells us you two are free fairies too?" Dimpleton asked, chomping down on a fresh handful of ant legs.

"That's right," Kelly said.

"And that you're related to Venuto?"

"That's right, but distantly related. This is the first time we've visited," she said.

"What do you think of our band?" he asked.

"It seems very nice," Kelly said.

Dimpleton beamed. "Your friend Bubbles thinks so too, but he won't admit it. We're taking bets on how long it will be before he petitions for band membership."

Beatrix laughed.

"Are you talking about me?" Bubbles asked suspiciously as he returned to the table with a plate piled high with ant legs.

"Whatever would give you that idea?" Dimpleton asked innocently.

Kelly was mostly silent for the rest of the meal while the fairies chattered amongst themselves about their plans for the rest of the day, which included arrangements for a game of tag in the underwater park. Dimpleton also spent a considerable chunk of time trying to convince Bubbles to go on a date with his cousin Bamblelina.

After breakfast Dimpleton and his brothers went their own ways, promising to meet Kelly and her companions an hour later for the game of tag. In the meantime, Beatrix and Bubbles led Stephanie and Kelly on the same tour of Glendenland that Dimpleton had given them the night before. They exited the mess hall into a wide hallway where many fairies bustled along purposefully. As they walked Bubbles pointed out the shadow archways leading to food storage, nectala production, fairy government offices, the hospital, and the medicine storage and creation bubble. Finally instead of just pointing to the archways he lead them through one and they entered a very large bubble containing a species of open-air market, except for of course they weren't really in the open air. There were many stalls with fairies selling all sorts of goods such as shoes, clothes, soaps and tonics, specialty candies and more. At the far end of the market there were some wooden structures and Kelly could see that in front of them fairies were selling furniture. Some shops were also hanging down from the ceiling in order to take advantage of the space overhead. Fairies could simply fly up to the hanging stalls to do more shopping. Bubbles informed them that the fairies made their purchases with fairy currency called glitterons. Kelly peaked over one fairy's shoulder as he bought a pair of golden silk slippers and felt a tug on the inside of her mind as she saw the pile of sparkling glitterons in his hand. The glitterons were little square golden pieces that bore a striking resemblance to the sparkling bits inside the snow globe Stephanie had given Kelly on her birthday. Stephanie, who was peeking over Kelly's shoulder, seemed to be thinking the same thing.

"Hey – we've got a bunch of those back at your house!" she exclaimed.

"You have a bunch of golden silk slippers?" Bubbles asked, eyeing the slippers the fairy was purchasing.

"No, glitterons," Stephanie said.

Bubbles eyes widened. "Whatever do you mean?" he asked.

"In my snow globe," Kelly answered.

"What's a snow globe?" Beatrix asked.

"It's a glass bubble with a model of a landscape inside, filled with water and hundreds of little white plastic flakes that swirl around and look like snow falling when you shake it," Kelly explained.

"But glitterons aren't white," Bubbles said as though he were trying to explain something very simply to a little child.

"Sometimes snow globes have glitter in them instead of white flecks. The snow globe I bought Kelly has glitter inside it and it isn't just any glitter. It's definitely exactly like those glitterons," Stephanie said confidently.

"You say globes of snow have hundreds of flakes inside?" Bubbles asked.

"Oh yes, there must be at least three hundred glitterons in your snow globe, don't you think?" Stephanie asked Kelly.

"Three hundred!" Bubbles nearly shouted, drawing a few sideways glances from nearby fairies in the market.

"If those really are glitterons in your globe of snow, we're *rich*," he added in a quieter tone of voice.

"Three hundred glitterons isn't that much money Bubbles," Beatrix said.

"It's certainly enough to buy some premium quality fairy dust," Bubbles answered.

"You wouldn't know premium quality fairy dust if it jumped up and kicked you in the buttocks!" Beatrix retorted.

"Would too!"

"Would not!"

"Well, we'll soon see about that, won't we. Once we go and get them and I buy some fairy dust," Bubbles said.

"I'm afraid we won't," Kelly interrupted. "We can't risk going inside my house just for the glitterons."

"You're seriously thinking about leaving them there for Miasmos's minions to find?" Bubbles asked.

"I don't like it, but it's just too dangerous," Kelly said.

"But, it's three hundred glitterons!" Bubbles protested.

"She's right Bubbles," Stephanie said.

Beatrix nodded in agreement. Bubbles pouted.

"Promise me you won't go anywhere near my house," Kelly said sternly to Bubbles.

Bubbles crossed his arms and stared at his feet, pouting even more.

"Do you promise?"

Bubbles nodded sullenly.

"Good."

They didn't do too much more exploring of the market because Bubbles was depressed he couldn't buy anything. Beatrix assured him that he would get some glitterons soon if he joined in the fairy community tasks like food collection, public area cleaning and dishwashing. These were just three of the many jobs that were rotated amongst the majority of fairies in Glendenland. The only fairies who were exempt from community job duty were fairies with specific full-time trades like healing. If fairies completed community duties for fifteen hours a week they received free food and medical care along with a small weekly stipend of glitterons. Fairies could make extra money by providing additional goods and services to other fairies or by completing extra hours of community jobs.

After exiting the market Bubbles said there was still a lot of Glendenland they hadn't seen but they had at least gotten a good idea of where the important places were. Kelly knew it would take her some time to be able to navigate through the mazes of unmarked hallways and archways of Glendenland without getting lost. They stepped into the nearest transport bubble and traveled back to the first transport bubble they had started from in the morning. From there they entered a series of winding hallways with periodic shadow archways on either side. These hallways were mostly devoid of fairies although they did pass a few, some of which nodded cordially to them.

"These are regular fairy residences," Bubbles explained. "We're almost at our quarters."

Bubbles opened the door to his and his sister's quarters by placing his hand in the middle of the shadow archway. Their quarters were quite similar to the ones Kelly and Stephanie were sharing, but the living room was smaller and contained a tiny stove, refrigerator, sink, and cabinets off to one side. After a few chilled glasses of nectala it was almost time for their game of tag with Dimpleton, Wimpleton, and Pimpleton.

A hop back through the transport bubble and a short walk later they reached the underwater park. The underwater park was a large bubble that could easily accommodate several hundred fairies at a time. The ground of the park was covered in soft moss and short grass. There were also some flowers and jungle gym playground structures spaced throughout the park. The park provided ample space for fairies to fly around in the upper parts of the bubble, and when they arrived Kelly saw many fairy families lounging about and talking as well as scores of younger fairies racing around in the air and chasing each other back and forth. Some fairies were playing Frisbee with small discs that looked quite a lot like human shirt and coat buttons.

Dimpleton and his brothers arrived a short while later and the game of tag began. It had the same rules as human tag except for they could fly as well as run. Kelly was pleased to find she could fly almost as fast as the other fairies, but she wasn't adept at the many types of acrobatics like somersaults, sudden dives, and quick changes of directions the other fairies managed with ease. Stephanie, on the other hand, performed all of these complex acrobatics without the least bit of effort. It was as if her artificial wings not only made up for muscle weakness but could also read her mind. Despite being "it" for more than half the game, Kelly had great fun and momentarily forgot all about Marcos Witherings and Miasmos.

After they were all tired out from the game and lying in the grass, Dimpleton suddenly sat up and told Kelly that Venuto was looking for her.

"How do you know that?" she asked.

"Fairy senses," he answered, speaking as though the answer were obvious. A few minutes later Venuto appeared at the entrance to the park, accompanied by his bodyguard. A few of the fairies closest to the doorway when he entered curtsied or inclined their heads respectfully, but then they went immediately back to what they had been doing. A couple of fairy children

85

waved at Venuto enthusiastically until he waved back. It didn't seem out of the ordinary for them to see a member of the royal family in their midst. Kelly was glad that the pomp and circumstance of the audience hall didn't seem to carry out into the rest of Glendenland. When Dimpleton had said Venuto was looking for her, she had been half-expecting Flimsly to enter the room first, blow on his horn, and announce that the honest and brave Prince Venuto Grand had entered the park.

Venuto spotted them and came over. He nodded cordially to all of them and then addressed Kelly.

"Would you please come with me?" he asked.

"Okay," Kelly said, getting up to follow him.

"The rest of you carry on with what you were doing," Venuto added before turning and walking back briskly in the direction he had come from. Kelly guessed he had said that to make it clear he only wanted Kelly to follow him, because Bubbles and Stephanie had looked like they were about to get up too. Bubbles sulked and Stephanie frowned.

"Don't worry, I'll fill you in later," Kelly whispered to them before hurrying to follow Venuto.

Kelly followed Venuto and his bodyguard to the nearest transport bubble. Once inside Venuto surveyed the map podium in the center of the room.

"Where are we going?" Kelly asked.

"That's what I'm trying to decide. We need a place where we are unlikely to be disturbed. Ah, this should be adequate." He pressed on a transport bubble near what Kelly thought was the audience hall, but she couldn't be sure. The shadow archway on their left turned sky blue and they walked through it. They left the archway on their right in the next transport bubble and walked a few meters down the adjoining hallway. Then Venuto led Kelly through another archway.

"Welcome to the Great Library of Glendenland," Venuto said as they entered a large bubble.

Kelly looked around. A female fairy with grey wings and grey hair pulled back in a bun sat at a large mahogany desk. She was the only fairy in sight. The rest of the library was silent and empty. Dark maroon sofas and armchairs populated the center of the library and stacks upon stacks of books filled the rest of the space. The only things that visually differentiated the Great Library of Glendenland from a human library were that Kelly didn't see any computers, and the stacks reached almost all the way to the domed ceiling. Of course fairies could just fly up to reach a book of their choosing and didn't have to depend on ladders like humans would have had to. Kelly knew she shouldn't be surprised that fairies had a library, but still she was a little bit surprised. She supposed her preconceived notions of fairies as simple creatures that just flitted around in the forest all day hadn't completely worn off.

"Over there is the history section. You will find it quite interesting, I can assure you. Those are the knowledge books. I suppose you might call them what's the word, oh yes, science books. And then there are the travel and art books over there." Venuto pointed to different stacks as he spoke.

"Is there a fiction section?" Kelly asked.

"Fiction?"

"You know, made-up stories that you read for fun."

Venuto looked like he found the idea of fiction curious.

"No, we don't have any books like that. We do have one compilation of human 'fairytales', but only because we found the name interesting." Venuto chuckled. "But we are going to another room, through here."

Venuto led Kelly through the stacks and to the back end of the library. He stopped in front of the far side of the bubble, but there was no archway that Kelly could see. He put his hand up to the unremarkable wall and in response to his touch a shadow archway appeared.

"Secret arch," Venuto explained.

Once Kelly, Venuto, and his bodyguard were through the arch, Venuto put his hand up to the other side of the archway and the archway marker disappeared. They were now in an almost empty domed room about three times the size of the living room of Kelly and Stephanie's guest quarters. The only pieces of furniture in the room were five square mats placed in a row on one side of the room. Venuto's bodyguard took up a statue-like pose by the invisible doorway and Kelly immediately forgot he was there.

"Now we can get started," Venuto said.

"Get started with what?" Kelly asked.

"My father has requested I give you magic lessons."

Kelly felt a rush of excitement. She couldn't wait to be able to do magic like all of the fairies could. But she was curious as to why Glenden had requested she have lessons.

"May I ask why he wants you to teach me?"

"He didn't tell me why, but I assume it's because he wants you to be able to fight Marcos Witherings."

Kelly thought that was a ridiculous idea. "Even the least talented fairy has more magic than I do. Wouldn't it be better for one of them to fight him?"

Venuto shook his head. "Only a very powerful fairy can fight a fadaman. You see, since fadamen are half-human, they possess the same protection as humans do from fairy magic. Humans have a thick skin that protects against fairy magic, and a fairy would have to work very hard to even have a tiny magical effect on a human. The fadamen possess this same shield, but at the same time they themselves have full use of fairy magic, as long as they are in their fairy forms. Since they have both power and an inborn shield, fadamen are very dangerous to fairies. They are also dangerous to humans because their magic can easily cut through the protective human shield."

"That's why Witherings told me that fadamen have the strengths of both species and few of the weaknesses," Kelly murmured.

"Exactly. Only a fadaman can fight on equal footing with another fadaman, since fadaman shields don't protect against fadaman magic," Venuto said.

"Yes, I'd already figured that one out," Kelly said, remembering how she had not had any sort of protective shielding from the electricity Marcos Witherings had shot at her.

"Now that you know how dangerous fadamen are, you might understand why my father is so concerned that Miasmos has a fadaman son. I think my father feels that having a fadaman on our side can't be a bad thing."

"But I'm no match for Marcos Witherings," Kelly said.

Venuto smiled. "Currently Witherings is much more powerful than you are because he has developed his powers, overcoming one of the weaknesses of the fadamen – the 'human fog'. But once you overcome the human fog you will be able to catch up to him."

"If you say so." Kelly wasn't convinced. "What's the human fog?"

"Fairies are by nature more in tune with the earth and its elements than humans, so they can intuitively use magic to some degree without a deep understanding of how it works. If they want to strengthen their powers they must practice and study, but otherwise they still have some basic instinctual command of magic. Full-blooded humans, on the other hand, are much less connected to the natural world, and having magical powers is no longer part of their nature, although it once was long ago. Human beings have a curtain of ignorance, a fog that prevents them from understanding the elements. With years of practice humans can remove this human fog and gain an understanding of the natural world and how the forces of nature work within themselves. But it would be against nature for humans to practice magic even if they were to reach such a depth of awareness where it became possible to do so. Since you are a fadaman, the ability to perform magic is a part of your nature, and once you turned fourteen the fairy side of you was mature enough to manifest itself. But unlike a full-blooded fairy, you can't instinctually use your powers. First you must get rid of enough of your human fog and gain sufficient awareness of the elements before you can use them."

"When you say elements do you mean the periodic table of elements?"

"No. I'm talking about earth, air, water, and fire."

"Oh, those elements," Kelly said.

"Yes," Venuto answered. "You must first be able to recognize the elements, to know how much of each element any particular object or environment has. You must understand how the elements interact with each other. You must be able to feel the elements and their presence. That is awareness. Only then will you be able to influence the elements. This awareness is what I'm going to teach you starting today."

Venuto instructed Kelly to sit cross-legged on one of the mats. He told her to sit with her back straight and to close her eyes.

"Before you can interact with the elements around you, you must be able to feel them inside of you. Every living being is a mixture of all of the elements and at any point in time we have different quantities of each element inside of us."

"I don't have any flames burning inside me, or any clumps of dirt," Kelly said, confused by what Venuto meant when he said she had different quantities of each element inside of her.

Venuto laughed. "That's quite right. The elements manifest within the body, and the world around us, in different ways. In addition to their solid and strong forms, such as flame, water, and clumps of dirt, there are also the fundamental essences of these elements. The fundamental essence is what you must understand. Fire's essence is temperature, and can actually be either hot or cold. Fire contains the entire spectrum of temperature. Air is movement, motion. Earth is the feeling of weight or solidity, and water is a binding, cohesive nature, in addition to wetness of course."

Venuto guided Kelly to survey different parts of her body systematically and to try to feel the different elements. He said that once she was good at feeling the subtlest elemental essences, then the next step would be to try to create and change the elements within herself. After that she would be able to finally connect her intention with the elements in the outside world. He gave an example.

"You see, I can call up the water elements in my body towards my hand, and they develop a sort of magnetism with the water elements in the air."

Venuto held up his hand and a mist of water vapor started to form in front of it. "Then if I call upon the cool end of the fire element, I can create ice." The vapor curled itself into a ball and froze, floating in front of Venuto's palm. "Then I can use the air element to make the ice move through the air." The ball of ice floated around the room. He made it look so easy.

"How do you think about all of those things at once?"

"It isn't really intellectual. To use a human example it's more like riding a bike. At first you have to think hard about all of the motions, but after you get comfortable with how it feels then you don't have to think about it consciously. Once you can feel the elements, you will be able to interact with them by feel, not by depending so much on the intellectual part of your mind," Venuto said.

"How long do you think it will take before I can do any magic?" Kelly asked.

"That depends on how thick your human fog is and on how much you work. I would say the shortest time before you can start to perform simple magic would be two weeks."

"Two weeks?" That seemed like a very long time.

"Maybe longer."

Kelly sighed.

"I have another engagement I must attend to," Venuto said. "I've set the archway so that you are approved to open and close it. You can come here and practice whenever you like. Our next lesson will be in one week. Until then practice what we went over today."

After Venuto left Kelly tried to practice some more, but this task was much harder than learning how to transform into a fairy had been. For that at least she had known exactly what to concentrate on. This was different – she had to try to do nothing and just be aware of the different sensations that corresponded to the different elements in her body. Her mind kept wandering away from the task and her shoulders and neck were aching. Her legs were numb. After a few more minutes she decided to give it up for the day.

She managed to find the secret archway by feeling her arm along the wall of the room until finally she touched the right spot and the archway became visible. She remembered how to get to the door of the library, but once out of the library and inside the hallway leading away from it, she wasn't sure which way to go. She succeeded in finding her way to the nearest transport bubble, which she remembered was only a few meters away from the entrance to the library. There she stood looking at the map. She didn't know which button to push because she still had no idea which particular rooms all of the unmarked circles on the map represented. Instead of risking getting lost by randomly selecting a circle, she decided to test the fairy senses of her friends. She closed her eyes and thought of Bubbles and Beatrix, mentally willing them to come to her.

A second later Bubbles, Beatrix, and Stephanie popped into the transport bubble.

"Wow, it worked," Kelly said, relieved.

"What worked?" Beatrix asked.

"Your fairy senses. I mentally called you here, didn't I?"

"Er, we ran into Venuto and he told us if we waited for you in the library you would show up sooner or later. We were on our way there right now," Bubbles answered.

"Oh." Kelly's face fell.

"So, what were you doing all this time? It's been almost two hours since you left us in the park," Stephanie said.

"Yeah, almost time for lunch," Bubbles interjected.

"I was having a magic lesson," Kelly explained.

On the way to the mess hall Kelly told her friends about her first magic lesson. They decided to walk the entire way instead of using the transport bubbles, to give Kelly more time to explain, because surely when they got to the mess hall Dimpleton, Wimpleton, and Pimpleton would be there and it was still supposed to be a secret that Kelly was a fadaman. About halfway to the mess hall they heard the sound of Flimsly's horn, but Flimsly was nowhere to be seen. Rather, the sound seemed to have come from the wall itself.

"What was that?" Stephanie asked.

"Shhh." Beatrix put her index finger up to her lips.

"Attention all fairies of Glendenland and respected guests," Flimsly's voice came to their ears from the walls, sounding some-

somewhat muffled. "His Grace the honorable, noble, wise and benevolent Glenden Grand has called a general meeting for this eve at 7:00 p.m. All fairies who wish to attend should arrive at least ten minutes early in the Great Hall. Thank you for your attention."

There was another sequence of horn notes before the walls were silent again.

"That was weird," Stephanie said.

"I wonder what the meeting will be about," Beatrix said.

"Ten glitterons says it has something to do with them Miamonians," Bubbles said.

Chapter 7
Miasmos's Search

The whole of Glendenland was buzzing with anticipation of the night's meeting. It was the only topic of discussion at lunch and theories as to its topic abounded. Dimpleton was convinced that Venuto was engaged and the meeting was to announce the identity of the lucky bride-to-be. Pimpleton and Wimpleton thought for sure the meeting would be to announce a raise in their glitteron stipends for community work, but Dimpleton said he didn't think that was an important enough announcement for a general meeting. Kelly overheard other fairies putting forth guesses ranging from an announcement of limits on nectala consumption to plans for building another underwater park. None of the fairies mentioned Miasmos or his minions; the Miasmonians didn't seem to be an issue for them at all. Kelly wondered how many Glendenians had even heard of Miasmos.

After an afternoon of more debate and another long game of tag in the park, Beatrix, Bubbles, Kelly, Stephanie, Dimpleton, Wimpleton, and Pimpleton headed for the Great Hall. The Great Hall was an apt name. It was the largest bubble Kelly had seen so far, even larger than the underwater park. The bubble was so large that Kelly wondered how boats traveling by on the river above didn't hit it. The Great Hall was filled with thousands of seats that rose up in rings like a baseball or football stadium.

"All of Glendenland can fit in this hall," Dimpleton stated proudly.

"How many fairies is that?" Stephanie asked.

"A little over four thousand."

There were already at least a thousand fairies in the hall, some having claimed the most desirable seats while others flew about and socialized before the meeting began. Dimpleton and his brothers led them towards an open row of seats near the speaking platform in the center of the hall. The thrones that had been in the audience hall the night before had been moved out to the speaking platform. Dimpleton waved to or called out his signature greeting *Hey-O!* to almost every fairy they passed. He seemed to know everyone. Kelly was glad Dimpleton was such a social butterfly because it meant that less fairies would stop to ask him who his new friends were, since they were probably so used to seeing Dimpleton with fairies they didn't know. Kelly was sure it would have attracted much more attention if Dimpleton had been a fairy with few friends and had suddenly appeared with four unfamiliar fairies in tow. Thankfully most of the fairies Dimpleton waved to didn't give more than a quick glance at Kelly and her friends, although she did notice that some fairies' eyes rested just a few extra seconds on her wings, which were presently unfurled because they had come straight from their second game of tag. Self-consciously Kelly folded her wings down onto her back.

"Dimpleton!" a high-pitched female voice called out. Dimpleton swiveled his head around to see who had called out to him. A few rows above where they were standing a short and cute blond fairy, almost as skinny as Dimpleton and with the same sand-colored wings, was waving both of her arms at them. Dimpleton grinned.

"Hey-O Bamblelina!" Dimpleton bellowed, taking a few great strides to reach her. The others followed.

"I saved you seats," Bamblelina said, flashing a bright smile. Her teeth were a startling shade of pure white.

Dimpleton introduced his cousin Bamblelina to Kelly, Stephanie, Beatrix, and Bubbles. Bubbles blushed when he was introduced and his pointed ears turned so red they were almost purple. Dimpleton insisted that Bubbles sit beside Bamblelina, which caused Bubbles to blush even more. Kelly ended up sitting between Stephanie and Dimpleton to the left of Bubbles and Bamblelina, and Wimpleton and Pimpleton sat on Bubbles and Bamblelina's right. More fairies continued to file into the room and the remaining empty seats were disappearing quickly.

"Do this many fairies usually show up for general meetings?" Kelly asked Dimpleton.

"I don't know. There have only ever been two general meetings since I was born. Usually the Great Hall is empty, except for the occasional musical performances or sports."

"What were the other general meetings about?" Stephanie asked.

Dimpleton's face grew somber. "They both happened thirteen years ago but I still remember them clearly. They were when the queen died," he said.

"How did she die?" Stephanie blurted out. Kelly hoped the question didn't offend Dimpleton. She thought it was inappropriate.

"She was murdered," Dimpleton explained in a low voice, glancing furtively about to make sure no other fairies were listening. "Someone poisoned a drink that was meant for Glenden but Queen Esmeralda drank it instead. All the evidence pointed to Peter Penadas, then the next heir to the throne. Peter was killed while supposedly trying to escape and his entire family, including his younger brother, mother, and all of his cousins, their spouses and children were banished. But some fairies have doubts as to whether Peter was really responsible." From the way he said the last sentence Kelly thought he was probably one of them.

"What do you mean Peter Penadas was the next heir to the throne? Wasn't Venuto the heir?" Stephanie asked.

Dimpleton shook his head. "No. You see until that point there had always been two ruling families of Glendenland, the Grands and the Penadas. In the year 1700 Glendenland was formed when the two major bands in the area, the Grands and the Penadas, decided to merge into one band. But so that both bands would have equal influence in Glendenland's future, it was decided that the governance of the band should pass from one family to the other and back again, instead of from father to son within one family. So the first king was Jonah Penadas and he was followed by Edmund Grand. Then came Merylyn Penadas, Gudama Grand, William Penadas, and finally Glenden Grand. Peter Penadas was William Penadas's eldest grandson, so it was his right to succeed Glenden Grand. But since he was killed and all of his family were banished, now there is only one ruling family and that makes Venuto the next heir."

"It doesn't seem fair that all members of the Penadas family were banished because of the actions of just one of them," Kelly said.

"Those were dark times," Dimpleton said. "I sincerely hope this meeting does not bring any news of a similar nature." Kelly felt a chill at these words, thinking of Marcos Witherings.

A moment later there was a loud fanfare as Flimsly appeared on stage, accompanied by four other fairies, two with horns like his and one with a trumpet. A hush came over the entire stadium as all of the fairies stared down at the stage expectantly. The two bodyguards came out next, and finally Glenden and his son were both announced and came onto the stage. Venuto sat in his throne but Glenden remained standing and glanced over the silent crowd. His face was devoid of any readable expression as it had been the night before.

"My fellow fairies," he began, his voice carrying loudly through the vast hall although unaided by a microphone. "I have called this meeting because an evil has arisen that threatens our peaceful existence."

A collective gasp arose from a large proportion of the fairies, but Kelly noticed Dimpleton was not among the fairies who gasped. Glenden continued: "Many of you may have no idea of the evil of which I speak, but others may have heard the rumors. You may have heard the whispers about free fairies gone missing, of energy being stolen from them and from humans. Some of you may have felt a growing sense of unease that seems to have no source; you may have sensed the perversions of magic being carried out. I regret to tell you that the rumors are true. This unease you may have felt does have a cause. The evil and mysterious fairy Miasmos is building an army. While none of us have seen him, or know from whence he has come, we know that he is gaining strength by feeding off of others and I fear he may be planning to attack not only other fairies but humans as well."

The mention of humans caused a series of worried and skeptical murmurs from the crowd. Glenden put up his hand for silence, which quickly followed.

"You may wonder how it is that Miasmos plans to attack humans. The answer is very troubling and I must admit I debated about whether or not to reveal it at this time. Miasmos has a fadaman son that he plans to use in his perverse quest for power. I have invited representatives from all the fairy bands in the rest of North America to come here for a council meeting. On the next full moon, exactly one month from now, the representatives who answer the call will gather here and we will collectively decide how to handle the threat. In the meantime, I request that any able-bodied and able-powered fairies who wish to join in our defense sign up for warfare training and group power coordination classes. Hours spent in these endeavors will count towards community duty or will be paid at the standard rate if in excess of the standard community hours. That is all for now. When the delegations of other fairies begin to arrive I expect them all to be treated with the utmost respect and courtesy."

Glenden and Venuto exited with the accompanying fanfare from Flimsly and his fellow musicians. Once they had gone the Great Hall erupted in a frenzied burst of conversation. Bamblelina, Wimpleton, and Pimpleton were talking animatedly with their neighbors on the other side of Bubbles. Kelly, Bubbles, Beatrix, and Stephanie were notably silent.

"This news doesn't seem to come as a surprise to you or your friends," Dimpleton said to Kelly.

"If I'm not mistaken it doesn't seem to come as much of a surprise to you either," Kelly answered.

A faint smile appeared on Dimpleton's face. "You are not mistaken."

Before Kelly had a chance to ask Dimpleton just what he knew about Miasmos, Bamblelina informed them that a special feast had been arranged in the mess hall in honor of the general meeting. They joined the masses of fairies who were headed for the feast. In the bustle Kelly lost sight of Dimpleton and his brothers but she could just see the top of Bubbles's head as he pushed past fairies he felt were moving too slowly. Bamblelina and Beatrix followed closely behind Bubbles. Kelly and Stephanie held hands so they wouldn't get separated. When they arrived at the mess hall it was packed with fairies who were excited about the feast and were also absorbing the king's announcement. Bamblelina, Bubbles, and Beatrix were no longer in sight, so while they waited in line Kelly and Stephanie eavesdropped on the conversations of nearby fairies.

"Are you going to sign up for warfare and group power co-ordination classes?" a short, plump female fairy behind them asked her companion.

"That's just a fancy way of saying to join the army. Surely I don't want to be in any war," her companion, a tall and skinny female fairy answered.

"I certainly will join. I think it's our duty," the short fairy responded.

"If it was our duty it would be required."

"Maybe it should be required," the short fairy said. The tall fairy laughed hysterically. "Maybe for male fairies, but not for females."

"Why not?"

The tall skinny fairy considered this question for a moment before finally answering. "I don't know, just because."

The two male fairies in front of Kelly and Stephanie both agreed they would join the group power coordination classes, but not so much out of a feeling of duty to protect the band but more because they thought it sounded better than a lot of the other community jobs like washing dishes and cleaning public areas.

"I don't think this Miasmos is really much of a threat anyway," one of them, a young male fairy with pale pink wings said to his neighbor. "If he were, don't you think we would have heard about him before now?"

"I've heard about him," a fairy with grey wings beside them piped in. "Free fairies are disappearing and talk says he's to blame."

"Did you ever actually know a free fairy who went missing, or did you just hear a rumor?" the skeptical pink-winged fairy asked.

"Er—"

"That's what I thought," the pink-winged fairy replied smugly. "It's all rumors, that's what I say. Especially this talk of a fadaman. Ridiculous. The old king's gone off his rocker, that's what I say."

"You shouldn't speak like that about the honorable, noble, wise and benevolent Glenden Grand," the grey-winged fairy retorted.

"What are you going to do about it?"

The grey-winged fairy pursed his lips and clenched his fists, and for a second Kelly thought she was about to witness her first fairy fight. But instead the grey-winged fairy just shouted: "Go to humanland!" and flew away.

It was immediately clear to Kelly that telling another fairy to go to humanland was a serious insult, because the skeptical fairy's face turned bright red in anger and he jumped up to pursue the other fairy. Perhaps there would be a fight after all, but the two fairies quickly disappeared from Kelly's view amongst the hordes of other fairies.

Kelly lost interest in the surrounding fairy conversations when she reached the serving table.

"Wow," Kelly heard Stephanie say beside her. The normal food for breakfast and lunch had already impressed Kelly in its choice and quality, but this was even more scrumptious. It was a true feast. There were chunks of fruits, cakes, breads, and different types of meat-like dishes that she heard other fairies referring to as grasshopper, ant, beetle, worm, and squirrel. There were casserole-type dishes and noodle dishes, and even though Kelly didn't know exactly what was in all of them they all smelt divine. She piled her plate high with a sampling of the dishes. When she and Stephanie finally made it through the line they managed to spot Bubbles, Bamblelina, and Beatrix in the nearby crowd and went to join them.

Bamblelina was talking energetically about taking warfare and group power coordination classes. "I can't wait. I've always wanted to learn how to do group magic," she said. "What about you two?" She turned to Kelly and Stephanie.

"We're just visiting the band," Kelly stammered.

"So? You can still take the classes if you want," Bamblelina said. "Bubbles is going to take them."

Kelly looked at Bubbles in surprise. He averted her gaze. Kelly thought he must really like Bamblelina. Otherwise she didn't think he would be the first to sign up for warfare and group power coordination.

"We'll think about it," Kelly said.

"Don't think about it too long; the classes start tomorrow morning first thing and you wouldn't want to miss too many of them." Bamblelina turned her attention back to the others, telling them what she thought the classes would be like.

"Good job," Stephanie leaned over and whispered to Kelly. "I got nervous when she asked that. I definitely can't join those classes because then they would figure out I can't do magic."

"Me too," Kelly said.

"At least you'll be able to do magic at some point," Stephanie said. "If you make magical progress by the next time she brings it up you can maybe say you thought about it and decided to join. I'll just have to say I'm still thinking about it."

"If she asks again just tell her you're a pacifist," Kelly said.

"Good idea." Stephanie smiled.

They stuffed themselves to the brim and when Kelly and Stephanie finally made it back to their quarters for the night Kelly's stomach was so full it almost hurt. Stephanie joked that if they ate like that every day they would both end up looking just like Bubbles in no time.

It was damp and dark and she was cold. Her head throbbed. She was in a dark room, somewhere underground. At the opposite side of the room was a small doorway, and a faint blue light was coming through it. It was magnetic. She wanted to go towards it but at the same time she was afraid. She crept forward until she reached the doorway and peeked through it. She saw what was causing the blue light. In the adjoining room there was a fairy with deep black hair braided down his back. His wings were a blazing blue and they were glowing, illuminating the room with the blue light. The fairy with blue wings had his hand stretched out in front of him, with his index finger pointing down at the crumpled form of a male fairy with tan wings and short, curly blond hair who lay on the ground writhing in pain a few steps away from the blue-winged fairy's feet.

"Tell me where he is," the fairy with glowing wings commanded, his voice rasped and scratched as if it were coming across an old radio full of static.

"I told you already, I don't know. Please stop. I don't know," the fairy on the ground pleaded.

"I'll stop when you tell me where he is," the blue-winged fairy responded, his wings glowing with a more intense light. His outstretched arm started to tremble slightly and the fairy on the ground screamed in anguish. The blue-winged fairy cackled mercilessly, clearly enjoying the pain he was causing the other fairy. Suddenly the blue-winged fairy became aware that he was being watched. He turned his head and his eyes met Kelly's. His eyes were the same blue as his wings and they were also glowing. Kelly was immediately struck by how much this fairy's face resembled that of Marcos Witherings, although Witherings lacked the pronounced age lines that the blue-winged fairy had around his mouth and eyes. Under the fairy's gaze, Kelly was filled with a feeling of coldness colder than anything she could imagine. It felt like all of her blood had turned into liquid ice. The fairy didn't move his mouth but she felt his words inside her mind.

"But you know where he is, don't you? You'll lead me to him."

The fairy's voice scratched the inside of her mind and the coldness she felt became almost impossibly intense.

"I know you've met him, I can feel it. Tell me where he is."

"Kelly, wake up!" Stephanie was beside Kelly's bed shaking her. Kelly jerked upright, breathing heavily, still with the impression of the fairy's cold blue eyes in her mind.

"Are you all right? You were screaming in your sleep." Stephanie looked worried.

"I'm fine, just a nightmare," Kelly answered.

"Some nightmare," Stephanie said. "What was it about?"

"I think it was about Miasmos," Kelly said. Stephanie listened intently as Kelly recounted what she could remember of the dream.

"Maybe it's your fairy senses," Stephanie said when Kelly had finished. "Maybe you can sense what he's really doing or what he wants."

"Maybe. But I have no idea who he was talking about. He's obviously looking for someone else too besides me."

It was still the middle of the night so Stephanie went back to her room and Kelly tried unsuccessfully to go back to sleep. She couldn't shake the image of Miasmos's eyes and every time she closed her eyes they were there. She lay staring at the domed ceiling of her room for the rest of the night.

In the morning Kelly and Stephanie went to breakfast without any of their fairy friends because Bubbles, Bamblelina, Dimpleton and his brothers were all at the group power coordination classes and Beatrix had come by early to tell them she was going to help with fairy food collection duty because she was dying to get some fresh air. On food collection duty fairies got to go outside and collect food from nature and also human markets, which was where they got the majority of their fruits and ingredients for cooking like salt, flour, and other spices.

Kelly and Stephanie both now knew the way to the mess hall, and once they arrived they saw the mess hall was reasonably full, but none of the fairies took any special notice of Kelly and Stephanie. Kelly noticed that Stephanie had changed her mind about not liking grasshopper cutlets and had helped herself to two from the serving line.

"What are we going to do all day?" Stephanie asked.

"I want to go back to the library," Kelly said.

When they were leaving the mess hall for the library they came upon Venuto, who was standing just outside the mess hall's main entrance.

"Good morning," he said. "My father has a plan to keep you two busy and to decrease the likelihood of Stephanie spreading 'human ideology'. I must confess I do find my father's worries a bit silly, but then again fairies can be quite curious so perhaps it isn't such a bad idea that you don't interact with too many of us."

"Does that mean we can't be friends with Dimpleton?" Kelly asked.

"Oh no, any fairies you happen to meet through Bubbles or Beatrix are fine to socialize with. My father just doesn't want you spending hours upon hours with many different fairies. He wants to keep your fairy contacts to a reasonable minimum, and asks that you not engage unknown fairies in unnecessary conversation."

"That seems fair," Kelly said. She was thankful that Glenden had allowed them to stay in Glendenland, and wouldn't want to do anything to make him change his mind.

"What terribly exciting plan does the king have in store for us?" Stephanie asked.

"He wants you to do community work like other fairies, but community work in medicine storage and creation, the place with the smallest number of workers. Since there are so few workers in medicine storage and creation there are shifts available when you two would be the only workers, thus leaving no opportunity for fairy chatter."

"I would have thought the library was the place with the smallest number of community workers," Kelly said.

"Yes, it has none. Hilda is a full-time worker in the library, and she is all that is needed," Venuto said. Hilda must be the fairy with the grey bun who had been manning the desk. "You will work in medicine storage and creation each morning and during other times of the day you are free to go about Glendenland as you wish. But remember if you do talk to other fairies to keep your cover stories straight. Don't give too many details because those are hard to keep track of. Shall we?"

They followed Venuto and his ever-present bodyguard to the medicine storage and creation bubble, which was right beside the hospital bubble. Kelly counted the shadow archways they passed on the way so that she could find her way back later. When they entered the bubble Kelly saw many rows of shelves that contained glass bottles and jars filled with different colored liquids and powders. Behind the shelves Kelly could just glimpse a clear plastic curtain with potted plants behind it. In front of the shelves were several tables, some with glass tubes and flasks on top filled with liquids in various stages of mixing. Others were covered with stray pieces of chopped leaves and piles of colored powders. A cauldron was steaming in a fireplace beside the tables.

"Helloooo," Kelly heard a high-pitched voice coo to them from amongst the shelves. A second later a homely, short, and slightly plump female fairy with light yellow wings appeared, carrying a jar of fairy dust. She wore an apron that had once been white but that was now speckled with different colored stains and clumps of various powders. "Are these my new charges?" she asked, gracing Kelly and Stephanie with a doting look.

"Yes. Kelly and Stephanie, meet Margretta, head healer of Glendenland," Venuto said.

"It's so nice to meet you. In all my years I've never been introduced directly to a human or a fadaman before." She smiled pleasantly.

"We're trying to keep the fact they aren't full-blooded fairies a secret for now," Venuto said.

"I figured as much. But of course it can't be a secret from me, healers can sense such things."

"Of course," Venuto said.

After Venuto took his leave, Margretta put her jar of fairy dust down on a table and wiped her hands on her apron. "Now come on, don't be shy. Come here so I can get a nearer look at you." She waved them closer.

Kelly and Stephanie gave each other apprehensive glances and walked forward. Margretta pinched Stephanie's cheek. "Why, you're just so cute!" she said.

"Thanks?" Stephanie answered uncertainly, rubbing her cheek.

"We should get to work. Today I'm making a soothing salve for burns. You two can start by grinding some of the ingredients."

Margretta directed them to a table near the steaming cauldron on which there were several grinding bowls and grinding stones along with piles of different ingredients. There were three different piles of dried leaves of varying sizes. There was also a pile of tiny black balls that resembled balls of unground pepper, although a full-sized human looking at the same pile would have said they more closely resembled poppy seeds. A pile of red balls of the same size rested beside the first pile, and a few yellow clumps lay on the far end of the table. Kelly thought the yellow clumps must be pollen. Margretta instructed that all the ingredients be ground as finely as possible so that the final product would be smooth and free of lumps.

Margretta occupied herself near the cauldron, stirring the mixture periodically and every now and then adding a pinch of fairy dust. The mixture gave off a light floral odor. Margretta had an endless supply of questions about human medicines and remedies. Stephanie and Kelly did their best to answer her questions but neither of them knew many technical details. Nevertheless, Margretta listened carefully to their explanations and was intrigued by many things they told her. One thing that surprised her was the fact that so many human remedies came in the form of pills. Margretta told them that there were very few fairy remedies delivered by pill. Most fairy remedies were either topical ointments or tonics, or were drunk or chewed. She was also surprised to hear that almost all human babies received vaccinations. Fairies had never had a need for vaccinations because they only suffered from minor illnesses similar to the flu or common colds. Mostly, fairies needed medical attention only when they had been injured, so the bulk of fairy medicine dealt with the treatment of burns, cuts, bruises, insect bites, bone breaks, and other injuries.

Long after Stephanie and Kelly's hands had started to ache from so much grinding, Margretta finally announced that their first three-hour shift was up. Kelly put down the grinding stone she was holding and shook out her hand. She and Stephanie got up and headed for the archway.

"See you tomorrow morning," Margretta called out to them cheerfully.

Once out of the room, Stephanie turned to Kelly. "I guess we didn't get out of summer labor, even though we aren't with our parents."

Kelly laughed, thinking of her mother's Christmas tree ornament project. But then she felt a stab of sadness. She envisioned Mindy all alone, not knowing for sure if her daughter was all right, probably reading and re-reading the note Kelly had left for Carmina to deliver to her.

They found their way back to the mess hall, and from there to the transport bubble beside it. Kelly studied the map for a few moments. She wasn't a hundred percent sure she remembered the transport bubble that Venuto had pressed the day before to get to the library. She picked the one she thought most likely and they walked through the archway that lit up. Once in the new transport bubble they exited through the door on the right, and walked a few meters down the hall. They went through the archway Kelly thought led to the library and thankfully it did. Kelly went to practice in the secret room, leaving Stephanie to peruse the library. About an hour later, after both of her legs had fallen asleep three times from sitting cross-legged, Kelly stopped practicing and found Stephanie asleep in one of the arm chairs with a thick volume entitled, *Chronicles of Glendenland, Volume III* in her lap. Kelly shook Stephanie awake.

"Did you know that 1920 was when the band decided to move underwater to live? Before that they had lived on the grounds of the White House, with their homes disguised in bushes and trees," Stephanie said. "Fairies don't like to live underground or underwater in general, but they didn't want to leave the land they had been attached to for so long and there were too many of them to stay hidden from humans above ground. Now they have a special charm on the water around Glendenland so that the city is invisible to humans that look down on it."

"What else did you learn?" Kelly asked.

"That's about as far as I got before I fell asleep," Stephanie confessed.

Kelly took the volume from Stephanie. It was almost as thick as the length of her hand and it was bound with dark brown leather. "How many volumes are there?"

"The books aren't in order, so I can't be sure, but there are at least five volumes of the *Chronicles of Glendenland,* at least seven volumes of *The History of Glendenland,* and at least three volumes of *Distinguished Glendenians,*" Stephanie said.

"Wow, you're an expert."

"I try."

Kelly followed Stephanie to the history section to put the book back, glancing at the other books along the way. Stephanie was right about the books not being in any logical order. A book called *Whales and Fairies, Encounters through the Centuries* was right beside another book entitled *A Complete History of Algerian Fairy Bands.*

"How do the fairies find the books they want?" Kelly asked.

"I don't know. I just remember that *The History of Glendenland, Volume III* was in between *A Fairy's Account of the Signing of the Human US Declaration of Independence,* and *Was Genghis Khan a Fadaman?*" Stephanie answered, taking the book back from Kelly and sliding it onto the shelf.

Kelly wondered if the books actually had a complex organization that she and Stephanie just couldn't figure out, or if fairies just put them back wherever they felt like. Looking more closely at the surrounding books, Kelly was surprised by how many of them dealt with human subjects. There was a book entitled *What George Washington Really Knew about Fairies* right next to two entitled *Fairy Involvement in the Human Vietnam War,* and *Human World War I, the European Fairy Perspective.*

"I thought fairies didn't like to associate with humans," Kelly said. "So why do they have so many books about human history?"

Stephanie shrugged.

"Hey look at this!" Stephanie exclaimed, pulling a hefty dark purple book off of the shelf and handing it to Kelly. It was called *Fadamen Through the Ages*. "Maybe it'll have some useful information, you know, about what kinds of fairies might have relationships with humans and stuff."

"I hope so," Kelly said.

"How does it start?"

Kelly opened the book and read aloud. "As the reader is certainly aware, fadamen are at the time of this book's writing a rare and elusive breed. The few that exist live largely in secret, often misunderstood by their fairy kinsmen. It was not always so. In ancient times in the old lands humans and fairies lived in harmony and fadamen were frequently found, and often revered. But as time passed and the rift between our species deepened, less and less fadamen were born, and questionable practices such as newborn fadaman infanticide began."

"What's infanticide?" Stephanie interrupted.

"It's when you kill little babies."

"That's horrible!"

"Ladies, I'm getting ready to go on lunch break so if you want to check out any books now would be a good time." The voice of Hilda the librarian coming from only a few steps away startled them both.

"I'd like to check out this book," Kelly said.

Hilda looked at the title. "All right, it will be due back in two weeks."

"Do we have to sign it out or something?" Kelly asked.

"Certainly not, I remember every book that is checked out," Hilda answered stiffly with her nose turned up in the air before she turned and walked away briskly.

"Was it something I said?" Kelly asked, thinking Hilda had seemed offended by her question.

Stephanie shrugged again. "We should probably go to lunch too," she suggested.

At lunch Kelly and Stephanie reunited with Bubbles, Beatrix, and Bamblelina, who had all had fun mornings in contrast to the hard work in the medicine storage and creation bubble. Beatrix said it had been wonderful to be outside again and she had even had a chance to stop by Carmina's house for a visit. Bamblelina talked excitedly about how they had created an enormous ball of fire by pooling all of their power together in group power coordination. They spent the rest of the afternoon playing darts in a common room in the fairy residences. After dinner they spent some time on the jungle gyms in the park and flying around, and after that they went to bed.

The next few days passed in much the same way. In the mornings Kelly and Stephanie helped Margretta in the medicine storage and creation bubble and visited the library so Kelly could practice her magic, and in the afternoons they played games with Beatrix and Bubbles. Sometimes in their games they were joined by Bamblelina or Dimpleton and his brothers. Kelly and Stephanie didn't have much contact with other fairies, except for the occasional exchange of a pleasantry with the fairies from group power coordination who came and said hi to Bubbles or Bamblelina, or with fairies from food collection duty who came to say hi to Beatrix. They didn't see much of Venuto, except for when he waved to them when they happened to cross paths or when he stopped by their quarters once in a while to check up on how they were doing.

Despite practicing magic daily in the library's secret room, Kelly didn't spend a lot of time further exploring the library. Although she had initially been quite excited to find the *Fadamen Through the Ages* book, it turned out to be a rather dry account of the daily lives of ancient and obscure fadamen. She didn't find it useful or even interesting to read about how a fadaman named George Mérida used to make the best hard-boiled eggs in central Spain or how another fadaman named Carol Bates used to spend her free time sewing baby dresses for the poor in London. The book was full of such tedious and non-magical details. Most of the other history books were similarly unenlightening. But during Kelly's practice sessions Stephanie managed to find a few books that were a bit more interesting, like the book of human fairytales Venuto had mentioned. The book was actually a Brother's Grimm compilation, which Kelly had never previously read. Another of Stephanie's finds was a book called *A Comparative Study of Generational Linguistics,* which despite the intimidating title turned out to be a colorful description of fairy slang. Stephanie was constantly putting her new linguistic knowledge to use, to the great amusement of Beatrix and Bubbles, who tended to break into hysterical laughter whenever Stephanie made exclamations like *That's a pile of burnt pollen!* and *She ate all the poppy seed*, which meant *That's a load of garbage* and *She's gone crazy*, respectively.

Before Kelly knew it they had been in Glendenland a week. Venuto stopped by the mess hall when she and Stephanie were at breakfast to remind her of her second magic lesson that afternoon. He sat and chatted with Kelly and Stephanie for a few moments, telling them that his father had already heard from three fairy bands that would be sending representatives to the council meeting in three weeks time. After a few minutes of chatting he got up and left.

"I think he's going to be disappointed later because I don't think I've made any magical progress at all," Kelly groaned to Stephanie once Venuto was out of earshot.

"Maybe you should buy a wand, we get our first glitteron stipend tomorrow."

"I don't think that would help very much."

"Excuse me," a voice behind Kelly said. Kelly turned to see a beautiful female fairy with delicate features behind her. The fairy had clear porcelain skin, like a china doll, with bright red lips and perfectly round circles of rosiness on her cheeks. She had light golden hair and her eyes were a brilliant sky blue. Her wings were presently unfurled and were a light pink, with gold lining the edges. "You two are visiting fairies, right?" she asked.

"Yes," Kelly answered.

"And you're relatives of Venuto's?"

"Yes."

"You don't look that much alike," the fairy responded.

"We're distant relatives," Kelly said.

The fairy still didn't seem convinced. "What relation exactly?"

"Why are you so interested?" Stephanie asked.

"Because I've studied noble fairy genealogy extensively and I'm not aware of any branch of the Grand family breaking off to become free fairies," the fairy retorted haughtily. "Nor am I aware of any other Grand family members having brown wings," she added, eyeing Stephanie's prosthetic brown wings with disdain.

"Then I'm afraid you haven't studied noble fairy genealogy enough," Stephanie snapped back.

"My father is the head of Glendenland's records section and I assure you the records are impeccable," the fairy said.

"Impeccable perhaps, but not entirely complete, it seems," Stephanie said. Kelly kicked Stephanie under the table.

The fairy narrowed her eyes and clenched her jaw. "I'll find out who you are sooner or later. I'm on to you. You've convinced Venuto you're related to him somehow because you must want something. But I won't let you hurt him, I won't!" The fairy jabbed her finger at Kelly and Stephanie with those words and then turned and stormed away. Several surrounding fairies had all fallen silent and were staring at them. Kelly shot them glares and they hurriedly stared down at their plates.

"What's up with her?" Stephanie asked.

When Kelly told Venuto about the encounter with the fairy at the start of her magic lesson he chuckled good-naturedly.

"That was Petania," he said. "Her family is a noble family and we grew up together. She's the closest thing I've ever had to a sister, and I must say she has always been quite protective of me. She just got back from a trip and I haven't had a chance to fill her in yet on who you two really are. She must have seen us talking in the mess hall and asked someone about you. They naturally would have told her you were my visiting relatives and thus she overreacted. Once I explain things to her I'm sure you will all get along quite well."

"I hope so," Kelly said.

"So, how is the practice going?" Venuto asked.

Kelly told him that she didn't think she had made much progress, but Venuto seemed pleased that she could concentrate for longer periods without getting distracted and that she could feel sensations in almost all parts of her body and identify which major sensation types corresponded to each element. He reminded her that the week before she had had trouble feeling any sensations at all. For next week he wanted her to try to feel the fire and water elements in her body and concentrate each one separately in the palms of her hands to see if she could attract the elements from her surroundings and make water vapor or flames in the air. Venuto said it was a very simple task because in actual practice one would generally call up a mixture of different elements at once, depending on the specific goal and the makeup of the surroundings. He hoped the task would be a good start and would help her become aware of the elements in the surrounding atmosphere. As they were finishing her lesson Kelly told Venuto about the dream she had had about Miasmos.

"Was that the first dream of that type you have had?" Venuto asked.

Kelly told Venuto about her previous dreams, including her very first dreams of flying around in a forest.

"Such dreams are no doubt a manifestation of your intuitive powers. Fairies, as you know, have what some call fairy senses. We are sensitive to what is happening to other fairies and we sometimes sense when something very significant happens in general."

"Does that mean I sensed what Miasmos was actually doing?"

"Not necessarily. After all there are three main types of dreams: dreams of the past, of the present, and of the future. Sometimes you may have dreams of the past, either your past or even another fairy's past. Other times you may have a dream about something that is happening at present. And other times you may have a dream of the future. But since the future hasn't happened yet, dreams of the future are not what will definitely happen. They just show one of many possibilities. With practice fairies can hone their intuitive powers and guide them. For example, we can hide ourselves from being sensed by other fairies and also in some cases we can communicate telepathically with other fairies, but that requires more intuitive power than most fairies possess. Such communication would be well within reach of a powerful fairy like Miasmos, though, so it isn't inconceivable that he might enter one of your dreams and try to communicate with you."

"You mean he was really talking to me? Is that dangerous?"

"I don't think you are in any real danger from the dreams, but it is good that you told me about them. Please let me know if you have any more."

"I will," Kelly promised. She thought for a moment about how to best phrase her next question. "When two fairies see each other in dreams does it mean they have any sort of special connection with each other?"

"It is definitely easier for fairies who already share a deep bond to communicate mentally over distances."

"When you say a deep bond, do you mean like a family bond?"

"Yes, that is one type of deep bond, why do you ask that?"

"I was just wondering if Miasmos and I could be related."

This question didn't seem to surprise Venuto. "You mean if he could be your father?"

"Yes," Kelly answered.

"I wish I could tell you for sure that you weren't Miasmos's daughter. But I'm afraid that based on wing color it is possible."

"What do you mean?"

"Miasmos has blue wings. Fairies with blue wings can have children with blue, purple, or silver wings."

"And mine are purple and silver," Kelly said, starting to feel sick to her stomach.

"However, your father also could have had purple or silver wings, or any combination of those two colors and blue," Venuto added.

"But from what I've seen of the fairies here none of those colors are very common."

"You are correct, those colors are quite rare. But even so there are still many fairies out there in this world with those wing colors," Venuto said, putting his hand on Kelly's shoulder reassuringly.

"How many?"

"Hundreds at least, maybe even thousands."

Kelly was glad to hear that there were in fact a lot of fairies besides Miasmos who could be her father. But Miasmos still hadn't been ruled out. Also, if there really were thousands of fairies out there with blue, silver, or purple wings, then finding which one of them was her father was going to be like finding a needle in a haystack.

"Is there any way to use fairy senses to find out who my father is?" Kelly asked.

Venuto sighed. "Since the father-daughter bond is a strong one, it is possible that as your fairy senses develop further you could start to have dreams or visions of him, but unfortunately the odds of that are less because you two have never actually met."

"Could another fairy with powerful fairy senses sense who my father was somehow?"

"Only if that fairy already knew your father well would he or she be able to sense you were his daughter. Otherwise, you and your father would have to be in the same room for another fairy to sense the relationship," Venuto said.

"So pretty much the only way to find him at this point would be to track down every male fairy in the world with blue, purple, or silver wings, put them in the same room with me, and have a powerful fairy walk around and figure out which one was my father. Somehow that's not very encouraging."

"Look on the bright side, at least your father doesn't have brown wings. Then the Great Hall wouldn't even be big enough to fit them all," Venuto joked.

That evening when Kelly and Stephanie were getting ready for bed they heard the sound of the chimes that meant someone was at their door. Kelly placed her hand against the wall to unlock the archway and to her surprise Petania walked into the room.

"I hope I'm not disturbing you, but Venuto told me who you really are and why you have a cover story. So I came to apologize, really I'm quite embarrassed," Petania began.

"That's all right," Kelly said.

"No hard feelings," Stephanie said.

"Hard feelings?" Petania asked.

"When you say no hard feelings it means you're accepting an apology," Kelly explained.

"Oh," Petania laughed nervously. "Um, that's all I came to say I guess. I won't bother you anymore." Petania turned to leave.

"You aren't bothering us," Kelly said. "You can stay for a bit if you'd like."

"That's all right, it's late. Maybe we'll see each other some other time." With that Petania started to walk towards the door.

"Wait a second, you said before that your father is the head of Glendenland's records section?" Kelly asked.

"That's right," Petania answered, stopping and turning to face Kelly and Stephanie again.

"And what kind of information is kept there?"

"Records, of course" she said curtly. Kelly and Stephanie looked at her expectantly, waiting for her to say more. "Like marriage certificates, birth certificates, death certificates..." Petania finally added.

"Is a fairy's wing color written on their birth certificate?" Kelly asked.

"Of course it is. Along with their birth weight, measurements, and eye color. Now, if you'll excuse me I really must be going." Petania swirled around again and left the room so quickly that neither Kelly nor Stephanie had any time to protest.

"I still don't think she likes us very much," Stephanie commented.

"I think you're right."

"Why all the sudden interest in the records section?" Stephanie asked.

Kelly filled Stephanie in on what she had learned from Venuto about what potential wing colors her father could have.

"So you want to look at all the birth certificates to track down fairies with blue, purple, or silver wings, to see if any fairy from Glendenland is your father?"

"It's an idea. But I doubt the records are public and something tells me Petania isn't going to want to help us gain access to them."

"There might be other ways," Stephanie said mischievously. Kelly recognized that tone of voice. It was the tone Stephanie's voice always took on when she was telling Kelly about sneaking out of her parents' house in the middle of the night or about forging permission slips for class trips her parents didn't want her to go on.

"Don't get any ideas," Kelly said. "We don't want to get kicked out of Glendenland, remember?"

The next afternoon they met Beatrix and Bubbles to go and get their first glitteron stipends. Perhaps to encourage fairies to spend their glitterons, weekly stipends were handed out at a table inside the main market. Bubbles could hardly contain his excitement as they waited in line to reach the table.

"First I'm going to buy me some silver slippers to match my bag," Bubbles said. "Then an underwater breathing mask so I can travel through the water, some perfume, a new wand, maybe some fairy dust—"

"We only get thirty glitterons each, Bubbles," Beatrix interrupted, shouting down to Bubbles from where she had been flying energetic circles above the queue of fairies.

"And your point is?" Bubbles asked.

"Thirty glitterons will buy maybe half those things, if you're lucky," she answered, as she completed three backwards airborne summersaults so fast that her image blurred in the air. Then she swooped down to join them, as they were the next in line to receive their glitterons. After the somewhat bored fairy manning the stipend table had handed them each their thirty glitterons, Kelly and Stephanie struggled to keep up with Bubbles as he sprinted through the rows of stalls in search of his items, and Beatrix happily flew around the stalls that hung from the roof of the market bubble.

Finally Bubbles stopped at a stall that sold slippers, hats, and cloth bags. He picked up a pair of silver slippers that had small bows on the tops near the toes.

"How much are these?" he asked the skinny and wizened old male fairy who sat behind the stall.

"Seven glitterons."

Bubbles gasped.

"What did I tell you?" Beatrix said cheerfully, having come down from the hanging stalls when she saw Bubbles pick up the silver slippers. Bubbles looked at the slippers he held in his hand, then he looked at his bag of glitterons. Then he looked back to the slippers. Then back to the glitterons. Finally he shoved the slippers into his sequin-covered bag and counted out seven glitterons to pay for them. Kelly bought a pair of simple pale green slippers and a matching bag for a total of seven glitterons. The slippers weren't as flashy as Bubbles's, but they were very comfortable and reminded her of delicate ballet shoes. Stephanie bought a dark burgundy silk bag for ten glitterons.

As they were leaving the stall something caught Bubbles's eye. "Hey, are those fairy sense necklaces?" he asked the stall owner. He was referring to a collection of thin golden chains hanging from a nail in the corner of the stall.

"Yes, top of the line, most recent models. Only five glitterons per pair," the stall owner replied.

"I'll take a pair," Bubbles said. Bubbles handed over the five glitterons and received two gold chains and a small round object from the stall owner in exchange.

"What are those?" Stephanie asked him.

"These are fairy sense necklaces," Bubbles said. "This is the charm." Bubbles held up the small object the stall owner had handed him with the chains. "It breaks into two parts like this, see? And one part goes on each chain." He broke the object apart, connected each half to a respective chain, and put one necklace on. Then he handed the other necklace to Kelly. Kelly looked closer at the charm and saw that it was a flat metal semi-circle, with a small, clear round stone in the middle.

"That stone in the middle will get hot and turn red if the wearer of the other half of the charm is in danger. That's why they're called fairy sense necklaces – they help your fairy senses if you don't have very good ones," Bubbles said. "They also help the wearer of the other half sense your location even when you aren't in danger. Since you are a *you-know-what*, you are harder for us to sense, and like I said the last time you were in danger we didn't sense it until you were deep in danger. Maybe this will warn us sooner."

Kelly was touched by this gesture. "Thanks Bubbles," she said and put on the necklace.

Next they visited a stall that sold underwater breathing masks. They sold for an expensive fourteen glitterons a piece, but considering they were something their lives would depend on when they were in use, Kelly and the others thought it was a reasonable price to pay. They all purchased masks because Dimpleton had told them that not only was it fun to swim in the river, but it was also a fast way to get from one place to another in Glendenland if there were lots of fairies clogging the hallways or using the transport bubbles. Also, since one could go in a straight line from one bubble to another underwater and didn't have to follow the shape of the hallways, for travel between certain bubbles it was faster to swim than to walk. Finally, to leave Glendenland, swimming to the surface of the river was generally the quickest way.

After their mask purchases Kelly had nine glitterons left, Stephanie had six, Bubbles four, and Beatrix sixteen. Beatrix said she wanted to save the rest of her glitterons until the next week so she could buy a beautiful dress she had seen in one of the hanging stalls for eighteen glitterons. Kelly also decided to save her glitterons, but Stephanie spent her last six on a large bottle of nectala and a chunk of honeycomb, which both she and Bubbles sipped and crunched on as they continued to walk around the market. Bubbles was determined to buy a new wand, even though Beatrix told him that he wouldn't be able to buy any nice wand for only four glitterons. They asked a passing fairy where they could buy wands and the fairy pointed them to one of the hanging stalls at the far end of the market. They flew up to the stall the fairy had indicated. It was one of the few stalls that were completely enclosed – instead of a hanging open platform it was a large square cube that hung down from the ceiling.

    They entered the cube through a curtain and found themselves in a small and smoky room, filled with mint incense that burnt on top of a little wooden desk. Behind the wooden desk sat another old and wizened fairy who looked like he could be the twin brother of the fairy who had sold them their slippers. The walls of the small room were lined with shelves stuffed full of long, thin wand-like objects. Some looked like the stereotypical magic wands – forearm-length polished wooden sticks. Others were more unique – like plastic rods of all different colors, wands that looked like they were carved from stone or jade, and a few absolutely gorgeous ones that were locked behind panes of glass. One of the locked-up wands had a crystalline texture that glinted as though it were being kissed by sunlight, even though at present it wasn't receiving any direct light. Another looked to be entirely made of gold, and another was a transparent clear color that reminded Kelly of Marcos Witherings's wand, except for this wand had a gold encrusted handle with a gemstone, possibly a ruby, in the handle. It took less than the blink of an eye for Bubbles to be drawn to the most expensive wands. He pressed his nose up against the glass and stared longingly at the entirely gold wand. He asked the wizened old fairy how much it cost.

    "Nine-hundred and fifty glitterons," the old fairy answered. Bubbles groaned.

"How about this one?" Beatrix suggested, holding up a dark wooden wand. It was plain but Kelly thought it would be a definite improvement on his toothpick.

"I don't like it," he said without even looking at it.

"It's only six glitterons," Beatrix said. "I'll loan you the two you need and you can pay me back next week."

"No, it's ugly!"

"I think it's nice," Stephanie said, taking the wand from Beatrix and extending it to Bubbles. "Here, try it."

Bubbles pushed Stephanie's arm away and headed for the door of the stall. The others followed. Kelly gave the old fairy an apologetic look.

"Have a nice day," the old fairy said politely.

As Kelly exited the stall just behind the others, she caught sight of Bubbles bumping straight into Petania, who happened to be passing by with Venuto at that very moment.

"Would it be too much to ask for you to pay attention to where you are flying?" Petania asked haughtily, dusting herself off from the collision.

"My apologies," Bubbles mumbled, his mind still clearly on the golden wand.

"Hi Kelly! How's the practice coming along?" Venuto asked when he spotted Kelly.

"Okay," Kelly answered.

"If you have any questions before our next lesson just let me know," Venuto said. "Also, I'd like for you all to join me tomorrow night for dinner in the royal dining hall. Since you are my relatives and visitors we ought to be spending more time together. Don't you think? We wouldn't want any fairies to think we weren't on good terms." Venuto winked.

"I really don't think anyone would notice how much time you spend together," Petania interjected.

"Well, after someone so publicly insinuated they weren't really my relatives, I think a show of unity is in order," Venuto said with a slight smile on his face.

Petania frowned.

"That's why of course you should come too Petania," Venuto continued. "And we should meet in the park first and walk all the way back to my quarters together, smiling and getting along quite well," he added. "How does seven sound?" Venuto asked Kelly.

"Sounds good to me, we'll see you then," she said.

"Bye." Venuto waved cheerfully as they parted ways. Petania didn't say anything.

"That Petania seriously has issues," Stephanie said as soon as Venuto and Petania had left.

"Venuto said she's protective of him," Kelly answered.

"A little more than protective I'd say," Beatrix said.

Chapter 8
The Key to Embralia

She was back in the underground tunnels. Miasmos and his son Marcos Witherings were standing side by side in the same room from the last dream, but the fairy who had been being tortured before wasn't there. Kelly felt like she was standing right beside Witherings and Miasmos, but neither one of them made any sign that they knew she was there.

"Did she tell you where he is?" Witherings asked his father.

"No," Miasmos said.

"But you're sure he has the Key to Embralia?"

"Of course I'm sure," Miasmos hissed.

"But how do you know his brother gave him the Key? Couldn't Peter have given it to someone else before he was killed?"

"Peter would have only trusted his younger brother to guard the Key. Besides, there was no time for him to give it to anyone else, even if—"

Abruptly Miasmos stopped and swirled around to fix his eyes on the place Kelly was watching from. His eyes changed from their bright blue glow to a brilliant orange, then the vision was gone.

Kelly sat up. She must have drifted off to sleep after lying down for a moment to rest her back. Before that she had been sitting cross-legged for over an hour while trying to create a magic fireball, so her back had understandably grown tired. Kelly resumed her sitting position and tried to concentrate on feeling the heat in her hand. She attempted to mentally guide all of the other feelings of heat in her body to join the heat in her palm while she simultaneously imagined the heat in her palm getting hotter and hotter. She felt some of the stray fire element in her toes streaming up her body to settle in her palm. She had been at this task on and off almost all day, but so far she had had no luck. But suddenly she noticed something – she wasn't just feeling the heat from inside of her body – she could also feel a heat in the air around her palm and forearm, as if the air around her hand was hot. It felt like she had just stuck her hand inside a stuffy car that had been sitting out in the sun with all its windows closed. The concentration of fire element in her hand was attracting surrounding fire element from the air. Then it happened. Kelly stared down as a few sparks appeared a few inches above her palm. Then a few more sparks appeared, and there were about eight bright orange sparks starting to swirl in the palm of her hand. Just as suddenly as they had begun they disappeared. Kelly had been so excited when she saw them that she had stopped concentrating on turning those few sparks into an actual ball of fire.

She tried again. This time it didn't take so long for the first sparks to appear, and in a few minutes she had a tiny ball of fire burning over her palm. She felt a subtle tingling sensation in addition to the heat, which she knew was the air element. She tried to direct this buzzing to move the ball of fire around, but she was only able to manage misshaping the ball a bit. She couldn't actually displace it.

"Wow, you're doing magic!" Kelly heard Stephanie exclaim from the doorway.

Kelly's concentration broke again and the ball of fire disappeared. "I know, I finally made a fireball." Kelly smiled. "And I think I almost know how to use the air element to move it around. I can't wait to show Venuto."

"Well you're about to get your chance. We have to go meet him in the park now for dinner or we'll be late. Bubbles and Beatrix are waiting outside."

They met Bubbles and Beatrix, who were both happy to hear of Kelly's first magical success. When they reached the park Venuto and Petania were already there, sitting together on the grass. When they arrived Petania jumped up to meet them, smiling on her way over.

"Hello, it's so nice to see you, how are you?" Petania asked in a saccharine-sweet voice.

"Fine thanks," Kelly said.

Venuto joined them and they started to walk back towards the royal quarters. Venuto's bodyguard was there as well of course but since he was always so quiet Kelly almost didn't even notice him anymore. Petania chatted amicably about her day helping her father in the records section of Glendenland as they walked along.

"Wait, so she likes us now?" Bubbles whispered to Kelly between his teeth.

"She's just putting on a show so that the other fairies think she accepted that Stephanie and I are Venuto's relatives."

"Oh," Bubbles said.

It was clear that Kelly was right because as soon as they reached the smaller and almost empty hallways closer to the royal living quarters, Petania abruptly fell silent. Kelly took the opportunity to tell Venuto she had succeeded in making a fireball.

"That's wonderful. I wasn't expecting you to make one that fast. I thought perhaps you might get a few sparks but not a full ball of fire. That's just great." Venuto beamed.

"It isn't that amazing Venuto. I was making balls of fire before I could walk," Petania said.

"Yes, but you aren't a fadaman are you?" he replied.

"No, but still. I don't think you need to get so excited about it."

"At our next lesson we can work on directing the elements through space," Venuto told Kelly.

They walked the rest of the way in an awkward silence. Venuto stopped in front of an unremarkable shadow archway. "This is the front entrance to the royal living quarters," he announced.

He placed his hand up to the archway and a series of chimes ensued.

While the doorway had been unremarkable, the inside of the bubble was certainly not. The floor was a polished light pink marble, and pots filled with beautiful plants and flowers balanced out the empty space between the plush sofa in the center of the bubble and the large armchairs that dotted the rest of the interior. At regular intervals along the bubble's circumference were a number of shadow archways. "This is the main reception room, basically the center of the quarters, and where visitors wait. Each of the shadow archways leads to a different main section. The one directly in front of us leads to the royal dining hall," Venuto said.

They followed Venuto through that archway and found themselves in a large bubble, about four times the entire size of Kelly and Stephanie's quarters. There was a fireplace on the far side of the bubble and a large square table that could seat at least fifty fairies stretched almost the entire length of the space. The wooden chairs around the table had beautiful deep red velvet cushions. A sparkling chandelier hung from the top of the bubble and swayed ever so slightly back and forth with the undulating movements of the bubble's surface.

"Please be seated," Venuto said. He motioned to the farthest end of the table, closest to the fireplace, where there were six place settings. Venuto sat at the head of the table, with Petania on his right and Kelly on his left. Stephanie sat across from Kelly, which put her right next to Petania. Bubbles and Beatrix sat to Kelly's left. They each had delicate china plates, silver forks, knives, spoons, cloth napkins, and golden goblets. Soon after they were seated the familiar fairy Flimsly appeared, this time carrying a bottle instead of his typical horn. He filled each of their goblets with a rich, dark red liquid.

"Is that wine?" Stephanie asked hopefully

"Grape juice," Flimsly answered. But it was the best grape juice Kelly had ever tasted. It was sweet and cool and just the right texture.

"How are things in medicine storage and creation?" Venuto asked.

Kelly told him about their work helping Margretta make the healing salve for burns and that they had also been helping to water and care for the variety of medicinal plants kept in the bubble. Next Bubbles talked a little about how his group power coordination classes were going. He said he especially liked it when the class broke into two groups and practiced fighting with each other, of course using non-hurtful magic. Each group mainly tried to spray the other group with large walls of water or to push the other group through the air by creating wind. There was a lull in the conversation when Flimsly brought them their succulent dinner because they were too busy eating to talk. They were served a delicious corn paste, cranberry sauce, bread, and squirrel steaks. They also enjoyed a salad made from the petals of an edible flower. After that came a scrumptious chocolate cake with a drizzling of dark chocolate sauce over the top. As they were finishing off the cake, Kelly asked Venuto if he had heard from any more fairy delegations.

"Right now four bands will be sending either their leaders or representatives to the council meeting. The Pixelori from New York City, the Rowenians from Tennessee, the Xianda from Texas, and the Bildensterns from South Dakota. I haven't heard from the Coppertoppins in California, but I doubt we will hear from them as in general they keep very much to themselves. But four out of the five major North American bands is a good number. We did send a messenger to the secluded fairy bands living in the national parks, but it's even more doubtful we will hear from them," Venuto said.

"Secluded fairies?" Stephanie asked.

"Fairies who've retreated to areas where they have absolutely no contact, or extremely rare contact, with humans. They wish to live free of the influence and destructive interference of humans," Petania answered. It was the first thing she had said since they sat down for dinner.

"What about smaller bands like the Catanori in Maryland, or free fairies?" Bubbles asked.

"What do you mean?" Venuto asked.

"Did you send any messengers to them?"

"No," Venuto said.

"You might consider it, I know a lot of them who would be willing to help get rid of Miasmos," Bubbles said.

"I will mention the idea to my father."

Bubbles smiled proudly and went back to gobbling up his third helping of cake. Petania played with her hair, looking bored. Kelly remembered the dream she had earlier.

"I had another dream with Miasmos in it," Kelly said.

Venuto leaned forward. "What happened?"

"Miasmos was still looking for the same male fairy but didn't know where he was. Actually it seems like he's more interested in something the male fairy has. Some key his older brother Peter gave him."

"Peter?" Petania asked. Kelly noticed that she had gone completely pale – the usually present perfect spots of rosiness on her checks had disappeared entirely. Bubbles paused with a forkful of cake an inch from his mouth and looked at Petania curiously.

"He must be looking for the Key to Embralia," Venuto said. He also had a grim expression on his face.

"What's the Key to Embralia?" Beatrix asked.

Venuto sighed. "Embralia was the name of an ancient city in the old lands across the sea. It was the home of the ancestors of the Penadas family, who until relatively recently were one of the ruling families of Glendenland. But as you might have been told, my mother was murdered by Peter Penadas, who was later killed in his attempt to escape. He didn't have the Key on him when he was killed so we believe he was able to pass it on to someone else."

"His younger brother?" Kelly asked.

"Most likely. But to answer your question Beatrix, the Key to Embralia isn't a regular key of the type you might use to open a door. It is a relic of deep and ancient magic that has been passed on from generation to generation in the Penadas family ever since the fall of Embralia 2,500 years ago."

Venuto went on to explain that 2,500 years in the past Embralia had been a splendid fairy city with at least 30,000 inhabitants. The ruling family, the Embers, lived in a large castle on the side of a tall, rocky mountain. The old king, Betardany Ember, was ailing and his one wish was to see his only daughter, Bethilda, married before he died. Bethilda was in love with the lowly farm fairy Petardo, unbeknownst to her father, but she was able to convince the king to hold a tournament for her hand in marriage. The tournament would be open to all male fairies, both rich and poor, and he who won the tournament would be able to marry the princess. Hundreds of fairies showed up to the tournament, in which they had to face magical obstacles and fight in magical duels. The princess's young love Petardo fought bravely and strongly, displaying an uncommon magical gift. Finally, after three long days the tournament was over, and the young farm fairy Petardo had won.

But just as Petardo was approaching the throne to receive a formal blessing to marry the princess, a dark hooded figure arrived at the castle. The new arrival said he was a prince from a faraway realm who had been traveling for many days to reach the tournament. The king told the fairy he was sorry but the tournament was over. Somehow the dark fairy convinced the king to extend the tournament to allow him to compete. It is not completely clear how he accomplished this feat, but perhaps in the king's old age the dark fairy was able to twist his mind. The king agreed to extend the tournament to one last challenge. He said there was an ancient stone of great power older even than the Earth itself, hidden somewhere in the deep forest on the other side of the mountain. As a young fairy the king had spent years searching for the stone, as legend said that the stone was the key to the mountain. It was believed that if the stone was placed on the right spot at the very top of the mountain, the mountain would open up, releasing all the ancient magic locked inside to whoever had opened it.

Petardo and the stranger, called Venalaz, set out the next morning. Nothing was heard from them for months. Spring past, then summer, fall, and winter. A whole year went by and even fairy senses gave no information because the deep forest on the other side of the mountain was shrouded in a thick perpetual fog that blocked them. The old king grew sicker and sicker and it didn't look like he would live much longer. Finally the stranger Venalaz returned with a small, polished black stone, almost fourteen months after he and Petardo had set out. The princess was distraught her love had not returned, and Venalaz told her that unfortunately her love had died. He claimed to have found Petardo's body in the forest close to the place where the stone had been hidden. Venalaz said that thanks to Petardo he had been aware of one of the magical traps guarding the stone. Princess Bethilda didn't believe her love was dead until Venalaz produced a necklace from his pocket, a necklace that the princess had given Petardo and that she knew he would never have parted with. Bethilda then knew that Petardo really was dead. But she didn't believe Venalaz's story. She suspected the truth, that Venalaz had killed her love. In fact, Venalaz had followed Petardo and waited until he had found the stone. Once Petardo had successfully retrieved the stone from its hiding place, Venalaz ambushed him, killing him and stealing the stone.

According to the rules of the tournament, the arrangements were made for the wedding between Venalaz and Bethilda. But the night before the wedding Bethilda killed herself by drinking poison. The news of his daughter's death proved too much for the old king and he died as soon as he heard it. Thus the throne of Embralia was empty, but Venalaz still hadn't married the princess so technically he had no right to the throne. Instead, Bethilda's young but brave cousin, Carlo, was the next in line. After all of his work to marry the princess, Venalaz was not willing to give up his chance to be king. Late that night he started to climb the mountain, aiming to place the stone at the top to get the ancient power from within. With that power he believed he would be powerful enough to overcome Carlo and his army.

Carlo heard of Venalaz's intentions and followed him. He caught up to Venalaz just as he had set the stone down in a small hole in a large boulder that sat on the peak of the mountain. The ground started to tremble and quake, and large rocks began to roll down the mountain. Carlo and Venalaz dueled as the mountain shook and a crevice started to open at its peak. Carlo managed to defeat Venalaz and quickly pulled the stone out of its position. The mountain stopped shaking. Carlo went back down to the city but found it was gone, having been completely buried in the rubble that had fallen from the mountain. Not a single fairy of all the thousands living in Embralia had survived, because the destruction had befallen them so quickly that those who weren't asleep in their beds hadn't even had a chance to unfurl their wings and fly to safety. Carlo, heartbroken, vowed that the stone should never be used because the destruction that would be unleashed by fully unlocking the mountain's power was too great. He therefore became the first guardian of the stone, and from that point onward the Embers were known as the Penadas because in the ancient fairy language "pena" meant suffering, and Carlo took that name to remind himself of the suffering the stone had caused his realm – the suffering that must be avoided in the future.

"Since that time the stone has been passed from generation to generation through Carlo's heirs, and has come to be known as the Key to Embralia. The exact location of Embralia is no longer known, but I am sure that if it were to be found, and if the stone were to be placed again at its peak, the mountain would open up the rest of the way and the ancient power inside would become available. Any fairy who received that power would be more powerful than any other fairy on Earth, but that power would come at a terrible price of destruction. This knowledge of certain destruction would deter most fairies from desiring it, but a fairy like Miasmos would not be deterred. In fact, he is probably more attracted because of it," Venuto concluded.

"If the stone is that dangerous why didn't Carlo just destroy it?" Kelly asked.

"He tried, but it was impossible. It can't be destroyed," Petania said.

It was very late by the time Venuto finished the story, so they said good-bye and left the royal quarters. Kelly's dreams that night were filled with the story of Princess Bethilda and her young love.

The next morning when Kelly and Stephanie arrived at the medicine storage and creation bubble, the bubble was filled with black smoke and there was soot all over the place. Margretta was standing in the middle of the room, waving her hand to clear the smoke away from her face.

"What happened?" Kelly asked, coughing as the smoke tickled her lungs.

"Hallo dears. Just had a little potion explosion I'm afraid. Looks like the honeysuckle nectar was past its use-by date. Would you two fetch some water and rags and help me clean this mess up?"

Kelly and Stephanie headed for the closest sink, near where the plants were kept, filled a bucket with water, and went to work scrubbing at the soot while Margretta examined the charred contents of the cauldron.

"Hey, look at your necklace," Stephanie said, pointing to the fairy sense necklace Bubbles had given Kelly.

Kelly looked down and saw that the clear circular stone had taken on a very slight pink tint.

"Is it warm?" Stephanie asked.

"No," Kelly said.

"Do you think Bubbles is in danger?"

"I don't think so. He said it would turn red and hot if the other wearer was in danger. It's still mostly clear, and it isn't hot at all."

"Kelly dear?" Margretta called from where she was scraping away at the burnt contents of the cauldron.

"Yes?"

"Would you go back and get me some lemon juice?"

"What does she want lemon juice for?" Stephanie whispered. Kelly shrugged.

"Where is it?" Kelly asked as she got up.

"The far wall, top shelf. You might need a chair to stand on, the shelves are too close together to fly in between."

Kelly grabbed a chair and headed for the shelves. Margretta had never asked Kelly to get anything off of any of the top shelves before, and as Kelly stood up on the chair she could see that it had been a long time since anyone had touched the items. All of the jars were coated in thick grey dust that completely obscured their name labels. Kelly reached out and wiped the dust from the label of the first jar. Scrawled in Margretta's sloppy handwriting were the words "Chopped pig ear, for skin cream." *Gross*, Kelly thought. She wiped the dust off the next jar. It read "Boiled watermelon juice, for shiny hair." The next jar's label read simply "Memory Restorative." That label perked Kelly's interest. Could it be a potion for restoring lost memories? A few jars later Kelly found the lemon juice, and she brought it over to Margretta.

"Thank you dearie," Margretta said as Kelly handed her the lemon juice. Margretta promptly removed the cork at the top of the jar and took a swig of the juice. "Nothing like aged lemon juice," she said, smacking her lips. "Would you like some?" She extended the jar to Kelly.

"No thanks," Kelly said. "When I was getting the lemon juice I saw another jar called 'memory restorative', what does that do?"

"It helps improve your memory, like if you need to memorize lists of potion ingredients. Maybe I should start taking it because it looks like it wasn't the honeysuckle's being expired, but rather my forgetting to add the cinnamon that caused today's potion mishap," Margretta said.

"So the memory restorative doesn't restore lost memories?" Kelly asked.

"Wouldn't that be nice." Margretta chuckled. "Unfortunately, once you forget something no potion can help you. Unless of course your memory was erased with a potion in the first place, then you would just need the antidote."

"There are potions that can erase your memory?" Kelly asked.

"Oh yes. Although you always need a spell as well to specify exactly which memories you want to erase."

"Do you have any of the antidotes?" Kelly asked.

"Why, was your memory erased?" Margretta asked nonchalantly as if she had been asking something as inconsequential as whether or not Kelly had ever played a game of tag in the underwater park.

"No, but my mother's might have been."

"I see. If you can bring me a sample of the potion that was used to erase her memory, then I could make an antidote. Otherwise, there's not much I can do," Margretta said matter-of-factly before downing the last of the lemon juice and turning back to the cauldron.

"How in the world am I supposed to get my hands on a sample of the potion?" Kelly commented to Stephanie as she rejoined her in cleaning up the mess from the explosion.

"Beats me."

By the time they had finished cleaning it was the end of their shift. They went to the mess hall for lunch and were soon joined by Dimpleton, Bamblelina, and Beatrix.

"Where's Bubbles?" Dimpleton asked.

"Don't know, I guess he's still on food collection duty," Beatrix answered.

"Too bad. I'm not sure how much longer the fried fly wings are going to last. They're a delicacy," Dimpleton said. He picked up one of the wings and chomped down on it. It crunched like a potato chip.

Kelly reached up to touch the charm on her fairy sense necklace. It was still cool to the touch.

"After we eat do you want to go for a swim in the river to try out your new breathing masks?" Dimpleton asked.

"We'd love to," Kelly replied.

After they finished eating there was still no sign of Bubbles. But they decided to go for the swim anyway. Kelly was nervous about entering the water as they approached the top of the mess hall.

"What if it doesn't work?" she asked as she slipped on her mask. It felt loose and far from airtight. Dimpleton assured her that once in contact with water the mask would form a seal and puff out a little bit, leaving a pocket of air that would be renewed continually with oxygen extracted from the water. Besides, she could just turn around and go back inside if she thought there was something wrong with it.

Dimpleton went first and Bamblelina and Beatrix went next. Stephanie and Kelly followed. Like Dimpleton had said, once Kelly was on the other side of the wall and out in the river, the mask made a seal against her face and a pocket of air formed. She breathed in and it was just like she had been breathing above water. It was amazing. They followed Dimpleton as he swam up a bit towards the surface. He then motioned for them to stop and turn around to look at Glendenland from the outside. Kelly could see the group of bubbles that formed the fairy city stretching across the bottom of the river. They swam for a full fifteen minutes or so in one direction and there were still more bubbles below them. Glendenland really was quite large, and Kelly wondered how it managed to stay hidden. Then she remembered that Stephanie had read it was invisible to humans. She wondered if Stephanie could see Glendenland below them or not, but she couldn't ask her friend because although they could breathe underwater using the masks they couldn't talk to each other.

Just then Kelly became aware of a pink glow in the water. She looked around to see where it was coming from, and realized that it was coming from her fairy sense necklace, which was now almost painfully hot to the touch and glowing a brilliant red. Bubbles was in trouble. Dimpleton, who had been swimming ahead, turned around and looked at the necklace as Beatrix starting swimming in panicked circles around them. Dimpleton motioned for them to follow him back in the direction they had come from, and now instead of swimming normally with his arms and legs he pumped his wings strongly in a backwards, arched motion, which propelled him through the water at great speed. Bamblelina, Beatrix, and Stephanie spurted after him, but Kelly dragged a bit behind for a few moments before she got the hang of the new arching wing motion. She caught up to the others just in time to see them enter the top of a bubble, which somehow she knew was the hospital bubble. Perhaps since she was able to do some simple magic now she was also able to sense which bubbles were which like the other fairies could, but she didn't stop to ponder that question because she was too worried about Bubbles.

She entered the hospital bubble and looked down. Even though medicine storage and creation was right next to it, she had never actually been inside the hospital bubble before. It was a large open space with many beds, but one side of the bubble was separated from the rest by a curtain, and that region contained several smaller curtained-off divisions within it. One of these small curtain rooms was full of frenzied activity, and Kelly stuffed her breathing mask in her bag and flew down to join the others.

Bubbles was lying on a table in the middle of the room, and was babbling incoherently and thrashing about. Kelly was surprised to see that Carmina was there, helping to hold down Bubbles while Margretta tried to examine him. Then it occurred to her that if Carmina was there it meant she must have been close to Bubbles when he was hurt. Kelly immediately knew Bubbles must have gone in search of the snow globe. She was furious with him but more than furious she was worried. She could see that the entire front of his shirt had been burnt off and his chest was covered in burns. He had a big gash on the side of his face. Beatrix was fluttering about nervously in the air above Bubbles, talking to him to try to calm him down, and Bamblelina and Dimpleton were standing at the end of the table looking on. Kelly noticed that Thomas was also there, standing quietly off in the corner of the room. She went to join him.

"What happened?" she asked.

"I just happened to be flying around looking for some flowers near your house, and I sensed that Bubbles was in danger. I flew up to see what was happening and found him on your front porch trying to fight off three of Miasmos's minions. I chased them away but he was badly injured. I got Carmina to help me and we brought him here, because neither one of us has the skills to treat him ourselves."

"Is he going to be all right?" Kelly asked as Bubbles let out a loud scream and tried to bite Margretta's arm.

"I don't know. His injuries are very serious, but I hope we got him here in time. What in the world was he doing at your house?"

Kelly explained that Bubbles had been after the glitterons in her snow globe. "I made him promise not to go there, but I suppose the temptation got the better of him."

"Self-control is not his strongest trait," Thomas said.

Kelly looked down at her fairy charm necklace. It was still glowing red but she thought it was just a small bit dimmer than before and it didn't feel quite so hot. Dimpleton turned away from the table and walked towards them, a very serious expression on his face. He reached out and grabbed Thomas's elbow.

"You and I need to talk," he said, pulling Thomas towards a gap in the curtain.

"If you'll excuse us a moment Kelly," Thomas said politely and followed Dimpleton through the slit in the curtain. Kelly's curiosity was sparked by this exchange and before she thought better of it she walked to the curtain and peaked through it. Dimpleton and Thomas were a few steps away on the other side of the curtain. She hoped they wouldn't sense that she was eavesdropping on them.

"What are you doing here?" Dimpleton asked in a low and anxious tone.

"I had to bring Bubbles here, there was no other choice," Thomas answered calmly.

"Even so, once you brought him here you should have left straightaway. Someone could recognize you at any moment. It will be a wonder if a powerful healer like Margretta didn't know who you were the instant you stepped into the room."

"She's too busy with her patient to take notice," Thomas said.

"Well, you better get out of here before she gets less busy."

"All right, tell Carmina I'll be waiting for her back at our home." Thomas pulled a breathing mask out of the cloth bag he carried over his shoulder, put it on, and flew up and exited through the ceiling. Kelly turned hastily away from the curtain and walked to the table where Bubbles lay. Why was Dimpleton worried about Thomas being recognized? Did it have something to do with why Thomas had left Glendenland? Why had he left? There was more to Thomas than met the eye, that was for sure. And for that matter there was more to Dimpleton as well. He portrayed himself as a happy-go-lucky, jolly sort, but there seemed to be a hidden depth under his outer shell of carefree frivolity. She wondered how much of Dimpleton's outgoing personality was an act, and at the same time she started to wonder how much of Thomas's apparent timidity was. While Dimpleton and Thomas had been talking, Margretta had somehow managed to sedate Bubbles, and he lay unconscious. Once Dimpleton returned and joined Kelly and the others at the end of the table, Margretta told them that she believed Bubbles would recover, but that he would have to stay in the hospital wing for at least two weeks.

"But now I need space to work so if you could leave me here alone with him for a few hours that would be nice," she added.

Beatrix, Bamblelina, Dimpleton, Kelly, Stephanie, and Carmina left the hospital bubble. Beatrix sniffled forlornly. Dimpleton told Carmina that Thomas was waiting for her at their home.

"I better go, then," Carmina said. "It is good to see you two again," she said to Kelly and Stephanie, "I just wish we weren't being reunited under such unfortunate circumstances." She gave them each a hug and left. The rest of them stood in the hallway, uncertain of what to do with themselves. Finally Dimpleton suggested they go to his quarters and wait until they were allowed to see Bubbles again. They spent the rest of the afternoon waiting nervously and sipping on nectala that didn't taste anywhere near as good as it usually did.

Chapter 9
Thomas's Secret

Margretta didn't let anyone near Bubbles that night or the next morning, and Kelly and Stephanie spent their morning shift alone in the medicine storage and creation bubble while Margretta watched over Bubbles. She had left them a note with instructions and several piles of seeds that needed to be ground up into fine powders. After their shift they found Beatrix and Bamblelina standing anxiously outside of the hospital bubble. Kelly noticed that Bamblelina's eyes were just as swollen and red from crying as Beatrix's were and her nose was a cherry red from frequent nose blowing.

"Any news?" Kelly asked.

Beatrix shook her head. Kelly and Stephanie managed to convince Beatrix and Bamblelina to leave their post outside the hospital bubble long enough to go to the mess hall for lunch. Neither Beatrix nor Bamblelina had eaten breakfast, and Kelly thought that perhaps the trembling of Beatrix's legs wasn't just from worry but also from a lack of energy.

On their way to the mess hall they crossed paths with a few fairies who knew Beatrix from food collection duty. They gave their best wishes for Bubbles to get better soon. Beatrix only managed to nod to them in response and Kelly could see that her lips were quivering as she struggled to keep back tears.

Kelly soon became doubtful about whether bringing Beatrix and Bamblelina to the mess hall had been a good idea. As soon as they entered the mess hall, it became apparent that in the time since breakfast, when only a small number of fairies who directly knew either Bubbles or Beatrix had been aware of Bubbles's injury, and that moment, every single fairy in Glendenland had heard the news, with varying degrees of accuracy. When they took a place in the serving line, they heard the fairies standing right in front of them launch into the subject.

"Did you hear about the fairy that's in the hospital wing? I heard the poor fellow was just minding his own business when fourteen evil fairies jumped on him out of nowhere," a short plump male fairy with brown wings said.

"I heard it was twenty," the male fairy's companion, a young female fairy with blond pigtails and yellow wings answered.

"But why would twenty fairies attack him for?" a third fairy, a skinny and bald old male fairy with grey wings, commented.

"How should I know?" the plump male fairy answered.

"I heard he was a spy trying to infiltrate the Miasmonian band," the young blond fairy said. "They set him on fire and all his skin melted off."

"That's not true. They froze him in a block of ice until his brain froze, and now he's gone crazy," the plump fairy said.

"Well, I don't know which one of you is right, but either way the poor chap will probably never recover," the old fairy said.

Beatrix burst into tears at these last words and all three of the gossiping fairies turned around to stare at her.

"What's wrong with her?" the young blond female fairy asked.

"What's wrong with you?" Kelly snapped back, patting Beatrix consolingly on the back. The blond fairy lifted her nose up in the air as she and her companions turned back around. After that incident they decided it was best if Bamblelina and Beatrix went back to Beatrix's quarters and if Stephanie and Kelly brought them their lunch.

A few hours later they were finally allowed to see Bubbles. He had been moved from the small curtained-off room to a bed in the main hospital ward. His chest and entire left arm were coated with a thick yellow paste that smelt like cinnamon. Margretta said that it was a special remedy for the type of burns he had received. She told them that Bubbles was in a healing sleep and wouldn't wake up for at least several days, but that if his loved ones were nearby part of him would be able to sense their presence and it would help his recovery.

"If he won't wake up for several days, how is he going to eat anything?" Bamblelina asked worriedly.

"A few days without food wouldn't hurt him," Margretta chuckled. "But not to worry. Every few hours, put a few drops of this in his mouth." Margretta held up a small bottle of a light blue cloudy liquid.

"What is it?" Kelly asked.

"An energy potion. Just a few drops provides the same energy as drinking two cups of nectala and eating a full plate of food," Margretta replied.

"Wow," Kelly said, impressed.

Dimpleton and his brothers came by to visit Bubbles a short while later, but they didn't stay for long. Then Venuto came by.

"Where's Petania?" Stephanie asked when Venuto entered the hospital ward.

"I believe she's in her quarters. Would you like me to get her?" Venuto asked.

"Oh no," Stephanie said quickly. "I was just surprised to see that she let you come here alone."

"What do you mean?"

"Isn't it obvious?" Stephanie asked.

Venuto scratched his head with a completely clueless expression on his face.

"You really have no idea, do you?" Stephanie giggled.

Venuto looked at her blankly.

"She likes you," Stephanie said.

"She's my best friend, of course she likes me."

"No, she *likes* you," Stephanie said.

Venuto still looked perplexed.

"She doesn't just want to be your friend," Kelly explained. "She wants to be your girlfriend."

Venuto laughed. "That's ridiculous. She's like a sister to me." He laughed some more. Then he suddenly fell silent. "Do you really think so?"

"I know so," Stephanie said. "You can call it human senses."

"Not just human senses. My fairy senses pick up on it just fine," Bamblelina interjected from her seat beside Bubbles. She was holding his left hand.

"Mine too," Beatrix added. She was holding Bubbles's right hand.

Venuto had started to look slightly uncomfortable, and he was shifting his weight from one leg to the other while his wings flapped nervously.

"How's Bubbles?" he asked, changing the subject.

Beatrix explained Bubbles's condition and also how and why Bubbles had been attacked.

"He's very lucky," Venuto said once Beatrix had finished. "It surprises me that the Miasmonians would attack him out in the open. They must be getting more confident. It's a good thing the council meeting is only a week and a half from now. I just hope the other fairy bands agree to help us."

Kelly was back in the room where she had met Marcos Witherings for the first time. She was in human form and sitting at the wooden table, facing the door. The door opened and Witherings walked in wearing a freshly pressed grey pinstripe suit and a light pink tie. Murk and Lurk flew one over each of Witherings's shoulders. Witherings carried a golden birdcage with a gem-incrusted handle. The fairy with tan wings that Miasmos had been questioning before was curled up in a ball on the floor of the cage. He looked to be in a fitful sleep.

"How do you like my new cage?" Witherings asked in his rasping voice. "I bought it with the glitterons from the snow globe your friend the fool so graciously pointed us towards." Witherings smiled smugly as he set the cage down on the table.

"Bubbles is not a fool," Kelly said. She felt her cheeks flush hot with anger.

"For a fadaman you have a surprisingly poor judgment of character. It's really quite disappointing." Murk sat down on Witherings's right shoulder and Witherings reached up to stroke Murk under the chin. Murk closed his eyes and made a sound that closely resembled a cat's purr.

"In spite of that and your numerous other shortcomings, I want to give you another chance to join me and my father," Witherings said.

"You're wasting your time."

"You do realize that if you don't join us, you'll be against us? And you know quite well what happens to those who are against us." Witherings gestured to the fairy inside the cage on the table.

"I'll take my chances," Kelly said.

"Ooh, is that confidence I hear in your voice?" Witherings asked. "Have you been learning magic?" His tone was patronizing.

He reached into his jacket pocket with a swift motion and pulled out his wand. He shot a string of sparks in her direction.

Instinctively Kelly put up her right hand and called up the surrounding air element to form a temporary shield to repel the sparks. The sparks bounced off the invisible shield, disintegrating harmlessly into the air.

Witherings laughed. "Not a bad start. But let's see how you handle this." He held up his crystal clear wand in her direction and paused dramatically.

Kelly felt afraid. She didn't know what was coming, but she knew it would be something horrible. She didn't know if she would be able to protect herself.

"Come on Kelly, if we don't leave now we won't have time for breakfast before our shift starts," Stephanie called out to Kelly through the wall to Kelly's bedroom.

Kelly rubbed her eyes tiredly. "All right, I'm coming."

It took a few hours for Kelly to shake the feeling of imminent dread that the dream had left her with. The dream had felt so realistic that she was convinced it had been an actual telepathic communication with Witherings. As Stephanie and Kelly headed to visit Bubbles after their shift, Kelly still had the image of Witherings's wand pointing at her in her mind's eye.

Bubbles continued in his healing sleep in the hospital bubble and Beatrix and Bamblelina continued at his side. They both had large circles under their eyes.

"How is he?" Kelly asked.

"The same," Beatrix sighed.

"Do you think maybe it would be good for you to go back to your community jobs? It might help you take your mind off worrying so much," Kelly ventured.

Bamblelina and Beatrix both let out horrified gasps. "But he might wake up at any moment, and how would he feel if he woke up all alone?" Bamblelina said.

"I guess that means you won't be coming to lunch then?" Stephanie asked.

"No, we're going to stay here. We'll steal a few drops of his energy drink," Beatrix said, a hint of mischief in her eyes.

"All right, see you later," Kelly said. As Stephanie and Kelly left the room Kelly reached up to feel her fairy charm necklace. She was happy to feel that it was only the slightest bit warm, which meant that Bubbles was no longer in mortal danger.

After lunch Kelly and Stephanie decided to head for the underwater park to play Frisbee. Dimpleton had lent them a human coat button a few days before and Kelly felt the need for a distraction from thinking about Bubbles and her most recent dream.

But when they entered the park they saw that they would not be able to play Frisbee as they had planned because the space was being used for a large group power coordination exercise. About five hundred fairies, divided into two groups, were taking part. One group wore red ribbons around their wrists and the other group wore blue ribbons. The groups were engaged in a mock battle. Individual fairies were shooting streams of water at each other from their wands and a large number of the fairies with red ribbons were working together to generate a steady stream of wind, which they aimed at the fairies wearing blue ribbons. Hovering above the action was a stern bald fairy with black wings dressed entirely in black. He looked quite a lot like Glenden and Venuto's bodyguards, and he wore a black eye patch over his left eye. Stephanie and Kelly stood just inside the archway they had entered, watching the exercise with interest. After a few moments the bald fairy with the eye patch blew on a shrill whistle and all of the fairies stood at attention.

"Very good," he said in a deep, rumbling voice. "Up until now we have been working mostly with non-painful forms of power, such as blowing tepid water and gentle wind at each other. We did make a huge ball of fire once, but we didn't hurl it at each other." The fairy set down on the ground and started to stride back and forth amongst the lines of listening fairies. "But it is important for you to understand the truths of battle. To understand what it is really like. So now I want us to fight for a few minutes with fire and ice."

The fairies exchanged worried glances.

"Begin!" the leading fairy shouted. He sprung into the air and hovered above the fairies, who stood uncertainly below him. "What are you waiting for?" he yelled down at them.

A small male fairy with a red ribbon tentatively shot a few tiny sparks at a nearby fairy wearing a blue ribbon. The sparks were so tiny that Kelly could tell they only produced a slight shock to the other fairy, probably somewhat like the shock one feels upon touching a metal doorknob after having crossed a carpeted floor in sock-covered feet. The fairy on the receiving end of the sparks shouted *Hey!* indignantly and shot back his own string of sparks, his sparks being slightly stronger than those he had received from his comrade. The fairy who had started the exchange blocked the incoming sparks and immediately sent more sparks in the other fairy's direction. Other fairies started similar exchanges and in a few minutes almost all of them were enthusiastically sending each other stronger and stronger sparks and even the occasional bolt of electricity.

"Where's the coordination?" the leader bellowed down at them.

In response to this question a group of about fifteen red-ribboned fairies joined together and formed a ball of fire in the air, subsequently flinging it at a group of blue-ribboned fairies.

The blue-ribboned fairies rushed together and shot jets of cool water at the fireball, which caused it to sizzle away into nothingness. The blue-ribboned fairies then responded in kind with their own fireball. The red-ribboned fairies didn't quite manage to stop it and about ten of them ended up frantically patting out flames that had sprung up on their clothes. This event irritated the red-ribboned fairies, and a large group of them gathered together and started to make swirling motions with their wands in the air, all pointing to the same spot above them. A smaller group of red-ribboned fairies took up positions in front of the larger group, protecting them from the attacks of the blue-ribboned fairies so they could continue to swirl their wands in the air.

It took Kelly a few minutes to realize what the red-ribboned fairies were doing. In the air above them a kind of mist started to appear, swirling around itself, like a clump of clouds twirling and twisting around each other. They were making a great ball of freezing cold vapor and were planning to fling it at the blue-ribboned fairies. Kelly could no longer quite see how many red-ribboned fairies were involved in making the great ball of freezing vapor because the teams had shifted positions and now most of the blue-ribboned fairies were in front of Stephanie and Kelly, blocking their view of the red-ribboned fairies. The ball of vapor grew very large, about the size of the living room in Kelly and Stephanie's quarters, and then suddenly it was hurtling towards the blue-ribboned fairies. Instead of calmly working together to deflect or diffuse the ball, the blue-ribboned fairies panicked and jumped out of the way. Before Stephanie and Kelly realized what was happening, there were no longer any fairies in front of them and the freezing mist ball was headed their way. Hastily they unfurled their wings but they weren't fast enough. The ball of mist washed over them before dissipating against the wall behind them.

Surprisingly, Kelly only felt a slight gust of cold air when the mist ball passed over her. It was as if she had opened the door on a cold winter day and then closed it again. She glanced at Stephanie, who seemed to be similarly unaffected. Then Kelly realized that all of the fairies were rushing towards her and Stephanie with horrified expressions on their faces.

"Are you all right?" she heard one of them shout.

"Quick, fall down and start shivering like you're freezing," Kelly whispered to Stephanie.

Stephanie and Kelly both dropped to the ground and started to shake as if they were very cold. Kelly looked up to see a crowd of fairy faces staring down at them. She could hear Stephanie's teeth chattering.

"I'm—so—co-co-cold," Stephanie said.

Kelly brought her hands up to her mouth and pretended to blow on them to hide the fact that she was grinning behind her hands at Stephanie's brilliant acting. Just then the imposing leader of the class pushed through the other fairies and glared down at them. Dimpleton was beside him.

"What the devil were you two doing there?" the imposing bald fairy demanded.

"We just wanted to play Frisbee," Kelly said innocently, shivering some more.

Dimpleton bent down and felt Stephanie's forehead, then Kelly's.

"They're very cold. I think I'd better take them to the hospital bubble," he said.

The imposing fairy nodded curtly and turned to the other fairies. "What have we learned here? You all," he said, pointing to the blue-ribboned fairies who had fled the frozen mist ball, "you all are cowards. And because of your cowardice these two poor bystanders got hurt!"

The blue-ribboned fairies cringed at his words.

"All back to your positions! Start again, and I don't want to see any cowards!!"

The fairies scrambled back to their positions. Meanwhile, Kelly and Stephanie continued to feign desperate coldness and Dimpleton scooped them both up, one under each arm. Kelly was impressed that despite his thin frame he lifted them with ease. Dimpleton carried them out of the park and down the hall leading to the hospital bubble. But before they reached the entrance to the hospital bubble Dimpleton turned abruptly and faced what Kelly thought was the outer wall of this part of Glendenland.

"Opa madabra," Dimpleton said. A shadow archway instantly appeared in the wall and he walked through it, still carrying Kelly and Stephanie. Once through the archway he put them down. They were in a large bubble that contained hundreds of wooden barrels. The faint smell of nectala filled the air and the archway they had come through was once again invisible. Kelly didn't have to ask Dimpleton to know why the stores of nectala might be in a hidden bubble. She was sure the temptation of so much nectala in one place would prove too much to resist for many fairies.

"You can stop pretending to be cold now," Dimpleton said to them.

"How did you know we were pretending?" Stephanie asked.

"You might have every other fairy around here fooled that you are fairies, but I can tell a fadaman and a human when I see them. Besides, a friend of mine asked me to keep an eye on you." Dimpleton sat down on top of one of the barrels, twisting his mouth to blow upwards at a stray piece of blond hair that had fallen down over his forehead.

"Was it Thomas who asked you to keep an eye on us?" Kelly asked.

Dimpleton nodded. "What were you two doing in the park? Didn't you hear the announcement last night that the park would be closed today for the exercise?"

"No. When was it made?" Kelly asked.

"Around midnight I think," Dimpleton answered.

"We must have slept through it," Stephanie said.

"Well, that was a close call. Good thing you thought quickly and pretended to be affected by the freezing mist. Otherwise there would have been some explaining to do."

"Who was the fairy giving the lesson?" Kelly asked.

"That was Milak," Dimpleton said.

"He looks like Glenden and Venuto's bodyguards," Kelly said.

"He was Queen Esmeralda's bodyguard before she died."

"Oh," Kelly said.

"How did he lose his eye?" Stephanie asked eagerly.

"Stephanie!" Kelly said.

"What?" Stephanie asked.

Dimpleton chuckled. "One day when he was a little boy he was watching a meteor shower and a meteorite fell into his eye. At least, that's his story."

"Wow, I'll think twice about watching meteor showers from now on," Stephanie said.

"The likelihood of the same happening to you is virtually zero," Dimpleton said.

"Still, I like my eyes," Stephanie answered, batting her eyelashes.

Kelly had been wondering a lot about Thomas ever since the exchange between him and Dimpleton she had witnessed the day Bubbles was injured. She was curious about why Thomas couldn't risk being seen in Glendenland. She could only think of one fairy who would be at great risk by showing his face in Glendenland, and the pieces fit. Miasmos seemed to be convinced Kelly had met the fairy he was looking for, but could Thomas really be Peter Penadas's little brother? She decided now was as good a time as any to try to find out.

"How do you and Thomas know each other?" she asked Dimpleton.

"We've been friends since we were little babies," he said. "Our families were good friends."

"You say they 'were' friends. Does that mean they aren't friends any more?"

"Er, yeah they aren't really friends anymore," Dimpleton said somewhat evasively.

"Could that be because his family isn't here any more?" Kelly asked.

"What makes you think his family isn't here any more?"

"They were banished, weren't they?"

Dimpleton's mouth dropped open in surprise but then he quickly tried to recover himself. He laughed nervously. "You don't seriously mean to say that you think Thomas is Peter Penadas's little brother Thomas? The name is just a coincidence I assure you, there are many fairies named Thomas."

"I didn't know Peter's brother was named Thomas, did you Kelly?" Stephanie chimed in.

"No."

"Well like I said, it's just a coincidence," Dimpleton said quickly.

"You're not a very good liar," Stephanie said.

Dimpleton sighed. "All right, you are correct. But you must promise not to utter even a word about his true identity to anyone. Even Bubbles and Beatrix. Not only would you be putting him in more danger, but anyone who knows his real identity is also in great danger."

"How many people know who he is?" Kelly asked.

"His wife Carmina and myself, one or two of his closest freefairy friends, and now you two. Hopefully some day he will be able to reveal his true identity publicly, but first we have to clear his name. I've been working these past thirteen years to try to discover who was really responsible for the queen's death. But I have not had much success," Dimpleton said sadly.

"How old was Thomas when the queen was murdered?" Kelly asked.

"We were both sixteen years old."

"That's awful," Stephanie said. Kelly nodded in agreement. She felt sorry for Thomas, and for Dimpleton too.

"He's lucky to have a friend like you that sticks by him," Kelly said.

"I'm lucky to have him as a friend," Dimpleton responded humbly.

At that point Dimpleton suggested they put on their underwater breathing masks and go back to their quarters by way of the river. He would go and fill Margretta in on what had happened so that she would tell Milak and anyone else who might ask that she had given them a healing tonic and sent them to rest in their quarters. He said that they should stay hidden away until dinnertime. They didn't want to raise any suspicions with an unusually speedy recovery.

Kelly and Stephanie spent a rather boring afternoon back at their quarters. Kelly entertained Stephanie for a few hours by creating balls of fire, ice, and water vapor in the palms of her hands, but soon Stephanie got bored and went to take a nap. Kelly kept practicing and by dinnertime she had managed to move a small fireball she had created about two feet away from her by sort of pushing it with the air element she channeled through her palm.

As soon as Kelly and Stephanie arrived at dinner they were immediately surrounded by many of the fairies from that day's exercise.

"Are you all right?" a short male fairy with bright blue eyes, orange hair, freckles, and orange wings asked anxiously. Kelly recognized him as being one of the blue-ribboned fairies who had scrambled out of the way of the freezing ball.

"Yes, we're fine," Kelly answered.

"We're awfully sorry," a skinny black female fairy with grey hair and grey wings said.

"Thanks," Stephanie said.

"What did it feel like?" a third fairy asked eagerly. Kelly recognized him as the unfriendly young male fairy with pale pink wings who had been skeptical of Miasmos's threat on the evening of the general meeting.

"How do you think?" Kelly asked sarcastically, not really feeling like talking to him.

The pink-winged fairy frowned and walked away, offended.

"That was a little harsh," Stephanie said.

"He asked a rude question, he didn't deserve a polite response," Kelly replied.

Once about twenty more fairies had come forward, apologized, and assured themselves that there was no lasting damage to either Kelly or Stephanie, Kelly and Stephanie were able to eat their dinner in peace. There was no sign of Milak and Kelly was glad of that. He was intimidating.

Chapter 10
The Council Meeting

The next week and a half passed uneventfully. Kelly's next two magic lessons went smoothly, and by the end of the last one she was able to create and fling small fireballs and ice balls all around the secret bubble where she and Venuto had their lessons. She had also managed to create electric sparks, but she couldn't quite create an actual electric current in the air. Venuto was pleased with her progress and told her that she was at least as good as an average fairy at magic. He suggested that she keep practicing without the aid of a wand, because he was of the opinion that wands bred laziness and dependence. Bubbles had still not awoken from his healing sleep, but Margretta wasn't worried. She said he would wake up any day now. Beatrix and Bamblelina had finally gone back to their community duty but had rearranged their schedules so that at least one of them could be by Bubbles's side at all times. As the council meeting approached, excitement and anticipation built up in Glendenland, and everywhere Kelly went she heard snippets of charged conversations full of speculation about which fairy delegations would actually show up and what the result of the meeting would be.

The night before the council meeting Kelly and Stephanie were returning to their quarters when they came upon an unusual sight. A petite female fairy was trying to enter the shadow archway across from Kelly and Stephanie's quarters. The shadow archway was locked, however, so every time the fairy tried to walk through it she simply bounced off the wall, which jiggled back into position. The fairy didn't notice Kelly or Stephanie because she was too intent on getting through the archway. She kept trying to walk through it again and again. Kelly and Stephanie stood uncertainly in the hallway, not sure of what to say. The first thing Kelly noticed about the fairy was the unusual color of her wings. They were a dark green, the color of evergreen needles, and they reminded her strongly of leaves because in addition to their green color they also had a shiny, almost waxy glint over their surface. The fairy had pale white skin, bright red hair, and Kelly could just make out a series of light brown freckles dotting the fairy's face and shoulders. The fairy wore a light brown, knee-length dress with thin spaghetti straps and a simple brown cloth bag hung from her shoulder.

"Excuse me," Kelly finally said. The fairy jumped back, reached swiftly into her bag and pulled out a small dagger. She held it up at them defensively.

"Calm down," Kelly said. "We're not going to hurt you. My name is Kelly, this is Stephanie."

"Hi, sorry, I startle easily," the fairy said, putting her dagger back into her bag. "My name is Gwendolyn."

"We noticed you were having a little bit of trouble with the archway," Stephanie said.

"Yes, I can't seem to go through. But my mistress is waiting for me and she'll be angry if I'm late."

"Your mistress?" Stephanie asked.

"The fair and just Riona, leader of Rowenia."

"You're a Rowenian?" Kelly asked.

"Yes, we've come for the council meeting your leader has called," Gwendolyn answered. "Are you Glendenians?"

"No, we're free fairies, distant relatives of Prince Venuto," Kelly said.

Gwendolyn's eyes widened. "You're nobility? I'm sorry I didn't know, your Graces." She proceeded to enter into a deep curtsy.

"No, we're not really nobility, you don't have to treat us any differently," Kelly said, feeling uncomfortable by Gwendolyn's sudden change in demeanor.

"But you're relatives of the prince," Gwendolyn said.

"Yes, but we're free fairies," Kelly said. "So really we're just normal fairies, not nobility."

"Whatever you say your Grace. I mean, whatever you say. Would you happen to know how to open the door?"

"You have to put your hand up to it and wait until you hear a set of chimes. Once you hear the chimes you'll be able to go inside," Kelly explained.

Gwendolyn put her hand up to the archway and the chimes soon followed. "Thank you!" she said before passing through the shadow archway.

"That was the first time I've ever been called 'your Grace'," Stephanie said.

"I hope you enjoyed it, it will probably be the only time," Kelly said.

"You never know, maybe I'll marry a prince someday."

"Just make sure it isn't Venuto."

"Don't worry, I can't do magic, remember? So that would be suicide."

Later that night Kelly woke up to find Stephanie sitting on the side of her bed shaking her shoulder. "Kelly, wake up."

"What time is it?" Kelly asked.

"Three a.m."

Kelly sat up, rubbing her eyes.

"I want to show you something," Stephanie said. Her eyes were sparkling in the dim light of the room. She reached into her pocket and pulled out a small white glove. "Try it on."

Kelly slipped the glove onto her right hand. It felt like it was made out of the same material as fake spider webs sold at Halloween. "What is it?"

"You know how when you want to open a locked bubble room you put your hand up to the archway, and if you're approved to open the archway it opens?"

"Yes," Kelly answered, wondering what Stephanie was getting at.

"Imagine you weren't authorized to open a particular archway but you needed to open it anyway. That's what the glove is for."

Kelly pulled the glove off of her hand and threw it to the side of the room. "I told you not to get any ideas about the records section. I can't believe you went behind my back and got some sort of secret glove!"

"I thought you'd be happy about it." Stephanie frowned.

"Where did you get it?" Kelly demanded.

"I bought it on the black market."

"The black market?"

"Yeah, that old guy in the wand cubicle doesn't just sell wands. Next time you go there you should ask to see his special collection." Stephanie winked. "And it wasn't cheap either. I had to steal a lot of fairy dust from the magic storage and creation bubble to pay for it."

"You stole from Margretta? I didn't think you'd ever stoop to stealing."

"Oh get down off your high horse already. Sometimes you have to bend the rules to get what you want, but I guess you wouldn't know that."

"What's that supposed to mean?"

"It's easy to take the moral high ground when you've never wanted for anything. Your mother always lets you do whatever you want, and she's so flighty she wouldn't even notice if you broke one of her non-existent rules."

"If that's what you really think then you don't know me at all," Kelly said.

"Oh I know you Kelly Brennan. You pretend you don't sneak out at night or cheat on tests because you think its wrong, but you want to know what I think? I think you're afraid."

"I am not afraid," Kelly retorted.

Stephanie picked up the glove from where it had landed on the ground and shook it in Kelly's face. "You know what this glove is?" Stephanie asked. Kelly didn't answer. "It could be the key to finding out who your father is. If you aren't afraid, then what are you? Apathetic? Do you even want to find your father?

You've hardly lifted a finger to find out who he could be since we've been here and when I try to help you all I get in return is you telling me I'm a criminal!"

There was a stony silence during which Kelly sat with her arms folded to her chest trying to come up with a sharp reply. She hated to admit it but Stephanie did have a point. What had she been doing to find out who her father was besides wishful thinking? Even though she didn't agree with Stephanie's morally ambiguous methods, they were actual methods nonetheless.

"Listen, the glove has a time limit on it," Stephanie said. "It'll only work for one more hour, so if we're going to do this we should get going, unless of course you prefer to stay here and fight some more. What's it going to be, are you in or are you out?"

It would be shame to let the glove go to waste, Kelly thought. "Okay, I'm in," she said. "But don't think I'm not still mad."

Kelly and Stephanie crept down the deserted hallways towards the records section. Kelly kept thinking she heard footsteps behind them, which caused her to look over her shoulder every few seconds. Stephanie just rolled her eyes each time Kelly looked over her shoulder and told her to relax. Finally they reached their destination.

"I think you should do the honors," Stephanie said, holding up the glove.

"Fine." Kelly grabbed the glove and put it on, then closed her eyes and thrust her hand up to the archway leading to the records section. There was no sound.

"What are you waiting for?" Stephanie asked.

"The chimes?"

"This is a glove for fairies who need to go undetected, Einstein. They don't exactly want their arrival to be announced by a sequence of chimes," Stephanie said before striding through the archway unimpeded. Kelly reluctantly followed.

The front part of the records section looked like a bank. There was a long counter with a glass partition, complete with little round circular holes for customers to talk through to the workers. Kelly and Stephanie found a gap in the far side of the partition and passed through it to a work area full of desks. Behind all of the desks were rows upon rows of grey metal filing cabinets, all of which were, of course, unlabelled.

"This is going to take forever," Kelly said, slipping the glove off of her hand and stuffing it into one of her pant pockets.

"We have two and a half hours before any workers arrive."

"You start on that side, I'll start over here," Kelly said. Kelly opened the first filing cabinet. There were at least a hundred unlabelled manila folders inside. *Are fairy senses really so strong that fairies don't have to label the folders?* Kelly wondered. She closed her eyes and tried to sense which of the folders contained birth certificates. She got nothing. So instead she lifted the first envelope out of the cabinet. It was a death certificate. She replaced it and moved on to the second folder. It was a marriage certificate. The third, another death certificate. The fourth was finally a birth certificate, but for a two-year-old female fairy with brown wings. After forty-five minutes Kelly was still on the first filing cabinet and had only found one fairy of the right age range and wing color to be a possible candidate. She sat down on the edge of one of the desks for a break.

"This isn't working very well," Stephanie commented, coming over from her side of the room. "I've found two possibles only, and they're both eighty-five years old, a bit old don't you think?"

"There must be some way fairies working here can find files quickly. I just don't believe they can tell where everything is just by fairy senses," Kelly said.

"You're a genius."

"What are you talking about?" Kelly asked. Stephanie pointed to something on top of the desk. It was a notepad. Kelly picked it up and examined it. It consisted of about a hundred blank death certificates.

"What's so special about this?" Kelly asked. Stephanie pointed to the top left corner of the top sheet on the notepad. Kelly squinted to read the tiny words "Fill in search information, then check box at bottom when complete."

157

"Look, here's the birth certificate notepad." Stephanie handed Kelly another notepad off of the desk along with a pencil.

"You really think just filling in this piece of paper is going to achieve something?"

"It wouldn't be anywhere near the most unusual thing I've seen in Glendenland," Stephanie answered.

"Right," Kelly said. The first box on the birth certificate template asked for fairy gender. Kelly filled in male. Then came the age, she wrote 30-85. Then came wing color. She wrote, blue, purple, or silver. She left the birth weight, measurements, temperature, and parent information boxes blank and checked the complete box at the bottom. No sooner had she checked the box than there was a series of loud clanging sounds as several drawers of different filing cabinets opened up all by themselves. Then manila folders started to fly out of the drawers, whizzing through the air and stacking themselves up on the corner of the desk. Kelly and Stephanie watched speechless as the stack of folders grew to be about a hand-length tall. Then as suddenly as the file retrieval had begun it stopped, and all of the drawers slammed shut in unison with one loud clang.

"Cool," Stephanie said. "How many are there?"

Kelly counted the folders. "Just thirty-five." She ripped the search sheet off of the notepad and tore it in half, giving one half to Stephanie. "You take these and write their names on the back of your paper." Kelly handed Stephanie half of the folders.

Kelly had only just opened the first folder when a soft cascade of musical notes reverberating through the bubble's wall greeted her ears. "The chimes!"

"Who comes to work this early, it's only four forty-five," Stephanie said. Kelly looked in the direction of the main archway and saw the center of the archway start to bend inward. Someone was in the process of walking through the archway.

"Quick, get under the desk," Kelly said. They ducked under the desk just in time to hear a set of heavy footsteps enter the room. The first set of footsteps was soon followed by a set of softer footsteps.

"This is a great big pile of burnt poppy seed if you ask me," a male voice said. "Getting dragged out of bed at four a.m. for some teenage mischief."

"A master glove went missing a little over an hour ago, and you know we have to check all sensitive locations for tampering whenever that happens," a female voice answered.

"That old liar. He said he was going to make a copy of a master glove, not steal an original," Stephanie whispered loudly.

Kelly put her index finger up to her mouth to warn Stephanie to be quiet.

"Let's get on with it so I can go back to bed," the male voice said. Both sets of footsteps were getting closer. Kelly could tell by the sound that the two fairies had already passed by the counter and were now somewhere in the first row of desks. "I'll check in the back," the disgruntled male voice said. The heavier set of footsteps pounded their way towards the back of the room while the lighter set of footsteps started to walk down the length of the first row of desks. Kelly and Stephanie were trapped; there was no way to escape without being noticed. Their best hope was to stay put. As the lighter set of footsteps got closer and closer Kelly and Stephanie pushed themselves as far back under the desk as possible. Suddenly a pair of brown boots appeared beside the desk. *Please don't look down*, Kelly thought.

"Hey, there's a pile of folders on top of this desk," the female fairy called out to her companion.

"So?" The male fairy's footsteps drew closer until there were two pairs of boots in front of Kelly and Stephanie's hiding place.

"It could be tampering. None of the other desks have any folders on top of them," the female fairy said.

I knew we were going to get caught, I can't believe I let Stephanie talk me into this, Kelly thought. She heard the light sound of sheets of paper being handled. "Who would want to break into the records section to steal a bunch of birth certificates? A worker probably just got sloppy and left them out."

"Still, maybe we should report it," the female fairy said.

"And wait here for the investigators? I don't think so. We only have a few more bubbles left to visit and I plan to finish quickly so I can go back to bed for a few hours before I have to wake up again. So unless we see something really fishy we're keeping our mouths shut. Got it? Now pick up those folders and put them back in a filing cabinet so we can move on to the next bubble."

Both sets of boots disappeared from in front of the desk. A filing cabinet opened and closed and then both sets of footsteps got softer and softer as the fairies walked away. Finally there was a set of chimes that signaled the fairies had exited the bubble and locked the archway behind them.

"Their fairy senses were so bad. We were less than three steps away from them and they didn't realize it!" Stephanie laughed. "Amateurs."

"This isn't a game," Kelly said. "We almost got caught." She was shaking all over.

"But we didn't. Where did she put those folders?" Stephanie headed towards the filing cabinets.

"Don't go near the cabinets. We're getting out of here."

"It's not like they're coming back. We still have time."

"It doesn't matter. We should never have come here in the first place. It was a bad idea and now we're leaving." Kelly reached into her bag and pulled out her underwater breathing mask. "Put on your mask," she said to Stephanie.

"You're really just going to give up when we're this close?"

"Put it on," Kelly demanded.

"Fine." Stephanie put on her mask and they flew for the ceiling. When they got back to their quarters they didn't say a word to each other. Kelly stormed to her room and flung herself down on her bed.

The next morning Kelly got up earlier than usual and went to breakfast by herself. But Stephanie soon arrived and sat down next to her as if nothing had happened.

"Good morning," Stephanie said, smiling. Kelly didn't answer. "You're not still mad about last night, are you?"

Just then Kelly noticed Gwendolyn standing by the serving line with a tray of food and looking around the mess hall. Kelly called out to her. She noticed that Gwendolyn received several curious glances from Glendenian fairies as she made her way to Kelly and Stephanie's table.

"How are you?" Gwendolyn asked as she sat down.

"Fine," Kelly answered.

"Glendenland is really very complex, I almost got lost getting here. We Rowenians have more fairies total, around 8,000, but we live more spread out. I'm not used to being in such an enclosed space with so many other fairies." Gwendolyn bit into a juicy grasshopper cutlet.

"Where do you live?" Kelly asked.

"We live in the forest in what the humans call Tennessee," Gwendolyn said. "We live mostly in the treetops."

"How many of you are here for the council meeting?" Stephanie asked.

"Just the queen, her bodyguards and her maidservants. There are six bodyguards, the usual number when the queen travels, and there are three maidservants. Minerva is always by the queen's side. As queen's attendant her job is to attend to our mistress's needs as they come about. Christalina is in charge of the queen's meals, and I'm in charge of helping the queen get dressed in the morning. I do her hair and her pretty face powders, and then at night I help her get ready for bed. Christalina and I have the easiest jobs because we get a lot of free time."

"What are you going to do with your free time today?" Stephanie asked.

"I don't know. I was going to explore Glendenland."

"If you want I can give you a tour, but first I have to go to my job in medicine storage and creation," Kelly offered.

"Yes, *we'd* be more than happy to give you a tour," Stephanie added. Kelly glared at her.

"You make medicines?' Gwendolyn asked, her green eyes sparkling with interest. "Can I come?"

"I don't see why not," Stephanie said.

Margretta was delighted they had brought a guest. She quickly put Gwendolyn to work helping to grind powders. Kelly was worried Gwendolyn wouldn't like having to help them, but to her pleasant surprise Gwendolyn seemed quite content. She peppered Margretta with question after question about each of the ingredient piles and their uses. Margretta enthusiastically answered her inquiries. Due to the lively conversation between Margretta and Gwendolyn, the shift felt much shorter than it usually did and soon it was time to go.

"Good-bye dears," Margretta said. "Oh and Gwendolyn dear, you will come again tomorrow?"

"That depends on the outcome of the council meeting. If the fair and just Riona decides to help in your cause then I shall be here tomorrow. Otherwise, I will be returning to Rowenia."

First they swung by the hospital bubble to see if there was any news about Bubbles. Kelly introduced Gwendolyn to Beatrix and asked Beatrix if she wanted to join them for lunch. Beatrix said she was going to wait for Bambelina to get back from group power coordination class first, so Kelly, Stephanie, and Gwendolyn went to lunch without her. Kelly tried to hide the fact that she was mad at Stephanie so that Gwendolyn wouldn't feel uncomfortable. So basically she just let Stephanie do all the talking. Gwendolyn's eyes widened in genuine concern when Stephanie recounted over lunch what had happened to Bubbles. Then they started the tour. As Stephanie explained the sites to Gwendolyn, Kelly reflected on her time in Glendenland so far. It was hard for her to believe they had been there an entire month. The time had passed so fast. Gwendolyn was duly impressed by the underwater park and the market, but she was most impressed when they arrived at their last stop, the library. She went straight to the section on medicinal plants and perused the books. She told them that Rowenia only had a small library inside the hollowed-out trunk of a massive old oak tree. They ended up spending the next few hours in the library and before they knew it it was almost four thirty, only half an hour from five o'clock — the time the council meeting had been set for.

"Oh dear, I'd better go!" Gwendolyn exclaimed when she realized the time. "I have to help the queen get ready for the council meeting!" Gwendolyn exited the library at a full-fledged sprint, calling *good-bye* to them breathlessly as she ran from the room.

"We'd better get to the Great Hall ourselves," Kelly said. "Otherwise there won't be any seats left."

When they arrived at the Great Hall it was already more than half full. Kelly squinted, trying to spot a good place to sit. There were so many fairies flying back and forth through the air that it was hard to see the available seats through them.

"Hey-O," Kelly heard Dimpleton's voice behind her. He gave her a pat on the shoulder. "How are you two lovely ladies doing this fine afternoon?" he asked cheerfully.

"All right," Kelly answered.

"Come on," he said, "my brothers are saving us seats down near the speaking platform."

They followed Dimpleton down to the seats he had mentioned. They sat down beside Dimpleton's brothers, saving one seat for Bamblelina or Beatrix. One of them would surely be coming, but they didn't know which one would be on Bubbles guard duty. Dimpleton's brothers had saved them seats very close to the speaking platform, in the fourth row. Kelly could easily make out the intricate details on Glenden and Venuto's thrones. There were also an additional six thrones set up to the left of the three usual thrones, four of which were a polished gold and two which resembled polished jade. The speaking platform had been covered with a lush rug patterned with winding deep green vines on a light blue background. In another fifteen minutes the entire hall was filled to capacity with fairies. Kelly spotted Petania below them in the front row, sitting stiffly in an elaborate pink lace dress. Beside Petania was an older fairy in a black silk suit. He also had light pink wings like Petania, and Kelly assumed that he must be Petania's father. The rest of the fairies in the first three rows below Kelly and her companions were very well dressed like Petania and her father, and Kelly noticed there was a higher proportion of less common wing colors like pink, blue, purple, and even metallic gold and copper in the first rows than in the rest of the Great Hall. Bamblelina was one of the last fairies to arrive, and once she sat down beside them Dimpleton commented that almost every Glendenian in Glendenland was present in the Great Hall.

That comment gave Kelly an idea. "Dimpleton, you have strong fairy senses don't you?"

"Just average really," Dimpleton replied modestly.

"Do you think—" Kelly was cut off by a loud fanfare as Flimsly emerged first as usual, leading a line of this time ten other musicians. Four of them carried trumpets and six of them horns. They were all dressed in bright red jackets and tight white pants – outfits that reminded Kelly of pictures she had seen of fox hunt attire. Their red jackets had large gold buttons that flashed in the light and Kelly could see that all of the instruments had been freshly polished. Flimsly stood in the front center of the speaking platform while the other musicians divided into two rows, five on the left and five on the right of the nine thrones on the platform. After their initial fanfare, the musicians started to play a festive march as Glenden and Venuto's bodyguards emerged to take their places behind their respective thrones. Once the bodyguards were in place the music stopped.

"All stand for his Grace the honorable, noble, wise and benevolent Glenden Grand!" Flimsly shouted. They all stood as Glenden entered the hall. He was wearing a golden crown on top of his head that had the shape of a delicate vine with golden leaves. His stunning green-flecked gold wings were unfurled and sparkling brightly in contrast to his deep purple velvet suit and black slippers. There was a dusting of golden glitter on his face that stood out against his dark chocolate skin and drew attention to his metallic golden eyes. He sat down in his throne.

"They're really going to the extreme for this; the only time you ever see Glenden wearing his crown is on his birthday or if a noble fairy gets married," Dimpleton whispered to Kelly.

"And please welcome the brave and honest Venuto Grand!"

Venuto arrived on stage wearing a suit of deep blue velvet with golden ruffles at the wrists and ankles. There was a dusting of copper-colored powder over his face that matched the color of his metallic copper wings. Kelly thought he looked a bit nervous. She saw Petania wave at him and he gave a very slight smile back at her that no one would have noticed if they hadn't been watching his face closely. Kelly guessed he wasn't supposed to show any emotion while on stage during a formal function. Venuto sat down.

"Please be seated," Glenden said. The spectators retook their seats. There was a pause during which all of the audience waited expectantly for the announcement of the fairy delegations. Finally after what felt like at least five minutes, but was probably closer to one minute, Glenden gave a slight nod of his head and Flimsly and the other musicians played another fanfare.

"It is the great honor of Glendenland to welcome the visiting fairy delegations," Flimsly recited. "Now we welcome the proud, the proper, the prudent, and pragmatic Pixelatus of the Pixelori!" As he made this latest statement Flimsly swung his arm out and up in the direction of the very back row of the Great Hall. Kelly and everyone else in the room turned back to look in the direction he had indicated. The Pixelori fairy delegation was entering the Great Hall through one of the back shadow archways and traveling in a brilliant procession down through the center aisle that led to the speaking platform.

At first Kelly couldn't see them all that clearly and could only make out that the Pixelori delegation consisted of fairies marching in rows of two down the aisle in tight formation. There were six rows of two, then a lone fairy form in the middle, and then six more rows of two. As they got closer Kelly could see that the fairies in the first six rows of the formation carried long wooden staffs that they smacked to the ground with each step. They all wore dark purple full body leotards that resembled modern dance costumes, and they all had closely cropped hair and their skin carried a very slight blue tint. Kelly couldn't tell if the tint was due to makeup or if it was the actual color of their skin. Even more intriguing than their blue skin were their wings. Their wings weren't all one color, or one main color with a bit of other color mixed in like the wings Kelly had seen so far. Instead, the Pixelori wings were divided into geometric shapes, all with different colors. It was like looking at a blown up picture of the back of a hand, with all the skin cells of different shapes and sizes, each cell with its own vibrant color.

When the first six rows passed by where Kelly and her companions were sitting, Pixelatus, the fairy in the middle of the procession, finally came into full view. Kelly's breath was taken away by his wings, which were the very first thing about him her eyes were drawn to. Looking at his wings was like looking into a kaleidoscope. They had divisions of color like the other Pixelori wings, but the divisions of color on his wings moved around, circling from one place to another. Kelly started to get dizzy from looking at his wings, so she looked to his face. Pixelatus had sharp, angular features and he was bald. He was wearing a thin silver band around his head, and he wore a tight silver leotard. When the Pixelori reached the speaking platform, two of the fairies with staffs took up a place behind the next throne on the speaking platform, while the other staff-bearing fairies stood in a tight row further behind them. Glenden and Venuto had both stood up for the Pixelori's entrance, and they each shook Pixelatus's hand before Pixelatus took a seat in the first of the six new thrones that had been placed beside the thrones of Glenden, the late Esmeralda, and Venuto.

"Now we welcome the fair and just Riona of Rowenia!" Flimsly announced.

The Rowenians entered from the same archway at the back of the Great hall. First came three male fairies carrying bows and cases of arrows on their backs. They were all bald like the bodyguards of Glendenland, but they had dark green wings like Gwendolyn's instead of the black wings of the Glendenian guards. They wore simple brown pants, brown boots, and white shirts. After the first three bodyguards came Gwendolyn, who was wearing a very pretty dark green silk dress that matched the color of her wings. There were two other female fairies dressed the same way behind Gwendolyn, and Kelly knew they must be Minerva and Christalina. One of them had dark green wings just like Gwendolyn and the first three bodyguards, but the other one had pale green wings.

The next fairy was clearly Queen Riona, and Kelly immediately understood why it was necessary to have a maidservant solely in charge of her hair and clothing. The queen had very long bright red hair that was presently piled up on top of her head in an elaborate twisted mound of at least a few hundred separate braids. Kelly thought Riona was very pretty. She had pale skin, green eyes, and a delicate, tiny nose that turned up just ever so slightly at the point – a nose that would have been the envy of many a human movie star. Riona wore an ornate white gown with a puffy skirt embroidered with rubies. The shoulders of her dress puffed out and were so large that Kelly didn't get a good look at Riona's wings until she had passed by and Kelly could look at them from behind. The queen's wings were the same dark green as the majority of the Rowenian delegation's wings, but around the edges they had a dusted gold border. Behind Riona the remaining three bodyguards finished off the group. Glenden, Venuto, and Pixelatus all kissed Riona's right hand before she took her seat next to Pixelatus.

"And now, the sharp, clever, and honorable Xanthus of the Xianda!"

The Xianda delegation only consisted of three fairies, Xanthus and two bodyguards. Xanthus was a very short and old male fairy. He had a white beard that stretched almost down to his bellybutton, but the hair on his head was closely cropped, causing what Kelly found to be a comical contrast. He had pure white wings and was dressed in a white, flowing robe.

"The bold and brilliant Gwilliam of Bildenstern!"

Gwilliam was quite young looking; he had curly blond hair and a baby face. His wings were bright orange, almost fluorescent, and he wore a bright orange suit of almost the same color. Kelly squinted to protect her eyes as he and his delegation of six similarly dressed Bildenstern soldiers passed by. Gwilliam took his seat in the last of the golden thrones, leaving the two jade-like thrones beside him remaining to be filled.

"And last but not least, the representatives from the smaller fairy bands, Catia of the Catanori and Belen of the Beleni!"

Catia was a tall and young female fairy with dark black skin and deep purple wings with flecks of gold in them. She wore a bright red dress. Belen was a short male fairy with pale skin and dark black shoulder-length hair. He had black wings and was dressed all in black, wearing black nail polish. Neither Catia nor Belen had brought any companions.

"Too bad Bubbles can't be here. He'd be tickled to know that because of his suggestion Glenden extended invitations to the Catanori and the Beleni," Bamblelina sighed sadly.

Once all of the visiting leaders were seated, Glenden addressed them and the audience.

"I wish to thank you all for your attendance. We have all gathered here today to decide how best to face the threat the Miasmonians have brought upon us. We shall now have the council meeting. Please, would the visiting leaders follow me. All residents of Glendenland please wait here for the results of the meeting." Glenden led the way as the other leaders and their servants and bodyguards followed him out of the Great Hall and through the shadow archway that led to the smaller audience hall.

"We don't get to see the council meeting?" Kelly asked Dimpleton, disappointed.

"Apparently not. I'd been hoping it would be public."

"So we just have to wait here until it's over?" Stephanie asked incredulously.

"I'm afraid so," Dimpleton answered. "Kelly, what were you going to ask me before?"

"I was going to ask if you thought you could sense if any of the fairies in this room are related to me."

"It is a big room, so it's a bit hard for me to tell from here. I'll be back." Dimpleton sprung into the air and flew all the way to the other side of the hall, where Kelly could see him starting to make his way around the rows waving and making small talk with fairies he knew, particularly the small number of fairies with blue and purple wings.

"What's he doing?" Stephanie asked. Kelly ignored her.

"Fine then, be that way." Stephanie pouted.

About fifteen minutes later Dimpleton was back. "I can say with certainty no one in here is related to you, at least not more closely related than a second cousin. I think around second cousin would be the limit of my sensing abilities."

"Thanks," Kelly said.

"I guess your father isn't a Glendenian then," Stephanie whispered to Kelly.

"Yes, and as you can see we didn't have to go on the black market to find that out."

"All right, I'll admit it. I messed up. Truce?"

"Just don't pull a stunt like that again," Kelly said. "At least not without talking to me first."

"Yes ma'am." Stephanie made a mock salute. Kelly laughed.

About twenty minutes later the Pixelori delegation came out of the audience hall alone. Pixelatus had a deep frown on his face and he burst into the air, flying for the ceiling. The rest of his delegation followed. As they reached into their pockets for underwater breathing masks they were greeted by boos from the onlooking fairies.

"What's going on?" Stephanie asked.

"They're leaving," Dimpleton said. "But I'm not surprised. They're a selfish bunch those Pixelori."

Pixelatus pointed his staff at the ceiling. A rainbow of bright-colored sparks shot out of it and formed a dancing pattern in the air, like fireworks. The Pixelori exited amid the flashing sparks, which took a few minutes to die down once the delegation had left.

"At least they put on a good show," Stephanie commented.

The next hour passed with no new information, and the audience started to grow a bit fidgety. At about two hours since the start of the meeting, the Xianda and the Bildenstern delegations both left at the same time.

"I guess they won't be helping either," Kelly said. "That just leaves the Rowenians, the Catanori, and the Beleni, doesn't it?" she asked Dimpleton.

"Correct. We will see how many of them will stay."

The council meeting dragged on for another four hours. Bamblelina left to check on Bubbles and Beatrix arrived to take her place. Some of the fairies gave up waiting and left, but at least ninety-five percent of them stayed in the Great Hall anxiously awaiting the meeting's results. Finally, at about eleven o'clock, the Rowenians came out onto the speaking platform, followed by Catia and Belen. At first Kelly thought they were all going to leave, but then Glenden and Venuto emerged on the platform as well and the Great Hall burst into cheers. The Rowenians, Catanori, and Beleni had decided to help. Kelly noticed that some fairies weren't cheering though, the young unfriendly skeptical male fairy with pink wings being one of them. Kelly suspected that it was because if the other fairy bands agreed to help that meant they agreed there was a real threat, and if there was a real threat there was likely to be a real confrontation. In the next few moments any fairy with those fears had them confirmed.

"My fellow Glendenians," Glenden began. "As you can see, these brave fairy leaders have agreed to lend the support of their bands to our cause." There was more cheering from the crowd. "Unfortunately, the Pixelori, Xianda, and Bildensterns were unable, or perhaps unwilling, to recognize the growing danger posed by the Miasmonians. Still, we have received more support than I had allowed myself to hope, and after serious consideration of disturbing new developments, we have decided that we must make our move against the Miasmonians in one week's time."

There was a surprised murmuring from the crowd.

"Isn't that kind of soon?" Stephanie asked.

"What new developments?" Kelly asked at almost the same time.

Glenden put his hand up to silence the loudening crowd. "Catia, leader of the Catanori of Maryland, will inform you of the new developments of which I speak, and I am sure it will erase any doubt from your minds about whether or not we should act." Glenden sat down and Catia took the floor.

"My band suffered an attack from the Miasmonians one week ago," she said. "Our band is small, with only five hundred members, and we are peaceful. About two hundred Miasmonians attacked us without provocation. We eventually caused them to retreat but when we counted our numbers thirty of us were missing. Their attack was disguised as a ploy to gain our territory but in fact they just wanted to kidnap as many of us as they could." She got teary-eyed and sat down.

"Thank you Catia," Glenden said. "As you can see, the Miasmonians are growing in strength daily, and becoming more confident. We must strike them now before they become too strong. It will take five days for all of the soldiers from the other bands to arrive. They will have two days of rest and preparations here and then on the night of the seventh day from today we will go to Miasmos's reign. Any able-bodied and able-powered fairy who will rise to the occasion and join the fight is asked to report to the park tomorrow to receive his or her uniform and battle wand. We will also need medical support volunteers. Any fairies wishing to help in that capacity should go and see Margretta tomorrow morning in medicine storage and creation. Group power coordination classes will be doubled in length and any fairy who will participate in the battle is excused from any community work in the coming week, unless they wish to continue both. Thank you, it has been a long evening, you may all take rest."

Glenden, Venuto and the fairy delegations, including Gwendolyn, exited amidst more fanfare from Flimsy and company. Glenden's suggestion of taking rest was the last thing anyone had in mind.

"No feast this time?" Stephanie asked.

"Doesn't look like it," Kelly said.

"But I'm starving," Stephanie complained. None of them had eaten dinner, since the council meeting had begun at five o'clock.

"I have some food in my quarters. Would you care to join me?" Dimpleton asked.

Beatrix declined because she wanted to go back to sit by Bubbles, and Dimpleton's brothers had already flown off to mingle with other fairies. So only Kelly and Stephanie followed Dimpleton to his quarters where he offered them brimming mugs of chilled nectala and squirrel fillet sandwiches. Kelly was actually glad no one else had joined them, because she was interested to hear Dimpleton's uncensored thoughts on the council meeting's results. She noted him as unusually pensive and quiet since the meeting ended.

"What do you think about the results of the meeting?" she asked him before starting in on her sandwich.

Dimpleton sighed. "I don't know. The attack on the Catanori by the Miasmonians worries me. The fact that they are kidnapping so many fairies can only mean one thing."

"What's that?"

"Perversions of magic. They are feeding off other fairies, stealing their energy to increase their own. I fear many in our band may be too naïve about what they are signing up to fight against."

"You mean you think we could lose?" Kelly asked.

Dimpleton didn't answer. Instead he got up and poured both Stephanie and Kelly more nectala.

"I should go and fill in you-know-who about the meeting," Dimpleton said, retrieving his underwater breathing mask from his pocket. "Just stack your dishes in the sink when you finish. By the way, there's some strawberry sorbet in the freezer, very tasty." He put on his mask and headed for the ceiling.

"Bye!" Stephanie and Kelly called out in unison.

"What do you think Thomas will think of all this?" Stephanie asked Kelly.

"I don't know," Kelly answered. She was worried by what Dimpleton had said. He didn't instill much confidence in her. If other fairies were naïve of perverse magic, what was she? Stephanie seemed to be reading her thoughts.

"You know, you've met Marcos Witherings, that's direct contact with the other side. You know more about what to expect than most anyone here."

"Maybe," Kelly said. But she doubted it. She remembered her last vision of Witherings, when he had held up his wand and she hadn't had a clue what was about to come out of it, just that it would be horrible.

Chapter 11
Queimada

Kelly could see Miasmos standing in a dark and damp hallway. Along one side of the hallway was a series of birdcages lined up, each with a fairy trapped inside. Miasmos stood in front of one of the cages with his hand extended out towards a small female fairy with yellow wings who huddled inside it. Miasmos's glowing wings filled the space around him with blue light. The fairy inside the cage was trembling and a thin cloud-like mist was rising from her body up to Miasmos's outstretched hand. He was sucking energy out of her.

"Father?" Marcos Witherings was walking down the hallway towards Miasmos. Miasmos put his hand down and the mist stopped rising from the fairy in the cage.

"What is it?" Miasmos snapped.

"The Glendenians, they're going to attack us!"

"Of course they are," Miasmos replied calmly.

"You aren't worried?"

Miasmos laughed. "Silly boy. I don't get worried. Besides, I want them to attack us."

"But they will outnumber us."

"If I didn't know you better I might think you were frightened." Miasmos fixed a penetrating gaze on Witherings.

"No, I'm just trying to think about what's best for us," Witherings stammered.

"Their attack is what's best for us. You'll see. They underestimate us. And I have a feeling a certain someone won't be able to resist showing his face at the battle, and once we kill him the Key to Embralia will be ours." Miasmos's eyes glowed an intense blue at this thought.

"But you can't deny that the Glendenians are powerful."

"Perhaps. But I have a powerful fadaman on my side."

"And they have her," Witherings reminded his father.

Miasmos's eyes flashed orange with anger. "Her? You're worried about her? She's a joke, just like her father!"

Kelly's heart started to beat faster. Her father?

"Still, I'd be more comfortable if she were out of the picture," Witherings said.

"Then take her out of it. Do something useful for a change." Miasmos turned back to the fairy in the cage and stretched out his arm again. Witherings stood looking at his toes.

"What are you waiting for? Out of my sight!" Miasmos demanded.

"Yes, father," Witherings hastily mumbled and hurried away.

Kelly woke up feeling very tired, as if she hadn't slept at all. She felt certain that in her dream she had telepathically glimpsed a real exchange between Miasmos and his son. She lay staring at the ceiling, trying to remember every single detail. Miasmos had said her father was a joke. If Miasmos hadn't liked her father, Kelly took that as a good sign. But who could her father be and how did Miasmos know him? Kelly was also disturbed by the fact that Miasmos hadn't seemed worried at all by the impending Glendenian attack. On top of that he had told Witherings to take her out of the picture. And if when fairies talked about taking someone out of the picture it meant the same thing it did when humans talked about it, then that meant he wanted her dead. When Stephanie walked into Kelly's room Kelly jumped up, startled.

"Whoa, easy now!" Stephanie said. "Just waking you up, you slept in again and it's almost time for our shift at medicine storage and creation."

"Will you tell Margretta I might be late? I need to go talk to Venuto."

"Another dream?" Stephanie asked. Kelly nodded.

"What happened?" Stephanie sat down on the edge of Kelly's bed.

Kelly told Stephanie what she had seen.

"At least you know that creep isn't your father," Stephanie said. Just then the door chimes rang.

"That must be Gwendolyn," Stephanie said. "We'll talk more later."

After getting dressed Kelly made her way to the entrance to the royal quarters and placed her hand against the shadow archway leading to the main reception room. There was a series of chimes and then a mechanical voice very similar to the voice of the lion statue spoke.

"State your name, fairy," the voice commanded.

"Kelly Brennan."

"State your business, fairy."

"I've come to see Venuto."

"Invalid business, please rephrase."

Not again, Kelly thought. Then she got an idea.

"I humbly request an audience with the brave and honest Venuto Grand," she said in a firm voice.

"Valid business. Please enter and wait in the reception room until you are called. Have a nice day."

Kelly walked through the shadow archway and sat down on the large sofa in the middle of the reception room. No sooner had she sat down than Flimsly appeared, dressed again in his bright red jacket and white pants.

"Come on now," he said to her. "You don't want to keep everyone waiting do you?"

"What do you mean everyone?" she asked as she followed him towards the archway that led to the dining hall where she, Bubbles, Beatrix, Petania, and Venuto had had dinner before. But Flimsly walked right through the archway without giving an answer, so she followed him through it to see that Glenden, Venuto, and the visiting fairy leaders Riona, Catia, and Belen were all sitting at the far end of the table. Glenden was at the head of the table, Venuto was seated on his right, and Catia, Belen, and Riona were all seated on his left. Minerva the Rowenian attendant was standing dutifully behind her mistress's chair, and Flimsly busily added another place setting beside Venuto. Kelly stood awkwardly just inside the doorway as all eyes turned to her.

"Sorry to disturb you, I was just stopping by to speak with Venuto," she stammered.

"Please, join us, we were just talking about you," Glenden said.

Kelly approached the table and sat down next to Venuto, feeling uneasy from Glenden's comment.

Venuto introduced Kelly to the others, who all nodded politely. Close up Kelly noticed that Riona was truly flawless — there wasn't even a hint of a blemish anywhere on her skin. She could also see that Catia had dark purple eyes that matched her wings, whilst Belen had light grey eyes.

During the brief introductions Flimsly had filled all of their goblets with freshly squeezed orange juice. It looked like Kelly had unwittingly stumbled into the royal breakfast.

"So you're the fadaman Glenden was just telling us about?" Riona asked.

"I suppose so," Kelly answered.

"If you don't mind me asking, how is it that you transform from human to fairy form? I've always wondered about that," Belen said.

Kelly explained the transformation process.

"Thank you, that's very fascinating," Belen said.

Flimsly brought out selections of cut fruits, ant legs, grasshopper cutlets, grits, biscuits, pancakes, and more.

"What was it you wanted to see me about?" Venuto asked.

"I just wanted to tell you about a dream I had, but it can wait until later." Kelly was a bit embarrassed to tell about her dream in front of the others.

"A dream?" Belen asked with interest. "I heard that fadaman senses can be quite powerful, is that so?"

"I don't really think mine are that powerful," she said. He looked disappointed.

"I don't see any reason not to tell about the dream now," Glenden said. "Please, let's hear it."

"All right," Kelly said. She told them about the dream, leaving out the part about her father. She only wanted to tell that part to Venuto. They were all quiet for a moment after she had finished. Glenden was the first to speak.

"I think this dream only further shows that we must strike now. The Miasmonians are clearly growing stronger and will already at this point be a challenge for us."

"I agree," Riona said. The others nodded. "With the five hundred soldiers I am providing, and the two hundred from the Catanori and Beleni, how many total will we have including yours?" she asked Glenden.

"We won't know the exact number until the end of today, but judging from the amount of fairies who were taking the group power coordination classes, I would say we will have close to 700 from our side. Meaning 1400 total."

"But we don't know exactly how many Miasmonians there are," Catia said.

"That's right, but our best information gives an estimate of between 600 to 1000," Glenden said.

"Are you going to fight?" Belen asked Kelly.

"Yes, I think so." She looked at Venuto for confirmation.

He nodded. "Yes, she's going to fight, but not amongst the main regiments. She will stay close to me during the battle. She's new at magic but is already as good as most fairies. She will be primarily useful in helping us fight the other fadaman. It would be much harder for us to fight him alone, but with her strength combined with ours we should have more success."

"I see," Catia said. "But I am curious about one more thing from your dream. Miasmos mentioned he thinks the guardian of the Key to Embralia might show up at the battle? Isn't he dead?"

"Before he died he passed the Key to his little brother," Glenden said. "His location is not known."

"Is there a chance the new guardian will show up at the battle?" Catia asked.

"Doubtful, he has been in exile for thirteen years and probably isn't even anywhere near Glendenland," Glenden said.

"Yet it is strange Miasmos would mention him," Catia said.

"Peter's little brother might feel like he still has a duty to help protect the Glendenians. He was after all part of one of the ruling families," Kelly suggested.

Glenden laughed. "Only someone new to Glendenland could say something like that. The Penadas don't know anything about duty or honor," he said, growing more somber. "All they care about is power, like Miasmos."

"Just because one of them might have been bad doesn't mean they all are," Kelly snapped before thinking about it.

"You seem pretty eager to defend someone you don't even know," Glenden commented coolly.

There was an awkward silence, during which Kelly held her tongue. She didn't like Thomas being talked about that way, but she didn't want to directly contradict Glenden or reveal that she knew Thomas.

"More orange juice?" Flimsly asked from beside the table, holding up the pitcher. During the rest of breakfast Kelly didn't say much. The others discussed technical details of when the new soldiers would arrive and where they would be housed. Venuto didn't speak much either. After about an hour Glenden thanked them all for coming and took his leave. Riona, Catia, and Belen got up to leave as well, but Kelly hung back for a moment because Venuto made a slight waving motion to her.

"You didn't tell us everything about your dream did you?" he asked once the others had left.

"No," she confessed. She told him about how Miasmos had mentioned her father.

"I'm glad, as I'm sure you are, to find out your father isn't Miasmos."

"I just wished Miasmos had said more about my father," Kelly said.

"Indeed."

Kelly turned to leave.

"Oh Kelly?" he called to her.

"Yes?"

"There isn't anything else you aren't telling me is there?"

"No," she said. She felt guilty lying to him, but she didn't know how he would react if he found out she knew Peter's younger brother. She couldn't risk telling him.

When Kelly made it to the medicine storage and creation bubble she found Stephanie and Gwendolyn busy grinding and mixing various ingredients for magical remedies. Margretta instructed Kelly to get right to work because they needed to redouble their efforts to produce as much medicine as possible before the battle.

"How did it go?" Stephanie asked.

"Not what I was expecting. I'll tell you about it later," Kelly promised. Just then a timid-looking young female fairy with brown wings entered the room.

"Hallo dear, this way," Margretta cooed. The fairy followed Margretta back into the shelves. Kelly looked at Stephanie inquisitively.

"A new recruit for medical duty. The tenth so far."

Every few minutes another fairy showed up to apply for medical duty, and Margretta would take them each back to the shelves and explain the medicines they would be taking to the battlefield, giving them brief instructions on how to administer the treatments to injured fairies. Stephanie sighed as she watched the most recent recruit leave the bubble.

"I wish I could go to the battle too," she sighed.

"Why, you can sign up for medical duty dear," Margretta said, having overheard her.

"I can?" Stephanie asked. "Even though I'm hu-, I mean, even though I'm not good at magic?" Stephanie glanced apprehensively at Gwendolyn but luckily she was intently grinding some pollen and hadn't noticed that Stephanie had nearly let slip she was a human.

"Of course dear, that's not a problem. Besides, you'll be safer than many others on the battlefield I'm sure." Margretta winked.

She was alluding to the fact that Stephanie possessed the inborn human protection against all but the strongest of fairy magic.

"Come on now, let me give you your orientation," Margretta said. Stephanie grinned and waved excitedly to Kelly as she followed Margretta back into the shelves.

As Kelly, Stephanie, and Gwendolyn left their shift and entered the hallway, a breathless Beatrix nearly bumped into them.

"Bubbawakynacomsehim!" she exclaimed, this time so impossibly fast that even Kelly's sharp fairy-form ears couldn't decipher what she was saying.

"Sorry?" Kelly asked.

"Bubbles is awake!" she said more slowly before sprinting back to the hospital wing. They quickly followed her. When they reached the hospital bubble they saw that Bubbles was sitting propped up on a pillow in his bed. He looked tired and a great deal thinner than he had been a week and a half before. Bamblelina was sitting by his side, looking at him adoringly.

"Hi Bubbles," Stephanie said.

"How do you feel?" Kelly asked.

"I'm hungry," Bubbles complained. Kelly smiled. Bubbles was back. "And I can't believe I missed the council meeting."

"You didn't miss much, I was inside and it was almost as boring for me as it was for the fairies waiting outside," Gwendolyn said. Kelly hadn't noticed that she had come into the hospital bubble with them.

"Who are you?" Bubbles asked bluntly.

"Forgive my brother's lack of manners," Beatrix apologized, shooting Bubbles a reproachful look.

"This is Gwendolyn, maidservant to Queen Riona of Rowenia," Beatrix said. "Gwendolyn, meet Bubbles."

"Nice to meet you." Gwendolyn curtsied.

Bubbles didn't say anything – he just eyed Gwendolyn suspiciously. Beatrix elbowed him in the side.

"Nice to meet you too," he mumbled.

At that moment Margretta arrived to check on her patient. She felt Bubbles's forehead, then checked his pulse.

"You're cured. Free to go," she said unceremoniously and left the room.

"Did you hear that? That's wonderful!" Bamblelina exclaimed. She kissed Bubbles on the cheek. Bubbles turned a deep shade of crimson.

"Let's go eat," Beatrix suggested.

News of Bubbles's release spread quickly, and at lunch he was continually approached by fairies inquisitive to hear his account. Bubbles basked in the attention and didn't correct any of the fairies who had twisted ideas of what had occurred. The rumors of his encounter with the Miasmonians had spun out of control, reaching almost epic proportions.

"How did you survive being attacked by fifty Miasmonians?" a young male fairy asked eagerly.

"I just kept fighting as hard as I could," Bubbles answered, stuffing a handful of ant legs into his mouth.

"Wow," the young fairy said, looking at Bubbles in awe.

"You know, you really shouldn't encourage them to think you fought so many Miasmonians," Kelly whispered to Bubbles after the young male fairy had left, to be replaced by a young female fairy child who just stood staring up at Bubbles with her mouth wide open. Her gaping made Bubbles uncomfortable so he stuffed an ant leg in the fairy child's mouth. She chewed on it without taking her eyes off of him.

"Why not? What's the big difference between three and fifty anyway?" Bubbles said.

"You don't want them to get an inflated view of how good you are at magic, do you?" Kelly asked him.

"I think it's a little late for that," Stephanie said.

"What do you mean?" Kelly asked. Stephanie pointed. Kelly saw that Milak, the imposing fairy with the eye patch who had been teaching group power coordination, was at the far side of the mess hall and heading straight for them.

"Are you Bubbles?" Milak asked as he reached them, not looking at anyone else at the table.

"Yes," Bubbles said uncertainly.

"Glad that you're back to full capabilities. I trust you will be coming by the park later to sign up to fight the Miasmonians?"

Bubbles launched into a coughing fit, having almost swallowed an ant leg the wrong way at the prospect of being in the battle.

"Of course he will, he's very brave," Bamblelina said from her spot beside Bubbles.

"Good man, good man," Milak said. "We need fairies with your expertise."

"But I don't have any expertise," Bubbles protested.

"Humble too? That's a rare quality these days, rare indeed. But any fairy who can face fifty Miasmonians alone and live to tell about it has just the expertise we need. I'll be expecting you later. Carry on," he said and walked away.

"I believe that would be what Kelly was trying to help you avoid," Stephanie said.

Bubbles groaned and put his head in his hands.

That night they had a welcome back party for Bubbles in one of the common recreation rooms near Dimpleton's quarters. Dimpleton and his brothers were there, along with Bamblelina, Beatrix, Kelly, Stephanie, and a bunch of fairies who had been taking group power coordination classes with Bubbles and Bamblelina before Bubbles got injured. There must have been close to sixty fairies there, and they cheerfully drank nectala and danced to the music played by Wimpleton and Pimpleton on a flute and a stringed instrument that resembled a banjo. The cheerful environment was contagious and Kelly was happy to see Bubbles awake and himself again. She thought it was adorable how he continued to turn beet red whenever Bamblelina gave him attention, which was pretty much constantly since she had been by his side every moment since the start of the party. After the party had been going on for at least four hours, Venuto and Petania arrived. Petania still gave Kelly and Stephanie somewhat frigid looks, but her smile was a little warmer towards Bamblelina. This difference made sense of course because Bamblelina was so absorbed with Bubbles it would have been impossible for her to be interested in Venuto as well. When Petania left Venuto's side for a minute to get herself a refill of nectala, Kelly took the chance to ask Venuto for an update.

"You didn't talk to her yet, did you?" she asked.

"Talk to who?"

"Petania."

"No."

"What are you waiting for?"

"I don't know. I just never seem to find the right time," he answered. Petania was on her way back with her nectala.

"Maybe you should stop waiting for the right time and just talk to her. What you think of as the right time might never come about."

Petania had gotten back with her nectala and she looked at Kelly coldly.

"If you'll excuse me," Kelly said. "I'm going to go see what Bubbles is up to." She went to join Bubbles, Beatrix and Bamblelina, who were all dancing in the middle of the room.

It was a dark, moonless night. Kelly was watching as if from very far away. She saw the outline of a cloaked figure on the rocky mountain face, climbing upwards. He continued to climb until he reached the top of the mountain. He reached into his pocket. Suddenly Kelly was pulled inward into the vision so that she was seeing the cloaked figure from only a few feet away. She recognized he was Miasmos and that he was holding a small black stone in his hand. Kelly looked down. The ground below them had a crevice running through it, about two feet wide, and just about as deep. The crevice marked the place where the mountain had started to open up before, some 2,500 years ago. Kelly tried to reach out to stop him but she wasn't really there so couldn't reach him. Miasmos bent down and placed the stone inside the crack. At first nothing happened. But then there was a deep rumbling sound from inside the mountain and the ground started to shake. Miasmos's eyes started to glow with a blue light that grew stronger and stronger as the shaking of the ground grew more violent. He put his hands up into the *air triumphantly and laughed a scary, cackling laugh. Lava started to shoot out of the ground, splashing all around him, but somehow he wasn't burnt by it, even as it touched his skin and flowed around his ankles. He just kept laughing and his eyes kept growing brighter and brighter.*

It was the sixth day after the council meeting. There was only one more day before the battle. The night after that night they would set out to attack the Miasmonians in their lair in the old tunnels off the metro system. All of the soldiers from the other bands had arrived the day before and were engaged in meetings and exercises with the Glendenians so that the different bands could get used to each other's fighting styles. Kelly had watched a bit of their exercises in the park, but after she had seen many of the great magical displays they were creating, she had gone back to the secret room in the library to practice her own magic. With each passing day Kelly became painfully aware of just how much magic she needed to develop, and since the day after Bubbles woke up she had been spending almost all of her free time practicing in the secret room in the library. Unfortunately she had to practice without Venuto's help because he was so busy helping to prepare Glendenland for battle that she had barely seen him since Bubbles's welcome back party. She felt her progress was slow, and she still had difficulty creating electric current. Up to that point she had only managed isolated bursts of sparks and brief flashes of current, and she couldn't sustain either sparks or current flow for much more than a second. Kelly had been sitting cross-legged trying to concentrate on the subtlest feelings of fire elements in her body when she had had the vision. She hadn't liked the most recent vision at all, but she reminded herself that visions of the future only showed one of many possibilities, not the only possibility. She hoped that the possibility she had seen would never come to pass.

That evening there was a feast in honor of the visiting soldiers, but it was a much more solemn event than the feast that had occurred a little over a month before when Kelly had first arrived in Glendenland. The impending battle was weighing down on everyone's mind. Bubbles was especially preoccupied.

He told them that Milak had just placed him at the head of a group of fifty fairies. He would have to lead the group in the battle.

"I don't know what I'm going to do," he said, having barely touched his plate of food.

"You're going to lead your group with bravery and expertise," Bamblelina said confidently.

Bubbles shook his head forlornly. "I'm not good enough."

"Milak wouldn't have put you in charge of a group if he didn't think you were good enough," Dimpleton said matter-of-factly.

"But he only thinks I'm good enough because he thinks I survived an attack from fifty Miasmonians."

"That's not the only reason. He's seen you perform excellently in the exercises all these last few days," Bamblelina said.

"Really?" Bubbles asked, a little bit of hope coming into his eyes.

"She's right Bubbles. Milak's not stupid. He knows you didn't really fight off fifty Miasmonians," Dimpleton said. "He made the group leader assignments through his judgment of our abilities alone, not on rumors." Dimpleton had also been assigned leadership of a fairy group.

Bubbles smiled. "So I really do have expertise," he said happily, scooping up a large forkful of mashed strawberries.

"Do you think we'll win?" Kelly asked Stephanie. They were back in their quarters after the feast, getting ready for bed.

"I don't know."

"Are you scared?" Kelly asked.

"More than I've ever been in my whole life," Stephanie admitted.

"Me too," Kelly said.

After lying awake for a long time Kelly eventually slipped into an uneasy sleep. The next morning they were awakened early by the chimes at their door. It was Bubbles, Beatrix, and Bamblelina.

"Come on, we're going to be late for Dimpleton's queimada!" Beatrix said.

"His what?" Kelly asked.

"His queimada, he said we could join his because we don't have a pot."

"What are you talking about?"

"You'll see. Come on, let's go!" Beatrix said impatiently.

Kelly and Stephanie hastily changed out of their pajamas and into day clothes and followed the others to Dimpleton's quarters. They entered through the archway that Dimpleton had left unlocked for them. Dimpleton, Wimpleton, and Pimpleton were already seated cross-legged on the floor. The furniture in the living room had all been pushed out of the way and on the floor in the center of the room was a silver pot. It was more like a deep bowl, with three legs supporting it so that its base rested a few inches from the ground. Dimpleton waved them closer, and Kelly, Beatrix, Bubbles, Bamblelina, and Stephanie joined the others on the floor to form a circle around the metal bowl. As they sat down Kelly noticed the bowl was full of what looked like nectala, but it also had grated lemon and orange peels on top. Dimpleton reached for a small sack beside him and emptied it into the bowl. It was sugar. Then he sprinkled on some dark brown grounds, which looked like coffee.

"What's that for?" Stephanie asked.

"It helps with the burning," Dimpleton said. He stirred the sugar into the liquid.

Stephanie gave Kelly a look that communicated *what in the world is he talking about?* Kelly shrugged.

"Who wants to recite the incantation?" he asked.

"Ooh, me, me, me!" Bamblelina said eagerly, waving her hand in the air.

"All right." Dimpleton handed her a roll of parchment that she unrolled as he pulled out a match from his pocket and lit it. "Ready?" he asked.

Bamblelina nodded. Dimpleton touched the burning tip of the match to the surface of the nectala mixture and it burst into bright orange flames. Bamblelina cleared her throat and then recited the incantation.

> *Forces of earth, air, water, and fire,*
> *We call upon you with this queimada.*
>
> *May these flames find the traces of those long lost,*
> *Call them here from mountain, river and frost.*
>
> *Prepared to face our challenge most dire,*
> *We will drink deeply from this queimada.*
>
> *These flames honor those who are here no longer,*
> *They'll lend us their strength and we'll be stronger.*
>
> *May our ancestors' spirits hear this call,*
> *If they fight beside us we will not fall.*

Just as Bamblelina was reaching the end of the incantation the flames took on a blue tint. Dimpleton pulled out a ladle and a goblet. He filled the goblet with some of the burning liquid and passed the flaming cup down the line. He filled more goblets until they were all holding their own goblets of the still-flaming liquid.

"Cheers," Dimpleton said, holding up his goblet and drinking from it. The other fairies enthusiastically followed suit, and then Kelly and Stephanie followed a bit more cautiously. Kelly was afraid she would get burnt by the flames, but as she lifted the glass they had almost extinguished and by the time she drank it the liquid was flameless. Her lips were met with a very sweet, full-bodied taste.

"That's what I call a queimada," Bubbles said appreciatively, smacking his lips.

"And how many queimadas exactly have you tasted?" Beatrix asked.

"You don't have to have had something before to know if it's good," Bubbles said.

"That's the spirit," Dimpleton said as he took Bubbles's now empty goblet and refilled it. They all drank another glass and when Kelly left with Stephanie for their last shift at magic storage and creation before that night's battle, she felt much lighter than she had been feeling before.

Chapter 12
Breaking Point

The light feeling didn't last for long. Kelly started to feel uneasy about fifteen minutes into their magic storage and creation shift. Kelly, Stephanie, and Gwendolyn were busy pouring liquids and creams from large storage bottles into smaller individual bottles for the medical volunteers to carry into that night's battle. There was a cauterizing spray for wounds that wouldn't stop bleeding, a warming draught for fairies affected by freezing mist, burn creams of varying strengths, smelling salts, and fairy dust, which Margretta said would help bring confused or disoriented fairies back to their senses. Kelly kept feeling the urge to look over her shoulder – she felt like she was being watched. Initially, she tried to explain the feeling away as battle nerves, but it kept getting stronger and stronger. Then, as she was screwing the cap onto an individual bottle of fairy dust, the bottle seemed to wobble and black spots started to appear around the borders of her vision. The black spots raced inward and everything went black.

She was once again in the room where she had met Marcos Witherings. He sat in human form across from her.

"So sorry to draw you away from such important tasks, but we need to talk," Witherings began.

"We have nothing to talk about."

"You might think differently in a few minutes," Witherings said. "I don't want you at the battle tonight."

"And I want you to crawl into a hole and die," Kelly retorted sarcastically.

"I'm afraid I can't oblige."

"Neither can I."

"Are you sure?" Witherings asked, reaching down to pick something up from underneath the table. He placed the object on the table. It was the golden birdcage with the gem-encrusted handle. But the fairy inside wasn't alone. Kelly let out a horrified gasp when she saw her mother, shrunk to fairy size, inside the cage. Mindy was sleeping.

"As you can see I have your mother here," Witherings said gleefully. "But don't worry, she's unharmed for the time being. Under the influence of quite a strong sleeping potion."

"Let her go," Kelly demanded.

"You're not the one to be giving orders, I'm the one with the bargaining chip. Here are my terms. I want a duel. You show up here, alone, in thirty minutes time. If you win, your mother goes free. If you lose, well, then she doesn't. If you don't come within thirty minutes, she dies. If you tell anyone else or don't come alone, she dies. Think it over, but don't think for too long, for your mother's sake. The clock starts now." Witherings pulled a stopwatch out of his pocket and pressed the start button.

Kelly started to get dizzy and everything went black again.

"Kelly, are you all right?" Kelly opened her eyes to see Stephanie's worried face above her. Kelly was lying on the ground of the magic storage and creation bubble.

"What happened?" Kelly asked as she sat up.

"You fainted. Stephanie used these smelling salts to revive you," Margretta said.

"Oh," Kelly said. Her mind was racing. She needed to think alone.

"Is it all right if I go lie down for a few minutes?" Kelly asked.

"Sure dear," Margretta said. "There isn't much work left to do so you don't have to come back if you don't feel up to it. You need your rest to be ready for tonight."

"Right," Kelly mumbled as she got to her feet.

"Are you sure you're okay?" Stephanie asked.

"Yeah, I'm just a little dizzy." Kelly headed for the door.

"I'll come check on you when the shift ends," Stephanie called out as Kelly left the room. Kelly didn't answer.

Kelly burst into her quarters and paced around the living room. She was convinced she hadn't imagined it. She had been telepathically contacted by Witherings and he had meant what he said. She knew he was waiting for her in the building where he had held her captive before. She didn't know how she knew for sure, but she did. Should she tell Venuto? Dimpleton? Bubbles? No, she couldn't risk it. Witherings might be able to sense it if she told anyone. There was only one thing she could do. She had to go and fight him. It was what he wanted and he would have the advantage – but she had to try to save her mother.

Kelly pulled her underwater breathing mask out of her shoulder bag and put it on. She took off her fairy sense necklace. She didn't want Bubbles's necklace to start glowing red to show that she was in danger, because if it did he would come looking for her. She hoped he would be too busy with other things to pick up on her being in danger without the necklace – and if he did sense anything she hoped his necklace not glowing would reassure him. She ran to her room and hid the necklace under her pillow. She exited through the top of her room and swam to the surface of the river. She snapped her fingers and changed into her half-invisible form, as it was still broad daylight. At least that way if any humans saw her they would be more likely to think they were hallucinating. Then she flew up into the air, staying close to the treetops as she zoomed at top speed towards the building where Witherings had her mother. On the ground below she saw many humans walking around, blissfully unaware of any of the problems amongst fairies or the danger Miasmos and Witherings posed to them. As Kelly got closer and closer to her destination, she felt more and more anxious. But there was no turning back now.

After nearly thirty minutes of flying Kelly spotted the building. She saw Grimes and Crisp sitting on a bench outside the entrance. They were both pretending to read the newspaper. She could tell they were pretending because Grimes was holding his newspaper upside down and Crisp was very obviously craning his head in all directions every few seconds. Kelly decided entering the building through the roof was her best bet. Scanning the rooftop carefully for any signs of Miasmonian guards, Kelly flew into the air duct that she had escaped from before. She flew down the duct and into the hallway. This time her developing fairy senses told her exactly where to go. She flew to the end of the hall and into the stairwell.

As soon as she entered the stairwell she instinctively put her right hand up to block a palm-sized fireball that was heading in her direction. After deflecting the fireball she looked in the direction it had come from to see Murk and Lurk hovering together at the base of the stairs. She swiftly shot a string of hot electric sparks at them. She was surprised at the strength of the sparks; they were stronger than any she had sent out before in practice. Murk and Lurk jumped out of the way, but a few sparks hit Murk's leg and he squealed in pain. Kelly took aim again. The second string of sparks hit Lurk squarely in the chest and he fell to the ground with a loud thud, writhing in pain. Murk looked down in horror at his injured friend, then he looked at Kelly with fear in his eyes. Kelly pointed her finger at him, but before she had a chance to send any sparks his way he turned and bolted, fleeing up the stairway. She had been expecting a little more of a fight from Witherings's loyal servants.

Kelly didn't bother following Murk. She continued down the stairway, past the moaning Lurk, and down the hallway that led to the interrogation room. She noticed that her mouth was dry and her palms were sweating as she approached the closed door. She reached out to twist the doorknob. The doorknob was almost as big as her entire fairy-form torso, and to turn it she had to grab it with both arms and flap her wings, using the force of her whole body. Though this maneuver was difficult, she couldn't risk changing into human form to open the door, because she would need to have immediate access to her powers as soon as the door opened. She heard a click, telling her that the door had been released. She let go of the knob and the door inched open.

"Do come in." Witherings's voice met Kelly's ears from inside in room. "You could have just knocked."

Kelly hesitated for a moment before cautiously entering the room. She held her right hand out in front of her defensively. Witherings was in his fairy form, standing next to the birdcage on the table. Kelly saw her sleeping mother inside the birdcage, along with the other fairy from her previous visions. That fairy, unlike Mindy, was awake and watching the proceedings with a mixture of fear and hope. Witherings had his wand drawn and was pointing it at Kelly as she came in.

"I've been expecting you," Witherings said.

"Is that so."

"I knew you'd come and try to save your mommy. Quite touching really, though foolish I'm afraid."

"We'll see about that," Kelly said. She shot a fireball at him from her right hand.

He flicked his wand in response and the fireball bounced away from him and hurtled back at Kelly. Kelly blocked it with her palm. Witherings then shot a bolt of electricity at her. She dodged it with a backwards summersault and it hit the doorframe behind her with a sizzling sound.

"Not bad," Witherings said. "Let's see how you handle the other elements." He flicked his wand and a jet of forceful water shot from it. Kelly quickly called on the cold end of the fire element and sent it out to meet the stream of incoming water. The water froze in midair and fell to the ground, shattering into a thousand pieces. Next Witherings started to shoot pointed icicles at her from his wand. One after another the sharp projectiles came at Kelly. She barely had time to think, but with a combination of dodging, blocking with the air element, and melting with the fire element, she was able to avoid being hit by any of the projectiles. After a few minutes Witherings paused, and Kelly caught her breath while trying to form a plan of attack.

"I see you have a basic control of the elements," he said, rubbing his wand against his jacket to remove the frost that had started to gather on its surface. "But you're going to need more than a basic control to fight me." He thrust his wand in Kelly's direction and a stream of flame flew out of it – he was using his wand like a blowtorch. Kelly put up both of her hands to block the continuous stream of fire but soon she felt her hands start to get hot. Witherings edged closer as he continued shooting the stream of fire from his wand. Kelly's arms started to shake under the pressure of blocking the flames. With all of her strength she called up a burst of water element and launched it at him, succeeding in momentarily stopping the flames as she jumped for cover behind one of the table legs. He was much stronger than she was.

But she wasn't going to give up. She took a deep breath and concentrated on feeling the atmosphere inside and around her body. She sensed a predominance of water element. She would use that. She took Witherings's idea and, pointing her arm out from behind the table leg, she launched an icicle at him. He shifted out of the way and the icicle shattered against the wall on the other side of the room. Witherings dove towards the table leg behind which Kelly was hiding, the stream of fire once more coming from his wand. Kelly darted out of his way, flinging icicles at him over her shoulder as she headed up towards the ceiling. Witherings followed close behind and she felt a flash of pain as a wisp of the flames hit her left foot, burning a hole in her slipper.

Having reached the ceiling, she changed direction and tumbled sideways in a series of summersaults in order to dodge the flames from Witherings's wand, thankful for the flying skills she had learned playing tag in Glendenland. She felt a tinge of satisfaction when one of her icicles grazed Witherings's left hand. But suddenly she realized Witherings was no longer behind her – instead he was heading straight for the cage on the table, the cage where Kelly's mother lay unconscious and defenseless. Kelly turned around and raced after him, setting down on the surface of the table. She was about to run at him, but she stopped short when she saw he had reached the cage. He stood next to it with his wand pointed directly at Kelly's mother. The male fairy in the cage with Mindy had pressed himself up against the bars on the opposite side of the cage, as far away from Witherings's wand as he could physically get.

"Enough fun and games," Witherings said. Kelly inched her foot forward. "Don't move!" Witherings's voice shook. Kelly stood still.

"I could kill your mother right now. I could burn her to a crisp in a second." He lifted his wand as if preparing to strike her mother.

"Don't, please," Kelly said. "I'll do what you want, just leave her alone."

"Ah, that's very nice, but I have to say I don't believe you," Witherings replied, still keeping his wand fixed on Kelly's mother. "You're just telling me what you think I want to hear, and then once I take my wand off your mother or turn my back on you you'll attack me. You're playing games, but you really shouldn't play games with people's lives. Do you know how you would feel if your mother were to die? Do you know what that would feel like?" He kept his right, wand-bearing hand pointed at Mindy, but pointed his left index finger in Kelly's direction. "Are you prepared for this?"

Kelly saw a thin white wisp of mist drift from his finger and float in her direction. When it hit her she fell to the ground in agony – but not physical agony, emotional agony. She felt a desperate sadness and pain that she had never felt before. Witherings had somehow hit her with pure suffering, and she felt her body shake with intense sobs as Witherings's laughter reached her ears as if from far away. Despite the intensity of the emotion, a small part of her mind was still clear and detached from what she was feeling. This part of her mind started to grow stronger and Kelly was able to think of an idea. She remembered the queimada from the morning when the fairies had called on the elements, asking them to find the traces of those long lost and bring them together. Kelly started to think about this now, but in a different way. Could the same principle be applied to the suffering one had caused to others? Kelly mentally wished for all of the traces left on the world by the suffering Witherings had caused

195

to gather together and come back to him. She wished that he would feel all the suffering that he had ever caused anyone. She felt her sobs subsiding and she stood up slowly, pointing her trembling right hand at Witherings. He looked at her with confusion, a confusion that quickly turned to panic as his eyes darted around the room.

Kelly saw what was causing his distress. A swirling fog was rushing into the room from the doorway. Inside the fog there were moving shapes and forms of fairies screaming and running, and faint cries were coming from the fog. The fog approached the table and started to swirl around Witherings, getting thicker and thicker. He pointed his wand at the fog, trying fire and ice but nothing worked against it. He tried to run from it, but it kept circling him. Then it started to disappear into him. He started screaming the most horrible screams that Kelly had ever heard. He fell to the ground and screamed louder and louder as the fog continued to enter the room and disappear into him. Finally it stopped and he lay on the table shaking, mumbling to himself and looking around with glazed eyes. Kelly approached him and kicked his wand out of his hand. He made no move to stop her. Something told Kelly that he wouldn't be much of a threat for a long time.

Kelly ran over to the cage to look at Mindy. The fairy, who had been watching silently up to that point, smiled weakly at Kelly as she arrived at the cage.

"Sorry I wasn't any help. I'm so weak I can barely stand, let alone throw icicles around like you can, that was something else," the fairy said in admiration.

"What's your name?" Kelly asked him.

"I'm Jonah. Who are you?"

"Kelly," she said.

"It's great to meet you, thanks for saving me."

"You're welcome." Kelly found herself smiling even though she was still worried about her mother. The cage was locked with a key so Kelly went back to Witherings and searched his pockets. She retrieved the key from his jacket pocket and opened the cage. She bent down and shook Mindy but her mother didn't wake up.

"Won't have much luck with that," Jonah said. "I heard him tell his father he gave her a hypnull potion."

"What's that?" Kelly asked, not liking the sound of it.

"It makes someone fall into a deep sleep that can't be reversed without the antidote, the antihypnull potion."

"And I don't suppose you have any antihypnull potion on you?" Kelly asked. Jonah shook his head. "I didn't think so," Kelly sighed. "And do you happen to know if he shrunk her with fairy dust, or with a spell?"

"A spell."

"That's just great," Kelly said, discouraged. Although on the bright side she didn't have to worry about her mother suddenly reverting to human size. She tried to figure out what to do next. Jonah certainly didn't look like he'd be able to help carry Mindy anywhere. Actually, he didn't even look like he'd be able to fly very far on his own. Kelly could carry them all if she were in human form. But she had to get her mother to Glendenland, because if anyone had the antihypnull potion it would be Margretta, and she couldn't exactly walk up to Glendenland in human form in broad daylight. Someone was bound to notice. Maybe she could hide Jonah and Mindy in a safe place and then get help from Glendenland? What if the Miasmonians found them before she got back?

She might be able to make it to Carmina and Thomas's house in human form. They would know what to do. But were the Miasmonians watching Stephanie's house? She would have to take that risk. The most immediate problem now would be getting out of the building. In human form she couldn't leave by the roof, so she would have to get past Grimes and Crisp, unless she could find an unlocked side entrance, but that might take too much time because she was expecting Murk would be back with reinforcements at any moment. She decided the quickest way to go would be through the front door, and she didn't think she'd have as much trouble dealing with Grimes and Crisp this time. She walked out of the cage and changed into human form.

"Whoa," Jonah said, impressed, coming out of the cage to get a closer look at her.

"Get back in the cage," Kelly said.

"Why?"

"Do you think you can fly for twenty minutes?"

"I guess not," he said and got back into the cage. "Where are we going?"

"To some friends who hopefully can help us." Kelly closed the door to the cage. The only problem now was that although Jonah could make himself invisible, Mindy was still perfectly visible inside the birdcage. Kelly looked around for something to cover it with. Her eyes fell on Witherings, who was still lying on the table. She turned back to fairy form, pulled off Witherings's jacket, and then held it in her hand as she transformed back into human form. Witherings's jacket returned to human size as she had hoped it would.

Jonah protested against being in the covered cage, because he wanted to see what was going on. So Kelly agreed to let him sit in invisible form on her shoulder. She picked him up and placed him on her shoulder, draped Witherings's jacket over the cage, picked the cage up, and turned to leave.

"Wait a minute," Jonah said.

"What?"

"What about him?" Jonah pointed to Witherings. "Are we just going to leave him here?"

"That was the idea."

"But what if Miasmos shows up and cures him," Jonah said worriedly. "Then he'd be able to fight in tonight's battle. I think we should take him as a prisoner."

"But if we take him with us, there's a huge risk that Miasmos will be able to sense where he is and come after us, isn't there?"

"I think there's just as much likelihood that Miasmos can sense us as he can sense him," Jonah said. "Either way we're in a lot of danger until we get in touch with other good fairies."

"All right," Kelly said. She picked up Witherings and put him inside the cage with Mindy. "I hope you're right."

She made her way to the front entrance of the building. She set down the cage just inside the door and Jonah hopped off her shoulder to sit on top of it. She peeked out the small window in the door to see that Crisp and Grimes were still pretending to read their papers.

"What are you going to do?" Jonah asked.

"I'm not sure." She ran through some possibilities in her mind, like setting one of them on fire like before. But then she got a much better idea.

"Will you check to see if Witherings has any fairy dust on him?" she asked Jonah. Jonah went into the cage and checked Witherings's pockets, but no fairy dust. Too bad. But there was another possibility. Kelly remembered that Lurk had been carrying the fairy dust that had been used on her the first time she had met Marcos Witherings.

"Wait here," she told Jonah. She transformed back into fairy form and flew quickly up to the stairwell where she had fought Murk and Lurk. Lurk was still there, whimpering. She felt a bit guilty as he cowered away from her when he saw her approaching.

"Don't hurt me!" he begged.

"I'm not going to hurt you, I just want you to give me your fairy dust."

"I don't have any," Lurk lied.

Kelly pointed her finger at him threateningly.

"Oh, you mean this fairy dust?" he said, producing the bottle from his knapsack. Kelly snatched it out of his grasp and raced back to where Jonah was waiting. She handed Jonah the bottle.

"When those two men come in here I want you to dust them, okay?" Kelly said.

Jonah nodded. Kelly transformed back into human form again and opened the door. Grimes and Smith stared at her in disbelief.

"Hello gentlemen, I believe your boss has had a bit of an accident. You might want to come take a look." Kelly went back inside and shut the door as Grimes and Crisp jumped to their feet and rushed towards it. Kelly transformed back into fairy form and hovered a few feet into the hallway and Jonah stood on top of the birdcage, poised just inside the door with the bottle of fairy dust.

Grimes and Crisp burst through the door, Grimes in the lead. Grimes stopped abruptly inside the door when he saw Kelly hovering in the middle of the hallway in fairy form and Crisp bumped into him from behind. This pause was just what Jonah needed, and he quickly poured generous amounts of fairy dust over Grimes's and Crisp's feet. Neither of the men noticed. Grimes reached out his hand to grab Kelly but she flew out of his reach. He stepped forward and tried again but at that moment the fairy dust took effect and he shrank to fairy size with a horrified expression on his face. Crisp was next, and seconds later they both stood in shrunken form, looking at each other in surprise. Kelly pointed her finger and unleashed a series of bright sparks in the fake agents' direction, more to frighten them than to hurt them. Grimes and Crisp started screaming and ran off down the hallway. Once they were out of sight, Kelly quickly transformed back into human form, picked up the cage and Jonah and exited the building, walking briskly. She didn't want to be around when the fairy dust wore off.

She turned down the first street, scanning the area nervously for any signs of Miasmonians on their trail, but she didn't see any. She walked fast. She hadn't gone more than two minutes when she saw the ghostly forms of two fairies approaching in the distance. To her relief she realized that they weren't Miasmonians; they were Thomas and Carmina flying at them at top speed, and soon they were just a foot away from Kelly.

"We were just on our way to see you," Kelly said.

"We know, we sensed you were in danger almost half an hour ago but we couldn't get here any faster," Carmina said. Thomas nodded politely.

"Jonah!" Carmina exclaimed when she saw Kelly's companion. The two embraced.

"You two know each other?" Kelly asked. Before either of them had a chance to respond Thomas spoke.

"Quickly, everyone in the bushes over there." He was pointing to a line of bushes by a tree on the side of the road, and he was listening intently to something none of the others could hear. "Kelly, put the cage down in the bushes and then transform, hurry!"

Kelly pushed the birdcage into a small space behind a low-lying bush. She transformed to fairy form and joined the others, who had already hidden themselves beside the birdcage. They huddled against the cage and Thomas motioned for them to be quiet. Kelly peeked out through a tiny space between the leaves. She saw the ghostly form of a Miasmonian approaching. The Miasmonian paused just a few feet away from their hiding place, cocking his head to the side, then he started to creep towards the bush. Thomas closed his eyes. Soon after, the Miasmonian turned abruptly as if it had heard something and flew off in the opposite direction. Kelly let out the breath of air she had been holding.

"What did you do to make it go away?" she asked Thomas.

"Weak minds are susceptible to suggestion. I simply suggested the idea that what he was looking for was on the other side of the city."

"What was he looking for?" Jonah asked.

"After Miasmos sensed the outcome of your fight with Witherings, he sent out over a hundred Miasmonians to look for him. That was only one of the first to arrive, I'm afraid there will be more coming," Thomas said.

"I knew they'd be able to sense him," Kelly said.

"Actually they aren't sensing him, they are sensing Jonah and your mother. You and Witherings are harder for fairies without exceptionally strong powers or a strong connection to you to sense because you are fadamen. Regular fairies like that one can't sense you," Carmina said.

"That's why only Miasmos was able to sense when his son went past the breaking point. If other nearby Miasmonians had sensed it, they surely would have shown up almost immediately at the place you were fighting," Thomas said.

"What should we do now?" Kelly asked.

"We need to get you, your mother, and Witherings back to Glendenland before the Miasmonians start showing up in groups too large for me to suggest to," Thomas said.

"But Jonah can't fly yet. So we'd have to carry him, my mother, and Witherings."

"We'll have to try," Thomas said.

"We might be able to manage for a bit, but the flight to Glendenland is at least twenty minutes," Carmina reminded her husband.

Thomas sighed. "There is a faster way to get to Glendenland."

Carmina gasped. "We couldn't."

"There is no other choice," Thomas said.

Chapter 13
Face to Face

"Let's see, we need a flat surface," Thomas said as he examined their surroundings. "The floor of the cage will work. Let's clear it out for a minute."

Carmina and Kelly gently carried Mindy out of the cage and laid her on the grass beside it. Then they carried Witherings and placed him beside Mindy. Kelly noticed that Witherings was drooling and repeatedly mumbling something that sounded like *I promise I'll be good mommy*. Once the cage was empty, Thomas stepped inside and pulled out a small bottle of fairy dust from his pocket. He started to pour it carefully on the floor of the cage and Kelly saw that he was making the outline of a large circle.

"What's he doing?" Kelly whispered to Carmina, not wanting to distract Thomas because he was concentrating so intently.

"He's going to make a temporary portal to Glendenland."

"Why did you say he shouldn't do it?" Kelly asked.

"Because only those members of the ruling families of Glendenland who might one day be king are supposed to know how."

Thomas had completed the circle and was now waving his hands in the air above it. Under his hands the air started to waver, giving the impression that the bars on the other side of the cage were wiggling.

"So if only members of the ruling family are supposed to know how, then they'll know whoever activated the portal is either a current member of the ruling family, as in, Glenden or Venuto, or a member of a family that used to be a ruling family," Kelly said.

"I didn't say that," Carmina said.

"She already knows who I am dear," Thomas called over his shoulder without pausing his intricate hand motions.

"In that case, yes, they'll know a Penadas of Thomas's generation activated the portal," Carmina said. "But I suppose there's not much we can do about it."

"Why of his generation?" Kelly asked.

"Since power used to shift from family to family, only family members of the generation next in line for the throne were taught the secret, and they in turn were bound by magic to only share the knowledge with the next ruling generation. Thus, Thomas and Peter learned how to make temporary portals from Glenden, and if history had taken a different course, one of them would have taught it to Venuto's future children."

A bright flash of light suddenly dropped from Thomas's hand into the circle. As the light made contact with it the inside of the circle changed. Instead of looking like the rest of the cage floor, it now resembled a piece of sky on a cloudless day, just like the archways in the transport bubbles in Glendenland when they were activated.

"You must go now. The portal will only stay open until the fairy dust is used up," Thomas said.

Kelly looked closely at the outline of the circle and saw that the fairy dust was rising up like smoke and disappearing. The outline was getting thinner and thinner by the second. Kelly managed to pick up her mother and Carmina and Jonah picked up Marcos Witherings. Carmina kissed Thomas on the cheek before she and Jonah stepped into the circle. They disappeared down into it.

"Your turn," Thomas said to Kelly.

Kelly approached the circle but paused when she saw there was still a little bit of fairy dust left.

"You aren't planning to go to the battle tonight are you?" she asked Thomas.

"That would be quite interesting." Thomas smiled slightly.

"Well if you were thinking about it you should forget it, since Miasmos is hoping you'll be there."

"Is he?" Thomas looked surprised.

"He wants the Key to Embralia and seems to think he has a pretty good chance of getting it tonight."

Thomas looked like he was considering this information, but he didn't say whether he was planning to come to the battle or not. "The fairy dust is almost out," he said.

Kelly stepped into the portal. She was instantly in free fall and before she could react she had landed on top of the heap that included Mindy, Carmina, Jonah, and Marcos Witherings. The sky blue circle in the air above them hung there for another moment, then vanished. It was only then that Kelly realized what part of Glendenland the portal had brought them to, and she couldn't think of any worse place.

They had landed right in the middle of the speaking platform of the Great Hall, which might not have been a problem if the Great Hall had been empty, but it just so happened that the Great Hall was full. Glenden was currently giving a motivational talk to prepare the fairies for that night's battle. Kelly, Jonah, and Carmina struggled to their feet in the crushing silence that had met their entrance. All of the fairies' eyes were on them. Venuto was clutching the armrests of his throne as if for dear life, nervously eyeing his father, who was standing only a few feet away from Kelly, glaring at her with clenched fists. Glenden's cheeks had filled up with air and he looked like he might explode. But within a few seconds he had composed himself and revealed the improvisational ability of a good leader in unexpected situations.

"My fellow Glendenians and honored guests," he said. "I had not told you about this matter before as the mission was risky and I did not want to get anyone's hopes up unnecessarily. Now I am pleased to announce that the secret mission has been a success.

"These three fairies bravely ambushed Miasmos's fadaman son when he was alone. He lies powerless before you. Alongside him you can see that they have rescued an innocent human captive of Witherings's. We must rejoice in this positive gain and the fact we will no longer have to contend with a fadaman in battle. But at the same time we should remember that the news of this capture will make Miasmos very angry, and we must expect the Miasmonians to fight hard tonight. You should all take advantage of the last hours before nightfall to get some rest. I now close this meeting."

"Come with me," he commanded to Kelly with clenched teeth before storming off the stage. Kelly followed, half-carrying, half-dragging her mother. Venuto got up to help her and Jonah and Carmina followed close behind with Witherings. They followed Glenden through the shadow archway that led to the audience hall. The visiting fairy leaders Belen, Catia, and Riona accompanied them, no doubt curious to hear what had really happened. As soon as they had all entered the audience hall, Glenden's wrath broke forth.

"Which one of you opened the portal?" he demanded, his gold eyes flickering with rage.

No one answered him. Jonah looked like he was about to pass out with fright.

"I've never seen you two before, was it one of you?" he asked, stepping closer to Carmina and Jonah. "Do you know that opening a temporary portal without authorization is a serious offense?"

"Father, they did capture Marcos Wither—"

"Silence!" Glenden shouted at his son. "Which one of you opened the portal?" he repeated.

"None of us opened it," Kelly answered, growing irritated with Glenden. She had nearly been killed by Marcos Witherings, her mother had been kidnapped, and all Glenden cared about was who had opened the stupid portal.

Glenden swirled around to look at Kelly, his crown tipping over to one side with the motion.

"What do you mean by that?" he asked.

"I mean exactly what I said. None of us opened it. One of our friends opened it for us."

"Your friend?" He looked confused.

"Thomas Penadas."

Carmina gasped, Venuto's mouth dropped wide open, Glenden stepped back like he had been slapped in the face, and Catia, Riona, and Belen continued to stand awkwardly to the side of the room.

"Thomas Penadas! How could you associate with that scoundrel?"

Kelly had had enough. "Thomas is not a scoundrel. He is a decent and honest fairy and he doesn't make assumptions about people based on their last names! Even if his brother had been the most evil fairy on earth, which I seriously doubt, it gives you no right to treat his family like you have!"

Glenden stared at Kelly in utter astonishment. "It is clear that your encounter with Witherings has left you stressed out and confused. Therefore I won't hold you responsible for what you are saying. But don't ever mention the Penadas name again! And mark my words, if Thomas even thinks of showing his face at the battle tonight Miasmos will be the last thing he has to worry about!"

With those words Glenden exited the room. Venuto stood looking a little unsure of himself, and Kelly couldn't tell how he felt about their knowing Thomas.

"Belen, Riona and Catia, why don't you help me take Witherings to the jail bubble?" Venuto finally ventured. The three of them lifted up the babbling, semi-conscious Marcos Witherings and left the room. Once the others had gone, Carmina, Kelly, and Jonah were left standing in the audience hall with the sleeping Mindy.

"What do we do with her?" Jonah asked.

"We should take her to the hospital bubble. And it might not be a bad idea for you to get checked out too," Carmina said to him.

When they reached the hospital bubble Margretta told them that Kelly's mother would be fine once she received the antihypnull potion. Margretta didn't have any in stock, however, and she said it would take about a week for the potion to be ready, since while it contained a relatively simple mix of ingredients it had to sit for at least six days before reaching full potency.

After Kelly told Margretta about her encounter with Marcos Witherings, Margretta told them she didn't think Witherings's future prognosis was very good.

"It sounds like the strain of all the bad things he ever did coming back to him all at once made him go crazy," Margretta said.

"Will he be crazy forever?" Kelly asked.

"He might recover at some point, but then again he might not. The fact he was affected means he still has some trace of a conscience left. Otherwise, what you did to him wouldn't have had any affect at all. So consider yourself lucky."

"I guess you wouldn't want to try the same thing on Miasmos then," Carmina said.

"Not unless you wanted him to turn all that energy back on you," Margretta said. "And judging from his son's use of perverse magic you can expect Miasmos to be capable of much more horrible things."

Jonah shivered, no doubt remembering some of those very things.

"Was what I did to Witherings a perversion of magic?" Kelly asked.

"No, you simply sped up a natural process. The suffering one causes others is bound to come back to them some day, it is the natural law," Margretta replied. "Even though some fairies like Miasmos might be able to put off the consequences for many years, even a lifetime in some cases, eventually their actions will catch up to them. In contrast, Witherings imposed undeserved emotional suffering on you, so that was a perversion of magic."

Kelly thought she understood, though it was a bit abstract. She imagined Witherings locked up alone, drooling and huddling in a corner under a tattered blanket. She couldn't help but feel a twinge of pity for him despite the things he had done.

"And you," Margretta said, having finally taken a closer look at Jonah, "you need an energy infusion! And no less than three days of rest."

"But the battle—" Jonah protested.

"Not another word about that. You can barely even stand up."

Jonah grudgingly promised he would rest and stay away from the battle.

"Good lad, now follow me for the energy infusion." Margretta led Jonah through a curtain to another part of the hospital Bubble.

Just after Margretta and Jonah had left, Bubbles, Beatrix and Stephanie bounded into the room. Bubbles was holding up Kelly's half of their fairy sense necklace pair.

"We were so worried about you! How could you just disappear like that without telling any of us about it?" Bubbles demanded. "And then on top of that you hid yourself from our fairy senses!" He was indignant.

"I hid myself?" Kelly asked, surprised.

"Quite well actually," Beatrix agreed. Kelly guessed that her intention that her friends not know of her whereabouts had somehow translated into a real blockage of their fairy senses.

"Sorry, but I didn't want any of you to get hurt," Kelly said. "And besides, Witherings said that I had to come alone or he would kill my mother."

"All right, we forgive you," Bubbles said. "But it you pull a stunt like that again I won't talk to you again until turtles fly!"

"You mean until pigs fly?" Stephanie asked.

"No, turtles," Bubbles said. He handed Kelly back her fairy sense necklace.

"Thanks Bubbles," she said. They embraced.

"That was awesome how you transported into the Great Hall," Stephanie said excitedly. "And the look on Glenden's face, that was priceless!" She laughed.

Kelly smiled. "I guess it is a little funny looking back on it."

"Tell us what happened, we want all the details," Stephanie said.

Kelly told them every detail of what had happened after she had snuck out of Glendenland earlier that day. Bubbles was especially impressed by her throwing icicles at Marcos Witherings.

"Usually it takes me a full five seconds to make an icicle, but it sounds like you were making them at least one per second," he said.

"And calling up all the suffering he had caused to come back to him, I never would have thought of that," Beatrix said.

"Well, Margretta said I'm lucky that Witherings still had a trace of a conscience left, otherwise it wouldn't have worked," Kelly told them.

Kelly heard Margretta's voice through the other side of the curtain. "Now remember, take three drops of this energy potion every two hours on the hour for three days. And for four days absolutely no running, no flying for more than five or six minutes at a time, and absolutely no lifting of heavy objects," she said. Then Jonah came through the curtain alone, carrying a small bottle of the same cloudy blue liquid that had sustained Bubbles throughout his healing sleep. Jonah had clearly already received some of the potion, because the color had started to return to his face.

"Jonah!" Beatrix shouted when she saw him. In a flash she was over by his side, hugging him and showering him with kisses.

"I guess he didn't run off with another fairy after all," Bubbles said.

After the reunion they all went back to their respective quarters to rest before the battle. Carmina and Jonah went with Kelly and Stephanie to their quarters, since they didn't have any of their own. When Kelly lay down on her bed she realized just how exhausted she was. She almost instantly fell into a deep sleep. She was awakened at nightfall by the sound of Flimsly's horn call traveling through the walls. Hurriedly she and Stephanie said good-bye to Carmina and Jonah before heading to the underwater park, where the fairies were lining up in their battle groups. Stephanie joined Beatrix, Gwendolyn, and the other fairies on medical duty. Kelly could see Dimpleton counting his group of fairies, and Bubbles was fidgeting beside Bamblelina in front of his group while Milak circled above them all, watching intently with his one hawk-like eye. Kelly was surprised to see that

Petania was also a group leader. She looked improperly dressed for battle in a light pink dress, but her group was very respectfully following her directions. Catia of the Catanori was once again dressed in a brilliant red, this time pants and a shirt, and she carried a case of arrows on her back. The other Catanori fairies were dressed in the same bright red and also carried cases of arrows. They would not be depending on magic alone that night.

Neither would the Rowenians. Kelly noticed that many of them had daggers at their belts. Queen Riona had replaced her usual elaborate garb with a simple pair of dark green pants and a white shirt. Her hair was braided and wrapped tightly around her head. The Beleni were all dressed in black like their leader Belen, who carried a crystal wand very much like Marcos Witherings's. Glenden's previous estimate of their numbers had been correct and Kelly thought there were about 1400 fairies forming the Glendenian allied forces. Kelly spotted Venuto and went to join him.

"Where's Glenden?" she asked.

"His arrival will be the sign for us to set out," Venuto answered.

"Oh. Where's your bodyguard?" Kelly asked, having noticed Venuto's bodyguard was nowhere to be seen.

"He's leading a fairy group."

"He won't be protecting you in battle?" It seemed strange to Kelly that Venuto wouldn't be unaccompanied by his bodyguard during the battle, since it would for sure be one of the most dangerous situations he had ever been in.

"I will be protecting myself," Venuto said. "Fairies never have bodyguards in battle."

"Why not?"

"I suppose because bodyguards are only around to protect you from surprise attacks, when your guard might be down. But in battle you're expecting to be attacked. Besides, it wouldn't be very brave to have a personal bodyguard in battle, would it?"

"I suppose not," Kelly said. She spotted both Venuto's and Glenden's bodyguards at the heads of their fairy groups on the far end of the park.

"Now that Marcos Witherings won't be at the battle, do you still want me to stay next to you or should I join one of the groups?" Kelly asked.

"You should still stay near me. Most of the fairies will expect it since they think you were sent on a special mission. Also, since they think you're my distant relative, it makes even more sense that you would fight by my side."

"I see," Kelly said. She was relieved she would be fighting beside Venuto.

A few minutes later they heard Flimsly's signature fanfare and Glenden entered the park with a flourish. He was carrying a long staff instead of a wand and he wore a shiny golden suit. Kelly didn't think that a bright golden suit was the best idea for a battle since it made him jump out quite visibly from his surroundings. She imagined he would be very easy for the Miasmonians to spot. Glenden pointed his staff upwards and sent out a series of bright yellow sparks before zooming towards the top of the bubble and disappearing out of it. Venuto and Kelly followed, Milak whistled, and all of the rest of the fairies sprung into the air.

They exited the river into the night. They flew high above the buildings towards where Glenden had sensed the Miasmonian hideout. They would be entering the underground lair by way of a human metro station. The flight took close to forty-five minutes. All of the fairies were in their transparent invisible-to-humans forms. Kelly looked just as transparent to any other fairy as the next in her half-invisible-to-humans form, and since it was so dark none of the fairies noticed Stephanie wasn't transparent. If any human had looked up at the allied forces from the ground, however, they would have been able to see Kelly and Stephanie, but due to the lack of light and the height at which the forces were flying, any such human would have surely thought they had merely seen a lone pair of birds, or bats.

Finally they arrived at the entrance to the station. It was still in operation and a handful of people were going in and out. Luckily it wasn't extremely busy and they managed to pass undetected by staying close to the ceiling, flying over the ticket gates and then down a long stairway that led to the train platform. Once at the platform, they hovered over the heads of the few people waiting for the next train. After the next train came and left, the platform sign informed them that the next train would arrive in five minutes. Five minutes would provide time for about half of them to pass safely into the tunnels. Glenden, Venuto, and Kelly entered the tunnel first. Behind them came Bubbles's, Dimpleton's, and Petania's groups, the Catanori, and nine more groups from Glendenland. Milak stayed behind to help guide the other groups after the next train.

They flew quickly down the dark tunnel as Glenden created illumination with his staff. About ten yards into the tunnel there was an indentation to their left that led to a small hole. The hole sat at the top of where an old door had been filled in with bricks. Glenden shot a continuous stream of hot electricity from his staff, tracing it around the outline of the old door. When he had finished tracing the outline, the remaining bricks blocking the doorway crumbled inwards, widening the gap so that at least fifty fairies could fly through at once. Quickly they flew through the entrance into a long arched hallway made completely of bricks. The place felt familiar to Kelly and she didn't like the feeling. They waited just inside the hallway for the rest of the fairies to arrive. Once they had been joined by the rest of the fairy forces, they followed Glenden as he led them further down the hallway. They were all very quiet and alert and Kelly wondered why they hadn't seen any Miasmonians yet.

The hallway soon ended and opened up to a large space that perhaps was originally going to be a subway station but was later abandoned. Old-fashioned lamps were set at even points along the walls, filling the room with a soft, eerie light. Kelly's heart skipped a beat when she saw what awaited them on the other side of the room. The far wall was full of a line of Miasmonians, all in tattered clothes and holding a variety of objects as wands such as toothpicks, twigs, and even a few paper clips. There were perhaps only 800 of them, a little over half of the Glendenian number, but the Miasmonians were staring at them with such stone-cold and fearless looks in their eyes that Kelly prepared herself for the worst. Kelly didn't see Miasmos. After a moment during which each side just stared at the other, the Miasmonians charged at them. The battle had begun.

The Miasmonians were sending a barrage of electricity bursts and fireballs at the allied forces. The allied forces scrambled into their group positions and deflected most of the attacks, starting to work together to form large fireballs in response. Bubbles's group produced a huge fireball and flung it at the Miasmonians, but to their surprise it only took about five Miasmonians to easily deflect it back at them, and Bubbles's group sprung out of the way as their own fireball came smashing back at them. Once the fireball flew past them, Bubbles's group quickly reformed and under Bubbles's direction began to create another fireball. Bubbles was remarkably calm and Kelly managed to feel proud of him amongst all the activity. There may have been less Miasmonians than Glendenians, but each one of the Miasmonians seemed to possess twice the power of a normal fairy. Kelly thought their unusual strength must have had something to do with the fact they had been stealing energy from others. Kelly saw that Petania's group had made a large ball of freezing mist that had managed to send about six Miasmonians falling down to the ground, shivering uncontrollably. Some cheers came up from her group at the fall of the first Miasmonians, but the cheers were short lived. Petania's group shifted to the defensive as a slew of irate Miasmonians flung icicles at them. Catia shot a series of arrows at the icicle-flinging Miasmonians, but most of the evil fairies managed to deflect the arrows with bursts of air.

Miasmonians weren't the only ones that had started to fall. Kelly looked down and saw Stephanie and the medical duty fairies flying about, attending to an increasing number of allied fairies. Kelly saw Stephanie not quite successfully dodge a fireball sent down at her from a Miasmonian, but the fireball bounced off Stephanie's arm harmlessly and Kelly breathed a sigh of relief. Kelly soon lost track of the rest of the battle as she concentrated on defending herself from Miasmonian attacks. She and Venuto were near the front of the group, close to the Miasmonians, and Kelly was sending icicles at the Miasmonians around them as Venuto shot them fireballs. She was constantly moving forward and backward to dodge and block fireballs, sparks, freezing mist, electricity bolts, and jets of boiling water. The sounds of the battle grew louder and louder as fairy group leaders shouted out frantic commands and injured fairies shouted in pain as they plummeted to the ground. Kelly could hear Milak's loud voice yelling signals to coordinate the group leaders. After a few minutes of fighting Kelly realized that Glenden had disappeared. She glanced around and out of the corner of her eye she saw a bright gold fleck disappear through an archway on the far side of the room. It was Glenden. He had taken advantage of the fact that all of the battle's activity was concentrated in the center of the room and had snuck along the side wall to the far archway. Kelly knew where the doorway led. Glenden had gone to fight Miasmos alone.

Kelly felt a slight sting on her arm as a Miasmonian electricity burst grazed her. She turned and threw a fireball at the fairy, hitting him squarely in the chest. He spun downwards towards the ground with his shirt on fire. During the time Kelly had been looking for Glenden, Venuto had shifted several yards away from Kelly. She saw that he was engaged with three Miasmonians. Kelly started to make her way towards him to let him know where his father had gone. But before she could reach him two Miasmonians flew in front of her and blasted her with a powerful jet of air. While the jet of air didn't break any of her bones, which it no doubt would have if she hadn't been a fadaman, she was still flung backward several feet. When she regained her balance she saw that Venuto was still fighting the three fairies, but to her dismay there was another fairy sneaking up behind him, aiming a toothpick at his back. She shouted to warn Venuto but her voice was drowned out by the surrounding battle cries.

As if in slow motion Kelly saw a bolt of electricity start to leave the tip of the fairy's toothpick towards Venuto's back. Just as the bolt was about to make contact there was a blur of wings as a fairy flew between Venuto and the electricity bolt. It was Thomas. Thomas managed to mostly deflect the bolt but since he had been forced to fly in so close between the evil fairy and Venuto to block it, the deflected bolt still caught Thomas on the top corner of his left wing. A hole started to burn in his wing but he didn't stop flying or fall down as Kelly had expected. Instead, while simultaneously shooting his own bolt of electricity at the Miasmonian, who turned and fled, Thomas reached up with his left hand and tugged on his wing. At first Kelly thought he was pulling the skin off his wing, but then she realized that he was pulling a cover off of his wings. The fibrous texture of Thomas's wings hadn't been because they were prosthetic – it had been because he had been wearing a prosthetic wing cover over his real wings to hide his identity. His real wings were amazing. They were a shiny dark blue with blazing gold flecks. Thomas seemed to grow in stature with his true wings revealed. Kelly heard some of the Glendenians behind her gasp as they paused to stare. Venuto had gotten rid of the three Miasmonians who had been attacking him and he turned to look at Thomas. Thomas and Venuto stared at each other, seeming to forget the surrounding battle. Kelly flew above them to deflect an incoming fireball that neither of them noticed. The Glendenians who had been close enough to see Thomas also seemed to forget about the battle, watching Venuto and Thomas with interest as they started to drop like flies.

"There's a battle going on, idiots!!" Milak roared. This reminder jolted the watching Glendenians back to attention. But Venuto and Thomas were still staring at each other intently. Finally Thomas extended his hand to Venuto. Venuto shook it. Kelly flew down to them.

"Glenden's gone to fight Miasmos alone," she said breathlessly. Venuto went pale.

"Is he out of his mind?" Thomas asked. "Which way did he go?"

"Follow me," Kelly said. She dropped down low, just above the injured fairies on the floor, with Thomas and Venuto close behind. She headed for the archway she had seen Glenden disappear through. They didn't have as easy of a time getting to the archway as Glenden had. A group of about fifty Miasmonians descended and blocked their path. But Dimpleton had spotted this development and he and his group flew down to confront the Miasmonians. As the Miasmonians were distracted by Dimpleton's group's arrival, Kelly, Thomas, and Venuto were then able to slip past them through the archway.

Kelly felt a bone-chilling coldness as soon as she flew through the archway. While the other brick tunnel had felt familiar, this one she definitely recognized. She had seen it in a dream, along with the pale blue light that was filling the archway at the end of the hallway up ahead. The blue light got more intense as they flew and the air grew colder. Finally they reached the end of the hallway, set down on the ground, and passed through the archway. The archway led to a circular room, and on the far side of the room Glenden was fighting Miasmos. Miasmos's blue wings were glowing intensely, lighting up the room, but his face was momentarily concealed as his back was turned towards them. They arrived just in time to see a bolt of electricity get past Glenden's defenses and hit him in the stomach. Glenden fell sideways to the ground and his staff clattered to the floor.

"Father!" Venuto shouted and started to move towards Glenden, but Thomas held him back.

"Don't do anything rash," Thomas said firmly. Venuto nodded. At that moment Miasmos turned around.

"So nice of you all to join us," Miasmos sneered, his eyes glowing blue with perverse enjoyment.

When Miasmos's face became visible Thomas's mouth dropped open in shock.

"Uncle Harald?" he said.

"I go by Miasmos now, Harald is such a boring name, don't you think?"

Thomas's eyes grew wide in horror. "You, it was you!" he shouted. This time it was Venuto's turn to hold Thomas back as Thomas tried to lunge forward, his face full of fury.

Miasmos laughed. "Yes, I was the one who poisoned Glenden's drink and framed Peter. With Glenden out of the picture and Peter gone, I would have been the next leader of Glendenland. You were still too young, and a few weeks later you were to have an unfortunate accident. But that witch Esmeralda had to go and ruin everything by drinking from his cup!" His eyes flashed orange at this memory.

"But why?" Thomas asked.

"Why? Because when your father died your brother was only a boy, he wasn't responsible. He should never have been entrusted with the Key to Embralia. No, I should have been given it, as your father's younger brother. It was my right, mine!"

"No it wasn't," Thomas answered more calmly. "The Key to Embralia chooses her own guardian, and she chose Peter, then me," he said, standing up taller. "You are a disgrace to the Penadas name."

"Everyone's entitled to their own opinion, yours just happens to be wrong," Miasmos said. "But no matter, soon the Key to Embralia will be mine!" Miasmos pointed his right index finger at Thomas.

"If you want the Key to Embralia, you'll have to come through me," Venuto said, moving to stand in front of Thomas.

"And me," Kelly said, moving to position herself at Venuto's side.

"My pleasure." A burst of flame shot from Miasmos's finger at them. Venuto extinguished it with a jet of frigid water. From behind them Thomas sent several icicle projectiles at Miasmos, but they all shattered in the air a few feet from Miasmos even though Miasmos hadn't moved an inch to deflect them. Kelly called up the fire element in the air around her and amassed a fireball about the size of her head, then flung it straight at Miasmos's face. This ball of fire also harmlessly dissipated into smoke as it reached a place in the air about an arm's length from Miasmos's face. It was as though Miasmos had some sort of shield around him.

"It's like he has a shield around him," Thomas said behind Kelly in consternation, echoing her thoughts.

"Is that all you've got?" Miasmos taunted them as he flew up into the air. They all alighted into the air as well. Kelly looked down and saw that Glenden had opened his eyes and was reaching slowly for his staff, but he was struggling a great deal in the effort and his lips were pressed together tightly as if he were in great pain.

Her attention was quickly drawn back to self-preservation as Miasmos started flinging fist-size fireballs at them with great speed. All three of them dodged and ducked the onslaught. Thomas fired back a few fireballs of his own, but it was all Kelly and Venuto could do to evade the fireballs coming in their direction. One fireball hit Kelly on the left elbow and she felt a sharp pain as it seared her skin. Miasmos's power was clearly strong enough to break through her inborn fadaman defenses.

Miasmos suddenly stopped flinging fireballs and hovered in position as Kelly, Thomas, and Venuto tried a variety of attacks with no affect. Miasmos laughed maniacally as their balls of fire dissolved into harmless puffs of smoke, their freezing jets of air turned and shot back at them, as Thomas's and Venuto's electricity bolts zapped away into nothingness and as Kelly's icicles shattered into thousands of pieces as they hit the invisible and so far impenetrable shield around Miasmos.

Then Miasmos raised his hand and a small puff of white smoke floated away from his finger. Kelly knew immediately what it was, but she didn't know how to stop it. The swirling white mist headed towards Venuto, who looked at it with a mixture of curiosity and trepidation.

"Don't let it touch you!" Kelly warned. Miasmos's eyes flashed orange and he pointed his finger at her. Nothing came out of his finger this time. Rather, his arm started to shake slightly and Kelly felt a sharp pain start in her stomach and quickly spread through her body. It was so strong that she couldn't keep aloft and she felt herself falling towards the ground. Thomas caught her before she hit the ground and set her down lightly before returning upwards to face Miasmos, whose hand was still pointing at Kelly. Kelly struggled to get up but she felt like she had been thrown into a pot of boiling water. All she was aware of was the terrible pain. Then suddenly the pain stopped. Kelly caught her breath and struggled to her feet to see that Thomas had moved closer to Miasmos and seemed to be making some progress on wearing down his shield. At least he was posing enough of a threat to have brought Miasmos back to fighting with normal magic. Venuto was flying around at full speed, dodging what were now five white wisps of mist chasing him. One finally got him and he let out a desperate wail of emotional suffering.

The other wisps turned and headed for Kelly. She did her best to dodge them while blasting them with fire, air, and water, but to no avail. The wisps continued to follow her. She tried pointing her finger at one of them and wishing that it disappear harmlessly, but that didn't work. Then she mentally willed the wisps to go back to where they had come from, but that didn't work either. Just then a wisp hit her and she felt a desperate sadness creeping up through her body. She fought to close her mind against it, but the sadness kept growing stronger and stronger. It was consuming her. All she wanted was for it to go away but it kept intensifying. Faintly she heard Glenden's voice in her mind. *Don't react, that gives it more strength.* Kelly closed her eyes and concentrated. She tried to objectively examine the physical tightness the sorrow created in her stomach and the warm, wet sensation her tears created on her face. Within an instant after she began to concentrate the sadness started to subside. She felt the next floating wisps of emotional suffering hit her in sequence, but now she had the secret to combating them. They made her sad for only a moment and then dissolved away when she didn't panic and react to them.

Venuto had also managed to overcome the wisp that had attacked him, and seconds later they were both flying up to help Thomas. Just as they reached Thomas's side Miasmos let out a jet of forceful air that flung all three of them backwards. They slammed into the wall. Both Thomas and Venuto were knocked unconscious to the ground by the impact, but Kelly was only made a bit dizzy. Soon she was on the ground beside Thomas and Venuto, however, as Miasmos pointed his finger at her again, shooting her more physical pain. This time it felt like all the blood in her body was freezing. She tried as hard as she could not to react, but this pain was so bad that it was impossible to observe objectively. She screamed.

"You are weak, weak!" Miasmos said, staring down at her.

To her side Kelly was dimly aware of Venuto stirring back to consciousness. Miasmos extended his other hand and Venuto started to scream. Thomas was still unconscious. Miasmos was so intent on Kelly and Venuto that he wasn't aware that behind him Glenden had finally fixed his hand around his staff and had struggled up into a sitting position. Glenden pointed his staff at Miasmos and a strong wind burst forth from it. Glenden was blowing away Miasmos's shield. Miasmos dropped his hand and started to turn around.

"Now! He has no protection!" Glenden shouted.

Kelly and Venuto both started to send strong streams of electricity at Miasmos. Kelly didn't know why she had sent electricity, since she hadn't had much success with it before, but somehow now she managed to sustain the current. Miasmos started to quiver as the electricity went into him. Thomas woke up and started to send his own electricity with Kelly's and Venuto's. Miasmos shook more and more, frozen in place by the power of their attack, unable to lift a limb in his own defense. His eyes grew oranger and oranger. Then something unexpected happened. He turned transparent as if he had gone into his invisible-to-humans form. Then the blue glow of his wings started to spread to the rest of his body. Kelly, Venuto, and Thomas all quickly stopped sending electricity at Miasmos as they realized that the energy was no longer staying within his body but instead it was passing through him. The electric current had almost reached Glenden on the other side of Miasmos before they stopped sending it. Then the outline of the transparent, blue Miasmos started to waver as his entire body began transforming into a cloud of bright blue smoke. *He's turning his entire body into the air element!* Kelly wouldn't have believed it if it wasn't happening before her eyes.

"Your time is short, very short. Enjoy it while it lasts!" Miasmos cackled as his body kept dissolving into smoke. After a few seconds only his face remained recognizable while the rest of him had become a swirling ball of blue smoke. Then his face too dissolved and the smoke cloud tightened into a smaller ball before racing through the air towards the door.

"He's escaping!" Venuto exclaimed, scrambling to follow Miasmos's cloud.

Glenden swung his staff around and blocked Venuto. "It's too late," Glenden said. Then he dropped his staff and clutched his chest. His face was contorted in pain.

"Father!" Venuto rushed to Glenden's side.

"My time—is up," Glenden panted.

"Don't say that, you're going to be all right," Venuto insisted.

"I'm sorry my son, I'm sorry," Glenden said. He looked over his son's shoulder, to Thomas. "I was wrong about you," he said.

Thomas bowed his head respectfully. Glenden smiled. Then he fell back and lay on the ground motionless.

"Father! No!" Venuto shook Glenden but Glenden didn't move. He was dead.

Chapter 14
Return to Humanland

A few moments later Dimpleton appeared at the entrance to the room, with members of his group standing in the tunnel behind him.

"Sorry for the delay, but we couldn't get past those Miasmonians until that strange puff of blue smoke blew out of here. When they saw the smoke the Miasmonians all scattered and ran for it," Dimpleton said. Then he caught sight of Glenden's body on the ground. His face fell. "Wait, that wasn't just any puff of smoke was it?"

"No, it was Miasmos," Kelly said.

Venuto wiped a tear off his cheek with the back of his hand. Dimpleton and Thomas picked up Glenden's lifeless body, and Venuto led the way back to the main battle area. Meanwhile, Dimpleton sent some members of his group to search the rest of the tunnel network for Miasmos's fairy prisoners. When they returned to the place of the main battle Kelly saw that the ground was almost completely obscured by the bodies of dead and injured fairies. She had never seen any dead bodies before that day, and she felt sick to her stomach when she laid eyes on all the contorted forms and vacant stares of the dead fairies on the ground. But at least the majority of Glendenian allied forces lying on the ground were simply injured as opposed to dead. Beatrix and Stephanie were both all right and completely absorbed in their medical duty. The rest of the allied forces had gathered in their groups and were hovering in wait. When they realized that Glenden was dead at least half of the fairies, including Petania, burst into tears.

Milak broke away from his position and flew up to Kelly and Venuto. The right sleeve of Milak's shirt had been ripped off in the battle, and there was a large red burn on his right shoulder.

"What's our status?" Venuto asked him.

"85 dead, 300 hundred injured, of those 25 critically," Milak answered. "Thanks to the fast action of the medical duty fairies, many deaths were avoided. The enemy wasn't as lucky. They lost at least 300, and the surviving Miasmonians fled in cowardice when they realized they could not win the battle."

"Thank you Milak," Venuto said. Milak nodded and went back to his place. Venuto turned his attention to the rest of the forces. "My fellow Glendenians and honorable allies. Due to your bravery we have been victorious. While unfortunately Miasmos managed to escape, he has been greatly weakened and his forces are destroyed. Alas, our beloved leader the honorable, noble, wise and benevolent Glenden Grand gave his life to defend us. We shall now return to Glendenland, and tomorrow afternoon there will be a general meeting in the Great Hall and the funeral." Venuto stopped talking, choking back tears, and signaled to Milak, who started to lead the troops back down the tunnels. Even though they had won the battle, Kelly didn't feel a great sense of relief or happiness. Glenden was dead, and Kelly had the feeling that although weakened, Miasmos was still very much a threat.

When they arrived back at Glendenland it was nearly sunrise. The return journey took much longer because of the number of fairies who needed to be carried back. When they arrived Kelly made her way to the hospital bubble to help take care of the wounded. Not all of the injured fairies had to be hospitalized, of which Kelly was glad, because if they had there would have been a serious shortage of beds. In the end only about one hundred fairies were hospitalized whilst the remainder, once examined, were given medicines and instructions and sent back to their quarters. It was mid-morning before Margretta finally insisted that Kelly and Stephanie get some sleep. Back in their quarters they didn't get much rest, however, as Jonah was waiting for them and wanted to hear all about the battle. A short while later they heard the sound of the chimes at their door. It was Bubbles, Beatrix, Bamblelina, and Dimpleton.

"Come on, we have to get to the meeting early because we have to sit up in the front rows with the other fairies who fought last night," Bubbles said.

Kelly and Stephanie followed the others as they hurried to the Great Hall. When they arrived Milak was instructing the arriving fairies where to sit, and he instructed Bubbles, Kelly, and Dimpleton to sit in the front row with the group leaders, whilst Beatrix and Stephanie sat in the second row with the medical duty fairies. The rest of the fairies who had fought in the battle filled in the next several rows behind the medical duty fairies, and fairies who hadn't been to the battle all sat in the further parts of the hall.

"Have you seen Thomas or Carmina?" Kelly asked Dimpleton as they sat down. Kelly hadn't seen Thomas since they had arrived back in Glendenland and when she and Stephanie had returned to their quarters Carmina hadn't been there, and Jonah hadn't known where she had gone.

"No," Dimpleton answered.

"Maybe they left," Bubbles said.

Fairies continued to file into the Great Hall, mostly solemnly, many of them dressed in black. The speaking platform was set up with the three usual thrones and the additional thrones for Riona, Catia, and Belen. Once the hall was full, Venuto and the visiting fairy leaders walked solemnly onto the platform, in the notable absence of Flimsly and his companions' music. Venuto and the visiting fairy leaders were all dressed in black robes. The audience was entirely silent. After the visiting leaders and Venuto sat down, Flimsly and his musician companions entered carrying a large and extremely heavy-looking coffin. The top was sealed, but everyone knew that Glenden was inside. The coffin was a green marble with golden flecks in it and was engraved with an intricate design of vines. Flimsly and the others set the coffin down on the speaking platform directly in front of Glenden's now empty throne. Curiously, Glenden's bodyguard was still standing in his usual position behind Glenden's empty throne, and Milak had taken up position beside the empty throne of the late Esmeralda. Kelly thought perhaps during funerals it was customary for prior royal bodyguards to stand at their old positions. Once Flimsly and the others had set the coffin down, Venuto stood up to address the crowd.

"My fellow Glendenians," he began. "We are gathered here today first and most importantly to honor the life of our great leader, his Grace the honorable, noble, wise, and benevolent Glenden Grand. He gave his life valiantly to protect us all and we will always remember him for his sacrifice and for his consistent and solid leadership over the course of his reign. Please join me in a moment of silence."

The fairies inclined their heads and closed their eyes. The silence lasted a few minutes, and the sadness in the room was almost palpable. Many fairies were sniffling and even a few were struggling not to sob too loudly during the silence. The end of the silence was signaled by the sound of a haunting melody. Kelly opened her eyes to see that the melody was being played by Flimsly on a wooden flute. After the music ended, Venuto spoke again.

"Now the honorable, noble, wise, and benevolent Glenden Grand will be taken to his final resting place beside his wife, the late Esmeralda." Flimsly and the other musicians picked up the coffin again, exiting the Great Hall in silence.

Kelly thought the funeral had been very short, since no one had given a eulogy and no fairies had gotten up to share memories of Glenden, but she soon learned that such memories were shared in a separate ceremony.

"Two weeks from now, as is tradition," Venuto said, "we shall gather here again to share our remembrances of the king and to hear the reading of his formal acts of leadership. Any fairy who wishes to write a commemorative song in honor of our dear leader should have it prepared in six days time so that the musicians will have time to learn it.

"We are also gathered here today to honor those who fought in last night's battle. Glenden was not the only fairy who died last night." Venuto recited the names of the other fallen fairies.

"Now, to honor the living. As is tradition, though many of you may not be aware of it since there hasn't been a battle for over thirty years, the day after a successful battle all those who took part are honored for their participation, and individuals who showed great courage are called onto the stage and awarded pendants by the leader of Glendenland. This ceremony will begin shortly, but first the new leader of Glendenland must be sworn in. This brings me to another announcement. I will not be the next leader of Glendenland."

Shocked murmurs arose from the crowd. Venuto put up his hand for silence in a commanding gesture reminiscent of his father. The fairies obediently fell silent.

"During the course of the battle I was present when Miasmos's true identity came to light. His real name is Harald Penadas."

There were deep intakes of breath from many fairies at the mention of the Penadas name.

"I was also present when Miasmos confessed to being the one behind my mother's death. I have absolutely no doubt that Harald Penadas acted alone out of a perverse lust for power and deep greed. Peter Penadas and the rest of his family were completely innocent, and there was no conspiracy as had been suspected previously," Venuto explained. "Additionally, even though he had been harshly exiled from our band, Peter's younger brother Thomas never turned away from his duty to our people. He bravely risked his life to assist us in the battle last night, even though he didn't know how he would be received by us. In light of this new information, the banishment of the Penadas family will be lifted, and the Penadas family will resume their rightful place as one of the leading families of our realm. As Peter's brother, Thomas Penadas is the next rightful leader of Glendenland. As was the tradition when both families ruled before, I, as the most senior member of the Grand family, will happily serve as the head advisor to our new leader. Without further ado I would like you would like you all to stand for his Grace the just, loyal, unwavering, and wise Thomas Penadas and his wife her Grace the intelligent and fair Carmina Penadas."

The fairies stood up. Some of them had dazed expressions on their faces, which Kelly took to mean they hadn't quite absorbed all of this new information. But as she looked around her she saw that many other fairies were smiling happily in expectation of greeting their new leader. Dimpleton had the biggest grin of all on his face.

Flimsly and the musicians came back into the hall first, having returned from carrying Glenden to his final resting place. They played a triumphant hymn as Thomas and Carmina walked onto the stage. Thomas was dressed in a light blue suit with silver flowers embroidered on it. His face was dusted with silver glitter and he was wearing Glenden's old crown. Instead of the usual long braid down his back, his hair was loose and it flowed down past his shoulders. Carmina was wearing a light yellow dress that matched her wings and a delicate golden tiara.

Dimpleton started to clap as Thomas and Carmina arrived on stage, and soon other fairies followed suit and the hall erupted with clapping and cheering. Carmina and Venuto sat down, Venuto in his usual throne, and Carmina in the late Esmeralda's. Now Kelly knew why Milak was standing behind that throne. He was Carmina's new bodyguard. Thomas stayed standing and turned to address the crown.

"Thank you for your warm reception. I am happy that the rift between my family and the Grand family has been healed. I am honored to be sworn in as your new leader, and the rest of my family will soon return to Glendenland. I wish to assure you that I will work in the interest of all of Glendenland and our allies, and I will make all decisions in conjunction with the able guidance of my head advisor Prince Venuto Grand. As my first act I would like to declare Glenden Grand's birthday a special holiday, during which there will be feasting and no work for any fairy."

This statement was greeted by enthusiastic cheering from the crowd.

"Now we shall begin the awards ceremony," Thomas said once the cheers had died down. "First I wish to sincerely thank the fairies of the Catanori, Rowenian, and Beleni bands for their partnership. We could not have triumphed without them. Our band extends our friendship to these bands and our eternal gratitude." Thomas presented each of the visiting fairy leaders with gifts. Riona received a golden bracelet, Catia received the golden wand that had so tempted Bubbles from behind the glass in the wand shop, and Belen was presented with a golden ring that had once belonged to Glenden.

"Next I wish to award individual fairies for their great service. First I wish to award Milak Montenegro for his capable direction of the Glendenian forces." Milak came out from behind Carmina's throne and Thomas placed a silver necklace around his neck. Next Thomas called about fifteen Glendenian fairies that Kelly didn't know personally up to the stage and presented them with necklaces as well. Then he called up a few fairies from the Catanori, Rowenian, and Beleni forces.

"Next, for great group leadership, I call Dimpleton Cloverdale forward," Thomas continued. Dimpleton proudly accepted his necklace.

"And finally, I would like for Bubbles and Beatrix Butterfield, Kelly Brennan, and Stephanie Portersfield to come up on the stage."

Bubbles sat dumbfounded when his name was called, and Kelly had to pull him up out of his seat and push him towards the stage.

"These fairies, although free fairies, fought beside us with incredible courage. Stephanie and Beatrix excelled in their medical service, and Bubbles led his fairy group with great expertise. Kelly showed bravery and skill beyond her years when she came face to face with Miasmos, fighting strongly beside Glenden, Venuto, and myself against him. Therefore I grant all of these free fairies honorary citizenship to Glendenland and present them with Glendenland's highest honor, the emerald heart," Thomas said.

He presented them with their necklaces. But their necklaces weren't silver like the other necklaces. They were gold. As they walked back to their seats Kelly looked at the pendant of her necklace. It was a beautiful bright green emerald in the shape of a heart.

"That concludes the awards ceremony," Thomas said. "Although not all fairies received special awards, I wish to reiterate that all fairies who fought made a valuable and esteemed contribution. A feast in their honor has been prepared. Please proceed to the mess hall." With those words Thomas headed off the stage, followed by Carmina, Venuto, and the visiting fairy leaders.

"I can't believe Thomas is the new leader!" Stephanie exclaimed once they joined the other fairies heading towards the mess hall.

"I know, I think it's great," Kelly said. She was very happy that Thomas's name had been cleared, and she was sure he would make a wonderful leader.

The feast went on for hours and they stuffed themselves with the mouthwatering food. After they couldn't possibly eat any more, some fairies started to play music and exuberant fairy couples danced around on top of the tables and did creative acrobatics in the air. Much nectala was drunk.

The next morning Kelly woke up surprisingly early, considering how long the feast had gone on the night before. Stephanie was still sound asleep, so Kelly decided she would go visit Thomas. About halfway to the royal quarters she came across Thomas and Venuto. Petania was also there, and she and Venuto were holding hands. As they approached, Petania gave Kelly a tentative, but for the first time genuine smile.

"Hi, we were just coming to look for you," Venuto said.

"I was just coming to visit you," Kelly answered.

"It seems your fairy senses are improving." Venuto smiled.

"Hi Kelly," Petania said.

"Hi." Kelly smiled.

"We wanted to ask you if you had thought about what you're going to do next," Venuto said.

"What do you mean?"

"Are you going to stay here or are you going to go back to humanland?" Thomas asked.

In her time in Glendenland Kelly hadn't really gotten around to thinking past the battle, but now that the battle was over it was a logical question, and as soon as it was asked she realized she already knew the answer.

"I think I'll go back to humanland. School starts again soon and I feel like I belong back there too, the same as I belong here."

"That makes sense, you do belong in both places, being a fadaman," Thomas said.

"Can I still come visit?" Kelly asked.

"Of course, you're always welcome here," Thomas answered. "The same goes for Stephanie. She can keep the prosthetic wings and ears she's been using, and so to visit she'll just need some fairy dust to shrink herself."

"She'll be happy to hear that," Kelly said.

"And you really have no excuse not to come visit frequently since your human house is only a half-hour flight away," Venuto said.

Over the next few days the visiting fairy leaders and their band members left Glendenland, and things gradually went back to normal in the underwater kingdom. The morning the Rowenians left, Gwendolyn stopped by Kelly and Stephanie's quarters to give them both Rowenian daggers as a going away present. She requested that they come and visit the kingdom of Rowenia sometime soon, and they promised they would try. Stephanie and Kelly spent their last days in Glendenland helping out in medicine storage and creation and the hospital bubble. Kelly knew she would miss living in Glendenland, but she took heart in the fact that she could come back as much as she wanted.

After a week the antihypnull potion for Mindy was finally ready. Kelly and Stephanie bid good-bye to Bubbles and Beatrix, who had decided to stay on living in Glendenland, and headed to meet Thomas, Carmina, and Venuto in the audience hall. They carried Kelly's still-sleeping mother with them. When they arrived, Venuto removed Stephanie's prosthetic wings and wing cover and collapsed the wings back into a ball, removed Stephanie's prosthetic ear tips, and put all of the items into a cloth bag. Kelly was intrigued by the fact that although the wings had been anchored into Stephanie's back for over a month, when they were removed the only evidence that they had been there was a line of tiny red dots on Stephanie's skin, like pinpricks. Venuto said they would disappear in a few hours.

"It feels weird not to have wings anymore," Stephanie said, wiggling her shoulders.

"You'll be using them again soon I'm sure," Carmina said.

Next Thomas opened a temporary portal into Kelly's living room, and Kelly, Stephanie, Thomas, Carmina, and Venuto stepped through it, carrying Kelly's mother. They lay Mindy down on the sofa. Venuto undid the shrinking spell that his father had performed on Stephanie. Stephanie returned to normal size, but her prosthetic wings stayed their same small size, fitting in the palm of her hand.

"Why didn't my wings get bigger? Everything else did, like my slippers." Stephanie frowned.

Venuto laughed. "Prosthetic wings have a protective spell on them to prevent them from changing size. Even under the influence of fairy dust they won't get any bigger."

Stephanie shrugged. "Oh well. It would have been interesting to try them out in human size though," she said.

Kelly was sure that if Stephanie had ever been able to try out her wings in full size the real Homeland Security would be after them in no time. Meanwhile, the temporary portal was dissolving quickly, so Kelly transformed to human size and Thomas reversed the shrinking spell Witherings had placed on Mindy.

"Are you going to tell your mother about fairies?" Venuto asked.

"I don't know," Kelly said.

"We think it might be prudent to wait awhile before telling her," Thomas said.

"Why's that?" Kelly asked.

"As you may know, if she can't remember who your father is it means her memory was erased. It is very difficult, and generally considered to be a serious crime to erase someone's memory, which means either a very evil fairy erased your mother's memory for a dark purpose, or a good fairy took the unusual step of erasing it for a very good reason. I would like to see if I can find out more about which of these happenings might have been the case before you tell her anything," Thomas said.

"But what good reason could there be for erasing her memory?" Stephanie asked.

"There are many," Thomas answered cryptically.

"All right, we'll keep it a secret for now," Kelly said. She thought finding out about fairies might be too much for her mother to handle at the moment anyway.

"Good. We'll leave you to wake her up then. Remember that Glenden's remembrance ceremony is next week. You'll be there, right?" Thomas asked.

"You can count on it," Kelly said.

Thomas inclined his head respectfully and stepped through the portal. Carmina hugged Kelly and Stephanie and then departed as well. Venuto waved good-bye and jumped through the portal, and the portal disappeared soon after. Kelly sat down on the sofa next to Mindy and unscrewed the cap off the antihypnull potion. It smelled like rotten eggs.

"That's foul," Stephanie said, covering her nose.

"Well, I have to give it to my mother. Will you hold her mouth open for me?"

Stephanie held Mindy's mouth open while scrunching up her nose in disgust as Kelly poured some of the viscous black potion into Mindy's mouth. As soon as the liquid touched Mindy's mouth, she started coughing and opened her eyes.

"Kelly! You're safe! I've been so worried." Mindy reached out her arms to her daughter and they hugged.

"Those horrible agents came by again last night looking for you, but I told them you weren't here, so they left. Then I went to bed and had the strangest dream. There was a little man with wings flying around me." Mindy's voice drifted off and she stared vacantly into space for a second. Then she shook her head. "Anyways, now you're here!" Mindy finished, smiling broadly.

"Yes, and you don't have to worry about those agents anymore Mrs. Brennan. Homeland Security had Kelly confused with another Kelly. The Kelly they were looking for was Kelly O'Brennan, not Kelly Brennan. Their documents had a typo," Stephanie lied.

"What? Those incompetent idiots. We should sue them!" Mindy stood up fast, then sat down, dizzy.

"I think we should just forget the whole thing," Kelly said.

"I suppose you're right," Mindy replied. "Are you girls hungry? Let me take you out to dinner. I'm sure you're both dying for a good meal after all that time hiding out in your friend's basement."

"Huh? Oh, right," Kelly said, remembering that in the note she had written to her mother she had said they were going to hide out in a friend's basement.

"I'd love to, but I should really be getting back home," Stephanie said.

"All right, say hello to your parents for me," Mindy said.

After Stephanie left, Mindy wanted to shower and change into different clothes for dinner, so Kelly waited for her mother in the living room. After a few minutes she switched on the TV. The familiar overly made-up face of Melanie Johnson appeared on the screen.

"Since Marcos Witherings's mysterious disappearance a little over a week ago, Senator Greg Allen has rebounded in the polls, and it seems he will have little competition for the democratic presidential nomination in the primaries at the start of next year. As far as his opponent's disappearance, Senator Allen declines to speculate. Reports that Marcos Witherings died of a drug overdose have been revealed as fictitious, and as of now authorities have no solid leads. They have asked that anyone with information come forward. More after the break, Melanie Johnson, evening news."

Kelly sighed. *They won't have much luck finding Witherings*, she thought. She switched off the TV when a tacky commercial with a singing donkey came on the screen. She had been away from TV for so long she wasn't used to it anymore. She looked down at the pendant on her emerald heart necklace, and then out of habit she checked the pendant of her fairy sense necklace. It was colorless and cool to the touch.

"What pretty necklaces," Mindy said, having reappeared in the living room ready to go to dinner. "Where did you get them?"

"They were birthday presents from Stephanie." This seemed to convince Mindy.

"I'll have to ask her where she bought them," Mindy said. "Shall we? There's a new Chinese place just down the street, so we can walk there." Mindy opened the front door.

Kelly got up and followed her mother outside. As they crossed the front lawn Kelly's ears were met with a serenade of horn honks as a car racing by her house cut off another car that had been about to turn onto the road. The driver of the car that had been cut off made an obscene gesture at the other driver. Kelly chuckled to herself. *Ah, humanland, sweet humanland.*